# A Colonial Reformer

## Vol. I

*by*

Rolf Boldrewood

Double9 BOOKS

# A Colonial Reformer
## Vol. I
**by Rolf Boldrewood**



ISBN: 978-93-71464-22-2

**Published by**

**DOUBLE 9 BOOKS**
2/13-B, Ansari Road
Daryaganj, New Delhi – 110002
info@double9books.com
www.double9books.com
Tel. 011-40042856

# ABOUT THE AUTHOR

Thomas Alexander Browne, known by his pen name Rolf Boldrewood, was an Australian author born on August 6, 1826, in London, United Kingdom, to Sylvester John Brown and Elizabeth Angell Alexander. Browne emigrated to Australia and became one of the country's prominent writers, particularly recognized for his works set in the Australian outback. His most famous work, Robbery Under Arms, a bushranging novel published in 1882, solidified his place in Australian literary history. He wrote under the pseudonym Rolf Boldrewood to create a distinct authorial identity. Browne's works often explored the harsh realities and the rugged life of early Australian settlers, reflecting the challenges, tensions, and moral complexities of the period. He also gained attention for his insightful depiction of colonial life and his contribution to the popularization of bush literature. Browne had a daughter, Rose Boldrewood, and a sister named Emma Brown. He passed away on March 11, 1915, in Melbourne, Australia, at the age of 88, leaving behind a legacy that contributed greatly to the understanding of Australia's colonial history through literature.

# CONTENTS

# CHAPTER I

When Mr. Ernest Neuchamp, younger, of Neuchampstead, Bucks, quitted the ancient roof-tree of his race, for a deliberate conflict with fortune, in a far land, he carried with him a purpose which went far to neutralise doubt and depression.

A crusader rather than a colonist, his lofty aims embraced far more than the ordinary sordid struggle with unkind nature, with reluctant success. Such might be befitting aspirations for eager and rude adventurers, half speculators, half buccaneers. They might fitly strive and drive—bargain and save—gamble, overreach, overwork themselves and one another, as he doubted not all colonists did in their proverbially hurried, feverish lives. But for a Neuchamp, of Neuchampstead, was reserved more chivalric exertion—a loftier destiny. As his ancestors had devoted themselves (with more energy than discretion, said tradition) to the refinement and elevation of the Anglo-Saxons—when first the banner of Tancred of Neuchamp floated over the Buckinghamshire meadows—so would his lineal descendant diffuse 'sweetness and light' among a vigorous but necessarily uncultured community, emerging from his unselfish toil, after a few years, with a modest competency, and the reputation of an Australian Manco Capac of the south.

Ernest Neuchamp fully endorsed the dictum that 'colonisation was heroic work.' He superadded to this assent a conviction that he was among the heroes destined to leave a glorious memory in the annals of the colony which he intended to honour.

For the somewhat exceptional though not obsolete character of reformer, he was fitted by natural tendency, derived probably from hereditary predisposition. The Neuchamps had always been leading and staunch reformers, from a period whence 'the memory of man goeth not to the contrary.' Of Merrie England they would have secured a much larger slice had they not been, after Hastings, more deeply concerned in inflicting reforms upon the stubborn or despondent Saxons than in hunting after manorial privileges with a view to extension of territory. Even in Normandy, old chroniclers averred that Balder-Ragnaiök, nicknamed Wünsche (or the wisher), who married the heiress of Neuchamp, and founded the family, converted a fair estate into a facsimile of a Norse grazing farm, maddening the peasantry, and strengthening his natural enemies by an everlasting tutelage as exasperating towards others as fascinating to himself.

Mr. Courtenay Neuchamp, who inherited, in happier times, the ancestral hall, in Buckinghamshire, was an easy-going man of the world, combining a shrewd outlook upon his own affairs with the most perfect indifference as to how his neighbours managed theirs. He was a better man of business than Ernest, though he had not a tittle of his energy or fiery abstract zeal. So far from giving credit to his ancestors, and their spirited efforts, he bewailed their misdirected energies.

'They were a lot of narrow-minded busybodies,' he would often remark, 'incapable of managing their own affairs with decent success, and what little power they ever possessed they devoted to the annoyance of their neighbours, people probably much wiser than themselves.'

'They had noble aims, to which they gave their lives,' Ernest would reply; 'I reverence their memories deeply, fervently, more—a hundredfold—than if they had left us the largest manor in the county, amassed by greed and selfishness.'

'So don't I; nothing can be more disgraceful than to see the representatives of the oldest family in the shire (for these Tudors are of yesterday) possessed only of an estate of less acreage than a tenant-farmer tills, with an inconvenient old rookery, hardly good enough for the said tenant-farmer to live in. I wish I had lived a few centuries earlier.'

'You would have enlarged our borders,' said the younger son, 'but at what a cost! We boast a long roll of stainless ancestors, each of whom was true to his God, to his king, to his plighted word, and who called no man his master, save his anointed sovereign. You would have been cursed with an unhappy posterity of spendthrifts, profligates, oppressors of the poor or trucklers to the rich.'

'Gra' mercy! as we used to say, for thy prophecies and predictions. I see no necessity for vice being necessarily allied to success in life. I believe sometimes it is rather the other way. But you were always headstrong; slave to imagination, that misleader of humanity. Go on your own path, and you may convert all the Papuans, Australians, New Zealanders, or whatever they are, that you are going to waste your life among, if you have sufficient breathing time before you are roasted.'

'I am going to New South Wales, in Australia, where they don't roast people any more than in Bucks. But you will never read up on any subject.'

'Why the deuce should I?' demanded the senior. 'What earthly benefit can I derive from the manners and customs of foreign savages. We have them of our own and to spare. If thereby I could persuade these pig-headed tenants of ours to farm in a more enlightened way, and pay interest on capital advanced for *their* benefit, or learn how to get old Sir Giles Windereach to sell us back that corner his father bought of Slacklyne Neuchamp, I wouldn't mind. Why else should I read beastly dry books?'

'Because you would learn to take an interest in your kind, and might then propose to yourself the healthful task of trying to improve them.'

'But,' said Courtenay, rather disrespectfully, 'why should I improve those classes, from which as a land-owner and very minor capitalist, I find it hard enough to defend my property as it is? Go and test a grocer in arithmetic, you will find him the more accurate man, and the readier. Try a labourer at his own cart, and see how he is at once your superior. Depend upon it, all this upheaval of lower social strata is bad. Some day we may find that we have freed internal fires and exploded social volcanoes.'

'I shall make the attempt where I am going, however,' said Ernest with decision. 'It may be that there are peculiar advantages in a new land, and a sparse population, without the crushing vested interests which weigh one to the dust in the old world.'

'Perhaps you may gather some of the dust of the new, which is gold, they say, if they don't lie, as most probably they do. Then you can rear an Australian Neuchampstead, which will be the third, under such conditions, built by our family, if old records are true. I wish you were taking more capital with you, old fellow, though.'

Here the elder man slightly relaxed the cold undemonstrative regard which his aquiline features usually wore, as he gazed for a few moments upon the ardent expressive face of the cadet of his house. 'It's another of the family faults that we can neither stay decently together at home, nor fit out our knights-errant worthily for the crusade.'

'My dear Courtenay,' said the younger son, touched to the depth of a delicate and sensitive nature by the rare concession of the head of the house, 'things are best as they are. You have enough which you require. I have not enough, which is an equal necessity of my nature. I should die here like a falcon in a corn-chandler's shop, pining for the sweep of her long wings against the sea-cliff, where with wave and tempest she could scream in concert. Hope and adventure are my life, the breath of my nostrils, and forth I must go.'

'Well, my blessing go with you, Ernest; I neither mistrust your courage nor capacity, and in any land you will probably hold your own. But I should have more confidence in your success if you had less of that infernal Neuchamp taste for managing other people's affairs.'

'But, my dear Courtenay, is it not the part of a true knight and a Christian man to lead others into the right path? *We* thankfully accept it from others. I think of the many needs of a new land, and of the rude dwellers therein.'

'I hate to be put right—colonists may be of the same opinion. *You* never can be induced to do anything that is suggested by another, or any Neuchamp, that I ever heard of.'

'Because we take particular care to be identified with the latest, and most successful practice in all respects.'

'Because we are always right, I suppose. A comfortable theory, but of which the public cannot always be convinced. I never try to convince them—I merely wish to be left alone. That is where I differ from you.'

'You will never gain, however, by your principles, Courtenay.'

'You will lose your fortune by following out yours, Ernest.'

The conversation having ended, as had nearly all previous discussions between the brothers, in each adhering steadfastly to his own opinion, Ernest went his own way with the cheerful obstinacy of his character. He selected a ship and a colony. He ordered a large, comprehensive, and comparatively useless outfit. He purchased several books of fact and fiction, bearing upon the land of his adoption, for reading upon the voyage, and girding himself up, he finally completed all necessary arrangements. He bade farewell to the old home—to the villagers, whom he had known from boyhood—and to his friends and kinsfolk. He did then actually set sail in the clipper-ship *St. Swithin*, comforting himself with heroic parallels of all ages and all shades of maritime adventure.

On the voyage out, he made acquaintance with several agreeable people. Of these, many were, like himself, sailing to Australia for the first time. Others were returning to the great south land, where they had probably spent their early years, or indeed been born. Among these, though he was not aware of the fact, since they did not advertise it, was a family named Middleton, consisting of a father, mother, and two daughters. These last were quiet and well-mannered, but decidedly amusing. Alice Middleton was handsome and lively; Barbara was rather staid, given to reading, and did not talk much, except with congenial people. She, however, could speak very much to the point, should such speaking be needed. With this family Mr. Neuchamp became on sufficiently intimate terms to confide his views upon colonial life, including his hopes of benefiting the citizens of his adopted country by the inculcation of the newest English ideas in farming and other important subjects. He did not find that readiness of response which he had looked for. This puzzled and slightly annoyed him, as from their intelligent sympathy in other matters he had confidently reckoned upon their co-operation. Indeed he had discovered the second Miss

Middleton in the act of smiling, as if at his enthusiasm; while the matron, a shrewd, observant person, went the length of inquiring whether he did not think it would be better to see something of the country, before settling the affairs of its inhabitants.

'My dear Mrs. Middleton,' replied Mr. Neuchamp with grave dissent, 'I regret that I cannot see the force of your position. My feeling is that one is far more certain to criticise fairly and dispassionately a new land and a new state of society, while one's impressions are sharply and freshly defined. Afterwards, the finer lines are effaced by use, wont, and local prejudice. No! depend upon it, the newly-arrived observer has many advantages.'

'Then you do not think it possible,' said Alice Middleton, 'that the new—arrival should make any mistakes in his inspection of the unlucky colonists?'

'If he has cultivated his power of observation, and his critical faculty, so that he can trust himself to be just and impartial, I do not see that it matters whether he may have lived one year or ten in any given country.'

'You will find that it *does* matter,' retorted his fair antagonist, 'unless you are different from every other Englishman we have ever seen.'

'Why, have *you* lived in Australia?' inquired he with accents of extreme surprise. 'I had no idea of the fact.'

'We have been there all our lives,' said Barbara Middleton, 'excepting for the last three years. Why should you think we had not been there?'

'I—really—don't know,' protested Mr. Neuchamp, now discovering suddenly that he was on unsafe ground. 'I thought you were English, and making the voyage, like myself, for the first time.'

'Don't apologise,' laughed Alice; 'you may as well say at once that you thought we were too much like ordinary English people to be colonists,' and she made him a slight bow.

'Well, so I did,' confessed our hero, too honest to evade the expression of his opinions. 'But you know, you're so—well—you do expect a little difference in appearance, or manner—'

'Or complexion?' continued his fair tormentor. 'Did you think Australians were—just a little—dark?'

'I recant, and apologise, and sue for pardon,' said Ernest, now completely dislodged from his pedestal, a horrid thought obtruding itself that similar discoveries would narrow his mission to most uninteresting dimensions.

This 'check to his queen' sobered Mr. Neuchamp for several days. He began to question the probability of influencing society in Australia to any great extent, if the component parts were like the Middleton family.

However, he reflected that people of cultivated tastes and unexceptionable manners were rare in any country. And when he thought of the vast interior with its scattered untravelled population, hope revived and he again saw himself the 'guide, philosopher, and friend of a guileless and grateful people.'

There were several landed proprietors who held great possessions in Australia among the passengers, with whom he made a point of conversing whenever such conversation was possible. But here again unexpected hindrances and obstacles arose.

Mr. Neuchamp found that these returning Australians were rather reserved, and had very little to say about the land in which so large a portion of their lives had been passed. They committed themselves to the extent of stating in answer to his numerous inquiries, that it was a 'very fair sort of place—you could manage to live there.' 'As to the people?' 'Well, they were much like people everywhere else—some good, some bad.' 'Climate?' 'Hot in some places, cold in others.' 'Manners?''Well, many of the inhabitants hadn't any, but that was a complaint almost universal at the present day.' The oppressed colonist generally wound up by stating that when he, Neuchamp, had been in Australia for a year or two, he would know all about it.

All this was very unsatisfactory. As far as these pieces of evidence went, the *terra incognita* to which, after such rending of ancient associations and family ties, he was even now voyaging, was as prosaic as Middlesex or Kent. These people either did not know anything about their own country or their own people, or, with the absurd indifferentism of Englishmen, did not care. He was partly reassured by one of the more youthful passengers, who had not been very long away from his Australian birthland. He considerately raised Ernest's spirits, and his estimate of Australia as a 'wonderland,' by certain historiettes and tales of adventure by flood and field. But when he introduced Indians, habitual scalping, and a serpent fifty feet long, Mr. Neuchamp's course of reading enabled him to detect the unprincipled fabrication, and to withdraw with dignity.

In due course of time, the vessel which carried Mr. Neuchamp and his purpose arrived at her destination. The night was misty, so that he had no opportunity of comparing the harbour of Sydney with the numerous descriptions which he had read. He was met on the wharf by the perfectly British inquiry of 'Cab, sir, cab?' upon replying to which in the affirmative, he was rattled up to the Royal Hotel, and charged double fare, with a completeness and despatch upon which even a Shoreditch Station cabby could not have improved.

Having renovated himself with a bath and breakfast, Mr. Neuchamp proceeded to view the component parts of the busy street from the balcony of the great caravanserai. On the whole, he did not see any striking departure from the appearance of an ordinary London thoroughfare. There were omnibuses raking the whole length of the street, fore and aft, as it were, well horsed with upstanding powerful animals; the drivers, too, had something of the misanthropical air which the true 'busman always acquires after a certain period. Hansoms rattled about, with the express-train flavour peculiar to that luxurious vehicle for the unencumbered. Well-appointed carriages, from which descended fashionably attired dames and damsels, drew up at imposing haberdashers for a little early and quiet shopping. The foot passengers did not look as if they were likely to contribute to any Arabian Nights entertainment either. They wore chiefly black coats, I grieve to say black hats, and serious countenances, exactly like the mercantile and legal sections of the city men in London. The labourers wore the same shoddy suits, the sailors the same loose or inexplicable tightened garments, the postmen the same red coat, the shabby-genteel people the same threadbare ditto; even the blind man, with a barrel-organ, had the same reflectoral expression that he had often noticed. All the types were identical with those he had hoped to have left ten thousand miles away. Certainly he did see occasionally a sauntering squatter, bronzed, bearded, and *insouciant*; but he, again, was so near akin to a country gentleman who had taken a run to town, or a stray soldier on leave, that he was upon the point of exclaiming, 'How disgustingly English!' when a slight incident turned his thoughts to the far and wondrous interior. Down the street, on a grand-looking young horse, at a pace more suggestive of stretching out through endless forest-parks than of riding with propriety through a narrow and crowded thoroughfare, came a born bushman. He was a tall man, wearing a wide-leaved felt hat and a careless rig generally, such as suggested to Mr. Neuchamp the denizen of the waste, whom he had hungered and thirsted to see. Here he was in the flesh evidently, and Ernest drank in with greedy eyes his swarthy complexion, his erect yet easy seat on his horse. However, just as he was passing the hotel, whether the gallant nomad was looking another way, or whether he had considered the hour, early as it was, not unsuitable for refreshment, the fact must here be stated that the colt, observing some triumph of civilisation for the first time (a human advertising sandwich), stopped with deathlike suddenness; his rider was shot on to the crown of his head with startling force. Mr. Neuchamp was preparing to rush downstairs to the rescue, when a quietly attired passer-by stepped up to the snorting colt and, with a gentle adroitness that told of use and wont, secured and soothed him. The gallant bushman arose, looking half-stunned; then, gazing ruefully at the crown of his sombrero, he felt the top of his head somewhat distrustfully, and with a word of thanks to the stranger, who held the rein in a peculiar manner till he was safe in the saddle, mounted and pursued his way after a swift but guarded fashion. 'My word, sir,' was his single remark, 'I didn't think he'd ha' propped like that—thank *you* all the same.'

Inspirited by this incident as showing a possibility of lights and shadows even upon this too English foreground, Mr. Neuchamp thought that he would deliver one of his letters of introduction to a merchant, whose advice he had been specially recommended to take in the purchase of land, or of whatever property he should select for investment.

# CHAPTER II

When the past is reviewed, and the clear sad lamp of experience sheds its soft gleam upon the devious track, then are all apparent the scarce shunned precipices, the hidden pitfalls, the bones of long dead victims. Then can we measure the tender patience with which our guardian angel warned or wooed into safety.

Here, where we loitered all heedless, flower-crowned, and wine-flushed, languished the serpent syren, heavenly fair, but deadliest of all. We had been surely sped. But an idle impulse, the tone of a passing melody, led to change of purpose, of route, and we stood scatheless anon, having tripped lightly among deaths as sudden and shattering as the lighted explosive.

At the diverging roads, where dumb and scornful sat the sphinx of our destiny, while we lightly glanced at the path whence none return, save in such guise that death were dearer, why did our heedless footsteps cling all instinctively to the narrow, the thrice blessed way?

And yet again, in the dark hour when we should have been watchful as the mariner on an unknown shore, who casts the lead over every foot of the passage through which his barque seems so easily gliding, how was our careless pride brought low, how sudden was the sorrow, how dreary the bondage, till we were ransomed from the dungeon of the pitiless one. From what endless weeping would not, alas, a dim knowledge and recognition of the *first false step* have saved us!

Such a false step Mr. Neuchamp was nigh upon adopting, with all its train of evil consequences. At the mid-day *table d'hôte* at the Royal Hotel, sufficiently welcome to him after the weary main, sat a florid, good-looking, smiling, middle-aged man, evidently a gentleman, and not less surely connected with the country division. He happened, apparently by chance, to be seated next to Ernest, who was immediately attracted by his bonhomie, his humorous epigrammatic talk, joined to the outward signs and tokens of the man of the world.

'You have not been very long in this part of the country?' said the agreeable stranger.

Ernest slightly coloured as he replied, 'I certainly have not; but I confess I don't see why I should be *affiché* as a new and inexperienced traveller. You and I are dressed much alike, after all,' added he, glancing at the other's well-cut travelling suit of rough tweed and the black hat which hung beside his own upon the pegs provided for lunch-consuming visitors.

'True, quite true,' agreed his new acquaintance; 'and it is not, perhaps, good manners to remark upon a gentleman as a species of foreign novelty. I remember a few years since chafing at it myself. But my heart warms to an Englishman of a certain sort. And we Australians learn to know the Britisher by all manner of slight signs, including a fresh complexion. I really believe, if you will pardon my rudeness in guessing, that you come from near my own county?'

Ernest explained the locality of Neuchampstead, upon which the affable stranger rose and shook him violently with both hands, exclaiming, 'I could have sworn it. Our people have been friends for ages. I come from just over the border. You've heard of the Selmores, of Saleham?' mentioning county people well known by name to Ernest.

'Now this is very delightful,' said his new friend, after all explanations had been made, 'and I shall take charge of you without any scruple. You had better change your quarters to the New Holland Club. I can have you admitted as an honorary member without a day's delay. I am a member; but I came here to-day to meet a friend, and have done so most unexpectedly, eh, my dear Neuchamp?'

So irresistible was Mr. Selmore, that Ernest felt absolutely carried away by the stream of his decided manner, his good stories, his pleasant sarcasms, his foreign reminiscences, and his racy description of Australian bush-life (he owned several stations, it would seem, himself). So it was natural that after a bottle of hock, of a rare vintage, ordered in honour of their auspicious meeting, that he should confide to Mr. Selmore his plans of life, his leading ideas, and the amount of capital which he was free to invest in some description of landed property.

After they had compressed more droll, confidential, and semi-practical talk into a couple of hours than would have served for a week on board ship, Mr. Selmore proposed a stroll down the street towards the public gardens, which he thought his young friend would find novel and interesting.

As they lounged down the principal street Ernest was struck with the change in the appearance of the crowd which thronged one side of the footway, between the bisecting cross-streets. The hard and anxious faces of the world's workers which had filled the pavement in the morning had vanished, and in their stead were the flowerets of fashion, the gilded youth of the land, the butterflies of society, the fair faces of daintily attired girls, the unworn features of those ornamental human types which comprise no toilers, whatever may be the proportion of spinsters.

Mr. Neuchamp, whose sensitive organisation was still more highly attuned by the voyage, gazed with much interest upon this novel presentment. Again he could not help asking himself, 'Have I really left Britain? Is this a colony, or a magically sliced-off section of London life? The swells are identical to the turn of a moustache, or the set of a collar. That girl's bonnet has not been two months from Paris, for I saw the fellow of it, which had only that day arrived, on Cousin Amy's head the week I left home. Allah is great! Have I come to reform these people? However, this is only the city. All cities are alike, except, perhaps, Tangiers and Philadelphia. Wait till I get fairly into the bush!'

Thus, looking with pleased eyes and wondering mind, Mr. Neuchamp hardly noticed that his companion, as he swaggered easily along, seemed to know and be known of every one. He, however, did not care to stop to speak to his numerous friends. As they passed on, some of them, Ernest commenced to observe, regarded Mr. Selmore and himself with an amused expression. Keenly alive to colonial criticism, though proposing to pour so many vials of the British article upon the heads of these unsuspecting Arcadians, he noted more closely the manner and bearing of the still undiminished number of the 'friends of his friend' whom they encountered. It might have been fancy, but he thought that he saw a keen glance, in some instances not altogether of mirth, bestowed upon himself.

They had reached a side street, along which they passed, when three young men, irreproachably attired for the ante-prandial stroll, blocked the way.

'Where are you off to in such a hurry, you old humbug?' said a tall handsome man imperiously. 'You *can't* have any business at this time of day.'

'Not so sure of that,' chimed in another of the party. '*I see you've got your black hat with you*, Selmore.'

Mr. Selmore looked straight into the speaker's eyes for a moment, and then gravely taking off the upper covering referred to, stroked it, looked at it, and replaced it upon his head.

'Yes!' he said, 'Evelyn, I have; I prefer them, even in this confounded weather. They make a fellow look like a gentleman if it's in him, and not like a man going to a dog-fight, like that white abomination you have on.'

The trio laughed more heartily and continuously at this rejoinder than Ernest thought the wit justified, to the enjoyment of which Mr. Selmore abandoned them without ceremony, merely remarking to Ernest, though good fellows, they were awfully dissipated, and he could not recommend them as friends.

Before quitting the business part of the city, where the handsome massive stone buildings gave an Italian air to the narrow streets, Ernest's roving eye happened to light on the name of 'Frankston,' legended upon a conspicuously bright brass plate.

'Ha!' said he, 'I remember something about that name. Is he a merchant—do you know him?'

'Yes,' said Mr. Selmore indifferently, 'he is a merchant, and a tolerably sharp man of business too. Takes station accounts; but I forget, you don't quite understand our phrases yet. He would be called more a private banker where you and I hail from. Why do you ask?'

'Merely because I happen to have a letter of introduction to him from a man I met abroad once, and I shall deliver it to-morrow.'

Mr. Selmore did not look sympathetic at this announcement, but he said little in contravention of his young friend's resolve.

'You must keep your weather eye open, if he gets you out to that pretty place of his, Neuchamp, or you will find yourself saddled with a big station and a tight mortgage before you can look round you.'

Ernest had more than once thought himself extremely fortunate in meeting with Mr. Selmore at so early a period of his colonial career. Now he was confirmed in that opinion.

'My dear sir, I shall be more than cautious in any dealings with him, I assure you,' he said warmly. 'Are these the public gardens? How different from anything I have seen before, and how surpassingly beautiful!'

They roamed long amid the glories of that semi-tropical park, rich with the spoils of the Orient and many a fairy isle of the Great South Sea. As the palms and strangely formed forest trees waved in the breeze fresh from a thousand leagues of ocean foam, as the blue waters glanced and sparkled through the clustering foliage, while they sat under giant pines and looked over the sea-wall and at the white-winged sailing boats flitting over the wavelets of the ocean-lake which men call the harbour of Sydney, Mr. Neuchamp freely acknowledged his wonder and his admiration. Stronger than ever was his faith in the destiny of a people with whom he was fixed in determination henceforth to cast in his lot.

Mr. Selmore had obtained his consent to dine with him at a well-known *café*, and thither, after visiting the baths, as the short twilight was deepening into night, they wended their way.

Upon entering the room the appearance of an extremely well-arranged dinner service was pleasant enough to view, after the somewhat less ornamental garniture of the table of a clipper-ship.

Ernest was introduced to two other friends of Mr. Selmore, also of the pastoral persuasion, and who looked as if town visiting was the exception in their rule of life.

The dinner passed off very pleasantly. The *menu* was well chosen, the cooking more than respectable, the wines unimpeachable. Ernest was sober from habit and principle. It would have been vain to have made the attempt to induce him to exceed. Still, with all reasonable moderation, it must be confessed that a man takes a more hopeful view of life after a good dinner, more especially in the days of joyous youth.

Mr. Selmore's friends were up-country dwellers, and it appeared that they were, in some sort, neighbours of his when at home. Much of the conversation insensibly took the direction of stock-farming, and Mr. Neuchamp found himself listening to tales of crossing flooded rivers with droves bound for a high market, or of tens of thousands of sheep bought and sold in a day, or the wonderful price of wool, while intermingled were descriptions of feats of horsemanship varied with an occasional encounter with wild blacks.

In the midst of all this, Mr. Neuchamp's ardour kindled to such a pitch that he could not forbear asking one of the last arrived strangers whether there was not any station for sale in their district that would be suitable for him.

One of the pastorals looked at the other in astonishment, when they both looked reproachfully at Mr. Selmore.

'You don't mean to say,' at length broke out the older man, whose assiduity to the bottle had been unabated, 'that you haven't told our young friend here that Gammon Downs is for sale, 'pon my soul it's too bad!'

'Why, it's the very place in the whole blessed colony,' said the other, 'for a new arrival—good water, good sheep, a nice handy little run, and the best house in the district.'

Mr. Neuchamp was so struck with the expressive and interrogatory looks of the two bush residents, that he bent a searching look upon Mr. Selmore, as if he had in some mysterious way been ill-treated by the withholding of confidence.

'Well,' at length spoke out that gentleman, with an air of manly frankness, '*you* know me too well to think that I should propose to sell one of my own runs to a friend, comparatively inexperienced, of course, though well up in English farming, on the very first day I had met him. There *are* people, of course, who would do this, and more—but Hartley Selmore is not one of that sort.'

'But it does seem a shame,' said the grizzled squatter, filling his glass, 'that if you have one of the best runs in the country, that you should refuse to sell it to this gentleman merely because he is a personal friend.'

'Thank you,' said Ernest warmly, 'you have interpreted my sentiments admirably. If this estate, or station, would be so suitable, why should we not come to terms about it like any one else?'

'So remarkably cheap too,' said the other man; 'but I suppose Selmore wants a lot of cash down.'

'I have only five thousand pounds,' said Mr. Neuchamp, 'and perhaps your property is far above that limit.'

'It *is* less than I thought of taking,' said Mr. Selmore thoughtfully; 'but, yes; I don't mind arranging for bills, at one and two years, which, of course, if you bought, could be easily paid out of the profits of the station. But pass the claret, we won't talk any more shop to-night. Just so far that my friends, who live near my place, are going up the day after to-morrow. They will be glad of your company, and will show you the wonders of the bush, including Gammon Downs. You can then, my dear Neuchamp, judge for yourself.'

This plan appearing to Ernest to combine the utmost liberality on the part of the vendor with special advantages to the purchaser, who could have abundant time to examine and deliberate about his investment, was promptly acceded to.

He departed at the close of the evening to the hotel, at which place he had decided to stay, notwithstanding the tempting offer of a club bedroom. Ernest Neuchamp was not minded to give up his habits of observation, and for the exercise of his pursuit he deemed the hostelry of the period more favourable than any modern club.

Human nature is so constituted that a project feasible, favourable, and merely needing the very smallest propulsion into action over night wears a changed aspect with the dawn. As Mr. Neuchamp regained his suspended senses in a hot and mosquito-raided upper chamber in the Royal, the idea of becoming at a plunge the proprietor of Gammon Downs showed less alluring than over the joyous claret-illumined board of yester eve. What if the name (given by the rude pioneers, it had been explained to him from some nonsensical circumstance) should be only too correct a designation for a delusive investment? What if Mr. Selmore were a little *too* obliging, confidential, and considerate for a true and generous vendor? What if his companions, who certainly appreciated the claret, were likely from friendship or interest to be leagued against the stranger? It behoved him to be careful. The slender resources of Neuchampstead had been strained to their utmost to supplement his younger brother's portion. Were this lost he could never regain his position. And though with the recklessness of a sanguine temperament, he would, without much regret, have addressed himself to the task of carving out a fortune with his own right hand in this land of promise, still he fully recognised the vast difference between a capital even of moderate amount and none at all.

Throwing on a few clothes hastily, he strolled off towards the baths, and after a leisurely swim in the cool translucent wave, he found his appetite for breakfast improved and his mental vision obviously cleared. He arrived at divers and various wise resolutions; and one of them was to call upon Mr. Frankston, the merchant. Two heads are better than one, decided Mr. Neuchamp sapiently, and Granville said that this old gentleman's head was an exceedingly good one, nearly, but not quite, as good as his heart.

Discovering with some difficulty the precise street, almost a lane, where he had suddenly descried the well-remembered name, he walked into this office about half-past ten o'clock, and inquired for the head of the house. The clerk civilly motioned him to a chair, telling him that Mr. Frankston was engaged, but would not probably be long, as the gentleman with him was Captain Carryall, in an awful hurry to put to sea.

In rather less than five minutes the door opened suddenly, emitting a loud burst of laughter, and a tall sun-tanned man in a frock-coat, whose bold bright eyes were dancing again with fun and covert enjoyment of an apparently very keen jest.

As more than one anxious-looking person had passed into the outer office, Ernest walked in, and found himself in the presence of a stoutish old gentleman, with a high-coloured, clean-shaved countenance, who was chuckling with great relish, and subsiding from an exhausting fit of merriment. His white waistcoat predominated much over his clothing generally, giving that colour, with the aid of a spotless domain of shirt-collar and shirt-front, an unfair advantage over his sad-coloured suit of gray tweed.

'Good-morning to you, sir,—won't you take a chair,' said the old gentleman with much civility. 'Very rude to be laughing in the face of a visitor. But that Captain Carryall told me the best story I've heard for ages. Picked it up at the islands last cruise. Awful fellow! You'd excuse me, I'm sure, if you knew him. How can I be of use to you, my dear sir?'

This last query belonged evidently to another region than the one into which the sea-captain, with his *cœur-de-lion* face, had allured him. So Ernest produced his card, and a note 'from their mutual friend, Mr. Granville, he believed.' The old merchant glanced at the signature, and without another look hurled himself out of his armchair, and seizing Mr. Neuchamp's hand, wrung it with affectionate earnestness.

'My dear sir—my dear fellow,' gasped he; 'I'd have given a hundred pounds if our friend could have been here, and heard that yarn of Charley Carryall's. Now, attend to me while I tell you what you've got to do. You'll have enough to amuse yourself till five o'clock, and then you're to come here with your trunk. The carriage will call punctually at that hour, and you're to come out with me to my little place, on the South Head Road, and confer upon me the very great obligation of staying with me till you go up the country—if you do go. Now, isn't that settled?'

'I am very sorry,' stammered Ernest; 'it is so extremely kind of you; but I have more than half promised to go up the country to-morrow to look at a station with a view to buying it.'

'And get sold yourself,' interjected Mr. Frankston. 'Not just yet, if you'll be my boy for a year or two. Whose desirable property is it?'

'It belongs to a Mr. Selmore, whom I met at the Royal Hotel,' answered Ernest, 'who was very kind, and gave me some very good advice.'

'Ha! ha! ha!' shouted the old boy, becoming very purple in the face; 'knew it was him—Gammon Downs, eh! Wonderful man, take in his own father if he was hard up, and suffer his venerable grandsire and maiden aunts to invest their last penny in a sour grass country, with fluky sheep, Cumberland and scab given in. Hanged if he wouldn't, and go to church immediately afterwards. Most remarkable man, Hartley Selmore!'

Mr. Neuchamp wondered how Mr. Frankston knew the name of Mr. Selmore's valuable estate, and how he had ever made any money, if he did nothing but laugh. Indeed, it seemed to be his chief occupation in life, judging from his conduct since they had met.

'Then you would not advise me to invest just at present?' inquired he.

'Not unless you wish to be in the possession of a small, *very* small amount of experience, and not one solitary copper at the end of twelve months,' said Mr. Frankston, with great decision. 'This is a bad time to buy, stock are falling. Don't begin at all till you see your way. If you meet Selmore tell him you've changed your mind for the present, and will write and let him know when it is convenient for you to inspect Gammon Downs. Five, sharp! old man;' and with a paternal glance in his quick twinkling eye, Mr. Frankston made an affirmative nod to his chief clerk, who then and there entered, and a farewell one to Ernest, who after he left the portals stood for a moment like a man in a dream.

'This is certainly a most remarkable country,' he soliloquised; 'with their outward resemblance to Englishmen, there must be some strange mental divergence not easily fathomed. I remember Granville telling me that this old buffer was a better father to him than his own had ever been, or some such strong expression; therefore I will at once decide to act upon his advice; Selmore and his winning way, notwithstanding. One must take up a position firmly or not at all. So I shall elect to stand or fall by this apoplectic old white-waistcoated guardian angel, as he proposes to be.'

'My dear Neuchamp,' said a cheery voice, while a cheery hand smote him familiarly on the back, 'you look absorbed in contemplation. This is the wrong country for that. Action, sir, action is the word in Australia. Now, do you know what I was doing when I ran against you?—actually going down to Bliss's livery stables to see if I could pick you out a decent hack. Burstall and Scouter are going to start early to-morrow, and of course you'll want a hack that won't frighten you after coming from the old country. With luck you'll be under the verandah at Gammon Downs on the afternoon of the fourth day.'

Ernest braced himself together, and fixing his eyes upon the somewhat shifting orbs of his agreeable friend, said with studied calmness—

'I shall be extremely sorry, my dear sir, to put you or your friends to any inconvenience on my account, but I have changed my mind, and do not think of leaving Sydney for a month or two.'

He was conscious of a stern, half-angry, searching gaze, which seemed to drag out of his countenance every word of the conversation with Mr. Frankston, before Mr. Selmore said grandly, 'I am sorry to hear that you have so suddenly altered your plans. I had written to the overseer at Gammon Downs to have everything in readiness to receive you, and Burstall and Scouter will, I know, be put out at losing the pleasure of your company. But of course if you have made other arrangements—only I am afraid that if you don't feel disposed to name a day for visiting Gammon Downs I may possibly dispose of it privately, and as the subject has cropped up (not at my initiation, you are aware), I do honestly think that no place in the country would have suited you half as well.'

Ernest felt sorely tempted to say that in a fortnight or three weeks he would be able to go up, but he remembered Mr. Frankston's suggestion, and rather coldly answered that he would write and inform Mr. Selmore when it would be convenient for him to inspect Gammon Downs. The inevitable smile, which was worn in all weathers upon the face of Hartley Selmore, had so little real sincerity about it after this statement, that when he had received a warm parting grasp, Ernest felt strongly convinced that he had fitted the right arrow to the string.

# CHAPTER III

In one respect at least it cannot be denied that the new country differs widely from the old. Events of important and fateful nature succeed each other with a rapidity so great as to affect the actor with a sensation of unreality. He soon learns, however, that this high-pressure transaction of life involves issues none the less exacting of consequences. He recognises the necessity of watchfulness, of prompt decision, and abandons himself to the accelerated rate of speed with a degree of confidence which he cannot help suspecting to be recklessness in disguise. It may be that ideas akin to this view of the subject passed through Mr. Neuchamp's reflective mind while waiting for the appointed time at which he was to meet Mr. Frankston at his office. But a few hours since he had been on the verge of a headlong and what now appeared to him a dangerous investment, in which his whole capital might have been swamped, and his plans for social and colonial regeneration delayed for years, if not wholly frustrated. Now, with an equally violent oscillation, he had abandoned one recent friend, and adopted another equally unknown; to-morrow he might be embarked upon another project with equal risk of proximity to a colonial whirlpool capable of swallowing an argosy. What was he to do in this frightful procession, where fortune and ruin followed each other upon the path of life like express trains?

Was there such a thing as prudence, hesitation, or delay in Australian business matters? He would not be so credulous again. Was this cheerful old merchant, whose speech was kindness, and whose eye was truth apparently, to be unreservedly trusted? He would hear what his counsel was like meanwhile; he knew his friend Granville to be clear-sighted and direct. He fully trusted him, and had good reason to do so. Yes—he would put his fortune on this die. *Vogue la galère!*

He had consulted his watch more than once before the hansom deposited him with a portmanteau at the office of Paul Frankston and Co., at two minutes past five o'clock. Just afterwards, a well-appointed carriage, drawn by a well-matched pair of bays, drove rapidly up to the door. As he was approvingly regarding the well-bred horses, he did not observe that a young lady inside was essaying to open the door of the carriage. Ernest, shocked at his unchivalrous conduct, rushed to the door, wrenched it open, and with a slight but deferential bow assisted her to alight. She walked at once into the office, followed by Mr. Neuchamp.

'I have been to Shaddock's, papa, for some books, and I thought I was late,' she said, throwing her arms round the old man's neck, unconscious that Ernest was immediately behind.

'You're generally punctual, puss, and so I won't scold her, Mr. Neuchamp,' said the old boy with his customary chuckle, as the young lady turned round and beheld with surprise the involuntary witness of her tribute of affection. 'Mr. Neuchamp, my daughter Antonia. My dear, this gentleman is coming to stay with us for a few months—for a year or two—all his life, perhaps, so the sooner you get acquainted the better.'

Then the young lady smiled, and hoped that Mr. Neuchamp would find their house pleasant, and become accustomed in time to papa's jokes.

'I can tell you it's no joke at all, miss. You know very well that if Mr. Granville would have had you, I should have ordered you to marry him forthwith. Now, Mr. Neuchamp is a great friend of his, and all we can do for him will be too little.'

'Mr. Granville was the nicest man I ever met,' affirmed the young lady. 'As for marrying, that is another matter. I daresay Mr. Neuchamp is coming to a proper understanding about your assertions, papa. How do you like the view, Mr. Neuchamp?'

As she spoke she leaned partly out of the carriage and gazed seawards. They were now driving upon a rather narrow and winding road, smoothly gravelled and well kept, much like a country lane in England. On the southern side the hill rose abruptly above them; on the lower side a dwarf wall of sandstone blocks occasionally protected the traveller from a too precipitous descent. Shrubs and flowers, as strange to Mr. Neuchamp as the flora of the far-famed bay, but a mile or two from them now, was to Sir Joseph Banks, bordered the road on either side in rich profusion. But the eye roamed over the intervening valley, over villas of trim beauty, clean-cut in the delicately pale sandstone, to the wondrous beauty of the landlocked sea. Blue as the Ægean, it was superior in its astonishing wealth of bays, mimic quays, and peerless anchorage to any harbour in the world. Crafts of all kinds and sizes floated upon its unruffled wave, from the majestic ocean steamer, gliding proudly to her anchorage, to the white-winged, over-rigged sailing boat, with her crew of lads seated desperately on her windward gunnel, to squatter out like a brood of wild ducks and right their crank craft, should fortune and the breeze desert them. Northward rose the 'sullen shape' of the great sandstone promontory, the North Head, towering over the surges that break endlessly at its base, and with its twin sentinel of the south, guarding the narrow entrance to the unrivalled haven. The fresh breeze swept through the girl's hair and tinged her cheek with a transient glow, as she said, 'Is not that lovely? I have seen it almost daily for years, but it never palls on me.'

'Beautiful as a dream landscape,' said Ernest from his heart. 'It makes one recall dear old Sir Walter's words—

'"Where's the coward that would not dare

To fight for such a land?"'

'We are a peaceful people so far,' said Mr. Frankston; 'but I fancy that we should take to war kindly enough in the event of invasion, for instance, and hammer away as briskly and as doggedly as our forefathers.'

'How many years have you been in this colony, may I ask?' said Ernest. 'Not long enough to shake off British feelings and prejudices, I am certain.'

'About ten years,' deposed Mr. Frankston confidently.

'Oh, papa!' said Miss Antonia.

'Well!' said the old gentleman, looking roguishly at her, 'I may have been here a *leetle* longer; but I am within the strict limits of truth in stating I have been here for ten years—there is no doubt about that.'

Thus chatting, they had arrived at a pair of iron gates, through which entering, they turned into the smoothest of gravel roads, which was obviously watered daily.

The grounds through which the upstanding bay horses bore them over the superb gravel, were extensive, but in perfect order. Many of the trees, chiefly of semi-tropical habit, were of great age, and their broad glossy leaves, faintly stirred by the sea-breeze, had a murmuring sound, which told the heart of an imaginative listener tales of a calm enchanted main of coral reefs, of palm-fringed, milk-white strands, and all the wonders of the charmed Isles of the Great South Sea.

They drew up at the door of a large old-fashioned mansion, built of pale sandstone and surmounted by an extremely broad paved verandah, looking like a section of an ice-house.

'Mr. Neuchamp!' said the old gentleman, 'this is your home as long as you are in Australia. I hope you like the look of it. It's exactly twelve minutes to dinner-time; so I recommend both of you to waste no time in dressing. James!'

A serious-looking man-servant advanced, and taking Ernest's portmanteau inducted him into a fascinating bedroom, with such a view of the sea that he was nearly led into forgetting the old gentleman's paternal admonition, and being late for dinner.

However, by putting on extra steam, after the important transaction of the tie was completed, he managed to re-enter the hall just as Mr. Frankston came skipping downstairs, and was immediately entrusted with the care of Miss Frankston as far as the dining-room.

The evening was warm, but the perfection of cookery, combined with the quality and temperature of the wines to prevent any deep feeling of inconvenience. Miss Frankston talked pleasantly and unaffectedly, while the old gentleman neglected no opportunity of interjecting a joke or telling some remarkably good story, for Mr. Neuchamp's benefit, of which his daughter did not always see the point.

After dinner Miss Frankston retired, with an assurance from her father that they did not intend to absent themselves for more than ten minutes, after which the serious butler brought in tenderly another bottle of claret, and departed.

'Fill your glass, Mr. Neuchamp,' said the old man; 'it won't hurt your head, nor your—any other part, I guarantee, for I imported it myself, and let us talk a *very* little business. What do you think of doing?'

'My intention is fixed to purchase a landed property, an estate or station, as you call them. Of course I can only begin in a small way, and that was why Mr. Selmore's place, Gammon Downs, seemed particularly suited.'

'Gammon Downs has ruined every man but Selmore, who has ever had anything to do with it. It's a sour, bad little place, in which you would have lost all your money in about a year, and would have had to sell, or give away, the stock.'

'And did Mr. Selmore know that it was a bad investment, an undesirable property, when he offered it to me?'

'I am sorry to say,' quoth the old gentleman, 'that he *did* know it, perfectly well; he knew that it has ruined half a dozen men, whose names I could give you.'

'And is he considered to be a gentleman, and a man of honour, in this part of the world?' inquired Mr. Neuchamp in tones of great surprise.

'Well, he *is* a gentleman—that is, if good birth, good manners, and a good education go to make one. But he has always speculated to the verge of his capital, and now, stock being rather low, he is decidedly hard up. But he is a wonderfully sharp hand, and he generally contrives to get hold of a "black hat" at least once a year, which has pulled him through so far.'

'A black hat?' demanded Ernest; 'and why not?—they seem common enough. And why should a hat, black or white, help him in any way?'

'You don't quite understand,' answered Mr. Frankston, with a twinkle of his fun-loving gray eyes, 'though it is more a bush expression than a town one, and rather slangy. A "black hat" in Australian parlance means a new arrival. And as people without colonial experience, like yourself, for instance, cannot be expected to understand the relative value of stock and stations, such a purchaser falls an easy prey to a talented but unscrupulous man like your friend Selmore.'

A light suddenly illumined the understanding of Mr. Neuchamp, whose faculties, like those of enthusiasts generally, were keen, if occasionally misdirected.

'So *that* was what his friend Evelyn laughingly alluded to when they met us yesterday. "I see you have your black hat with you," he said.'

'By Jove! you don't say so; did Evelyn say that?' laughed the commercial mentor; 'just like him; for two pins he'd have warned you not to believe a word he said. Fine fellow, Evelyn! And what did Mr. Selmore say?'

'He only smiled, took off his own hat—an ordinary "Lincoln and Bennett"—stroked it, and put it on his head again.'

'Capital, capital! O lord! that was Selmore all over. You can't easily match him. He has the devil's own readiness. Deuced clever fellow he always was! It's a pity, too, really it is. If he were not so desperately cornered, I believe he's a kind-hearted fellow in the main. But when he has bills to meet he'd take in his own father.'

'Thou shalt want ere I want,' as that famous freelance, Mr. Dugald Dalgetty, formerly of Marischal College, remarked, thought Ernest; but he said, 'It seems then that my small capital was very nearly appropriated to the retirement of Mr. Selmore's bills payable, which was *not* my primary intention in choosing a colonial career. My dear sir, I shall never be sufficiently thankful for your kind advice. What would you advise me to do now, if I may trespass further on your great kindness?'

'My dear boy, as Granville's friend, I look upon you as my son temporarily; and if I had a son who had just completed his education and wished to purchase station property, I should say to him, this is a country and stock-farming is a profession not to be understood all at once. Before investing your money spend a little time in learning the ways of the people of the country and of the management of stock before you invest a shilling.'

'And how long do you think a man of reasonable intelligence ought to be in gaining the requisite knowledge?' asked Ernest, rather dismayed at the prospect of a lengthened term of apprenticeship.

'Not a day less than two years,' answered Mr. Frankston decisively. 'My advice to you is to travel for a month or two through the interior, and then to locate yourself on some station where you can acquire the details of practical management.'

'But will not that be expensive, and what could I do with my money in the meantime?'

'It will not be expensive; and as to your money, you can lodge it in a bank, where you will receive interest at current rates. You can select any of our Sydney banks, which are quite as safe as the Bank of England. I shall then be happy to give you introductions which will secure you a home and the means of acquiring the necessary knowledge.'

'Thanks, a thousand thanks,' quoth Ernest, much relieved; 'at any rate I shall feel safe. I shall gladly take your advice; and the sooner I am off the better.'

'Better stay a month with me,' urged the kind-hearted old boy; 'there is plenty of time for you to learn all about stock, and how to distinguish between Gammon Downs and a run that, if it doesn't make a fortune all at once, will not ruin you under five years at any rate.'

But the man to whom he spoke had not crossed ten thousand miles of ocean, torn up old associations, and severed himself from the inherited life of an English country gentleman, to linger by the wayside. So he made answer—

'My dear sir, I feel that if I have left many good friends behind I have found one as kind and more effectual in help and counsel. But my purpose is fixed. I cannot rest without I feel that I am on my way to its fulfilment. With your permission I must leave town next week at farthest.'

'Well, well—I am not sure but that you are wise. Sydney is an easy place to spend money in, and there is nothing like buckling to when there is work to be done. I must see and pick you up a horse.'

'Do you know,' said Mr. Neuchamp, with an air of slight diffidence, 'that I much prefer to walk; I shall see more of the country and be less hampered, I imagine, on foot.'

'*Walk! walk!*' repeated Mr. Frankston, rather taken aback; 'don't think of it.'

'Why not, may I ask?'

'Because in this country no one walks. It is too hot for that sort of thing, and it is not exactly the thing for a gentleman.'

'But,' pleaded Ernest, 'I am a tolerable pedestrian; many a pleasant walking tour I have had in England, and indeed on the Continent. Is there any danger?'

'None, that I am aware of—but I would certainly advise you to get a horse, or a couple; they are cheap enough here.'

'You won't be offended if I say that I really prefer walking. It is a capital thing in many ways; and I shall not get a chance of seeing Australian life without conventional spectacles so easily again perhaps.'

'Please yourself, then,' said Mr. Frankston; 'I am very much in favour of letting people alone, particularly in unimportant matters; you will find out for yourself, I daresay, why I advised you to commence your journey on the outside of a good horse. You won't take any more wine? Then we'll go and get a cup of coffee from Antonia.'

They found that young lady ensconced in a large cane chair upon the balcony in front of the drawing-room, gazing dreamily over the dark glimmering waters.

'You will find coffee on that round table, Mr. Neuchamp; and you, papa, will find your cigar-case on that ledge. Mr. Neuchamp, if you like to smoke, pray do so; I have no dislike to it in the open air.'

Mr. Neuchamp did not smoke. He held it to be a waste of time, of money, of brain-power; leading likewise to a false content with circumstances, with which the true man should wage ceaseless warfare. So he brought his chair near to that of Miss Frankston, and as the old gentleman lighted his cigar and leaned back in much comfort at some distance, he felt fully disposed for a little æsthetic talk.

'What a glorious night,' he remarked, 'with this faint fresh sea-breeze! how grand the effect of the darkly bright water, the burning stars, and this superb cloudless heaven!'

'It is so indescribably glorious,' made answer Miss Frankston, 'that I feel incensed with myself for not delighting in it more freshly and intensely. But it is thus with all familiar marvels that one has seen all one's life.'

'All one's life?' repeated he.

'I was born in this house,' said she simply, 'and have sat on a chair like this, and gazed on the sea, as we are doing now, when I was a small lonely child.'

'Oh! dreamy and luxurious southerner,' laughed he. 'A life of lotus-eating! Has it affected the tenor of your mind with any indisposition to exertion or change?'

'As far as I can pretend to know, it has had the reverse tendency in my case. I have always had a passionate desire to travel. I am my father's own daughter in that respect, he says.'

'And where has Mr. Frankston chiefly been?'

'Where has he not been? When he was young he managed to get away to sea, and roamed about the world splendidly; he has been to New Zealand, of course; all over the South Sea Islands; besides having travelled to England and the Continent, the East and West Indies, Russia, America, China, and Japan.'

'You quite take my breath away. Your papa is a perfect Marco Polo. But why should he have gone to England?'

'In order to see it, of course. Every Australian with sufficient brains to comprehend that there are more streets in the world than George Street would like to do that.'

'And was Mr. Frankston born in Australia? I thought he told me that he had been ten years here.'

'So he has been, and fifty more. He did not say *only* ten years. He likes to joke about being taken for an Englishman, and says it is because he has a red face and a white waistcoat.'

'Well, I do not see the resemblance on those grounds,' made answer Mr. Neuchamp guardedly. 'But really, your papa is so exactly like an old gentleman of my acquaintance, who is a very Briton of Britons, that I took it for granted that he must be English.'

'So he is English, and so am I English; only we were not born in that small great country. But you *must* think that there ought to be some distinguishing manner, or accent, about Australians, or you would not exhibit surprise at the resemblance.'

'If I ever had such an absurd idea, I am now entirely disabused of it,' said Mr. Neuchamp gallantly; 'and I must hope that in a short time to come I may be taken for an Australian, of which at present there is not apparently the least prospect.'

'Indeed, there is not,' replied Miss Frankston; 'pray excuse my smiling at the idea.'

'But why should I be so advertised, apparently by my whole personal effect upon society, that the waiters at the hotel are as aware of the fact, the cabmen, the persons whom I pass in the street, as if I had "passenger's luggage" marked on my shirt-front? It is not entirely my complexion, for I see blonde people in every direction; nor my clothes, nor my speech, I hope.'

'I do not know, indeed. I cannot say. There must be some difference, or people would not notice it. But you must not imagine that because you are known to have just come from home that anything short of a compliment is intended. Indeed,' said the girl with some diffidence, 'it's quite the other way.'

'I am delighted to hear you say so,' returned Mr. Neuchamp, 'and it will comfort Wilhelm Meister during his "Wanderjähre."'

'Kennst du das Land?'

sang she. 'Are you fond of music, Mr. Neuchamp? for I think I shall go in and give papa his nightly allowance of harmony. He refuses always to go to bed until I have sung to him. You had better keep him company.'

Mr. Neuchamp did so, the air of the balcony and the sight of the wondrous Southern Cross being as yet more attractive than the lady of the castle and her song.

'That's right,' said the old gentleman, lighting another cigar and composing himself to listen. 'Pity you don't smoke; it's an added pleasure, and one hasn't too many in this world. It's a luxury that lasts—one of the few things you can do as well when you're old as when you are young.'

'I must differ from you,' returned Mr. Neuchamp. 'I think it often leads to the wasting of valuable time, but I bow to your greater experience.'

'And greater age; and you are right to be on the self-denying side for the present. But ask yourself what an old buffer like myself can do with his evenings more profitably. My eyes—not so good as they were thirty years since—have generally had a fair day's work before dinner-time. Cards, talk, and a moderate smoke make up an old man's evening. When I look at the sea here—and she always was a good friend to me—hear Antonia sing and play—bless her heart! and smoke a very good cigar, it is rather a cunningly mixed enjoyment, you must own. Now she's off!'

The last statement was made simultaneously with the first notes of a song which floated out through the opened French windows, and proved to Mr. Neuchamp—a fair connoisseur—that his hostess had a fresh, true, soprano voice, and rather unusual execution. As he sat listening to song after song which Miss Frankston bestowed upon them with an utter absence of apologetic affectation, as the stars burned more brightly in the cloudless southern sky, as the wavelets kept their rhythmical murmurous monotone, he involuntarily asked himself if he had left *all* the social luxuries in the other hemisphere.

'This is pleasant,' said the merchant, after a long silence of words, with something between a sigh and a shake; 'but there are such things as breakfast and business for to-morrow. We must end the concert. Make for that small table in the corner.'

Upon the piece of furniture referred to there stood a silver-encrusted inviting spirit-stand, with a bottle of iced Marco-brünner.

'You must allow me to thank you for your songs, Miss Frankston,' said Ernest; 'whether the surroundings completed the witchery I cannot tell, but I have rarely enjoyed music so much.'

'I am glad you like my singing,' said she simply; 'we see so few people that I am not always sure whether my old music-master and myself extract the correct expression in much of our practice.'

'I can assure you of the correctness of your rendering,' promptly assented the stranger-critic. 'I heard the last song you were good enough to favour us with sung the week before I left. It had just been published. And I certainly prefer a slight emendation, which I think you have made.'

'Most satisfactory!' said she, with a mock inclination of respect; 'and now good-night. Papa and breakfast wait for no man.'

# CHAPTER IV

Few things are pleasanter, in their way, than staying in an agreeable house, while the welcome, the local recreations, the allotted leisure, are alike in the fresh bloom of unexhausted enjoyment. Your justifiable curiosity as to your friends' intellects, experiences, and power of amusing you is for a while unsatiated. All is new and delightful; to be savoured with the full approval of conscience. The gardens are enchanted, the ladye peerless fair, the stranger knights courteous, the host an incarnation of appreciation and generosity. All this glamour lasts undiminished for the first fleeting week or two, possibly survives the month. Then the process of disenchantment commences. Either you have business external to the castle, or you have not. In the former case, you begin to feel darkly fearful of neglect, and conscience, if you keep one, self-interest if you do not, commences to be 'faithful,' even to inconvenience. If you own no care, or tie, or duty, which may not be postponed to the 'Cynthias of the minute,' and still prolong your stay, you cease to be a guest and fall into the more prosaic *rôle* of *habitué*, inmate, lodger, amenable to family rules and to criticism. Then the fair ladye, if she be the sole cause of detention, is at times sharply scanned, lest the proverbial chandelier bear hard on the value of the entertainment. On the whole, a state of perpetual arrival at the mansions of favourably prejudiced strangers, combined with comparatively early departure,—unerringly anticipating the first shade of social satiety,—would probably comprise most of the pleasurable sensations permissible in this imperfect existence.

Mr. Neuchamp had, from the first, no thought of trenching upon even the border of this 'debatable land'; for after a very short trial of this pleasant life he told Miss Frankston that if he stayed for twelve months, he should still find new objects of interest. He thereupon completed the painful process known as 'making up one's mind,' and arranged to leave for the interior on the following day. Not that he was peculiarly sensible to any state of uncertainty. His enthusiastic temperament saved him from indecision. Having, with what he believed to be sufficient care and circumspection, elaborated a plan, he was uneasy and incapable of enjoyment until an advance in line was made. His, the fervid temperament, which delights itself with intensifying the action of all warfare, declared against circumstance, ever the foe of generous youth and ardent manhood.

So impatient was Mr. Neuchamp to hear the first shot of his campaign fired, that he had the stern virtue to refuse to remain another week for a certain picnic, at which all the notabilities of the metropolis were to be present, and at which the purest form of social pleasure might be anticipated.

'My dear Miss Frankston,' replied he, when urged upon this subject by Antonia, 'I grieve that I cannot consistently comply with your kind request. But I feel myself so rapidly turning into a mere town lounger, that I am sure another week or two would complete the transformation, and my moral ruin. For besides, unfortunately'—here he smiled at his expressed regret—'I fixed to-morrow for my departure from your most pleasant and hospitable home, and I *never* alter my plans.'

'I should be very sorry to wish you to alter them for our sake,' said the girl, unable, however, to suppress a slight tone of pique. 'No doubt you will be much happier exploring the highway across the Blue Mountains, which, of course, will be a great novelty to you. But I should not have thought a few days would have made any difference. You will find it dull enough at Garrandilla, where you are going.'

'Dull!' said he, 'dull! in the heart of a new continent, a new world, with untold stores of new plants, new companions, new experiences, the outset of a new life. My dear Miss Antonia, how *can* it be dull to any person of ordinary intelligence?'

'Well,' answered she, smiling, 'perhaps it is I who am dull for thinking so. Most young men who have left our house for the interior have been of that opinion. But I will not attempt to cloud your anticipations. Only, I really *do* think you ought not to walk.'

'Why not? What possible difference can it make how I get over the twenty or thirty miles a day before I reach the station, to which your father has so kindly given me letters of introduction? Such jolly walking tours as I have had in England and Wales, in Ireland, and one lovely vacation tour in our old home, Normandy.'

'What a charming thing to be able to see the place where one's ancestors lived a thousand years ago!' said she eagerly. (Mr. Neuchamp, having let slip the admission of the early settlement of his family in that rather stirring Norse colony, had been cross-questioned upon the subject.) 'How you must have enjoyed it! That's the worst of Australia—there's nothing a hundred years old in it, except a red-gum tree. But seriously, you may find yourself exposed to inconveniences by walking, like a labouring man. It is not the fashion in our country for gentlemen to walk.'

Miss Antonia had entirely settled the matter by the last observation. Fashion had been through life one of the deadliest enemies to the peace of Ernest Neuchamp. In his own country he had alarmed his relatives and scandalised his neighbours by his wild defiance of that successor of Thor and Odin, as he profanely termed the social belief of decorous Christians. Was he to bow the knee to this false god in a strange land, which at least he hoped to be pure from the idolatries of the effete civilisation from which he had fled? Not so, by St. Newbold! the patron saint of his house. He smiled with great gentleness as he answered, with half sad but most irrevocable decision—

'My dear Miss Frankston, I did not become a colonist with any idea of being trammelled by usages or customs. You will pardon me, I am sure, if I retain my first intention.'

'Most certainly,' said she. 'I shouldn't wonder if you had a friend or two in England who called you obstinate. But you will tell me some day how you got on, and whether there was *any* small portion of reason in the advice given you.'

'I shall for ever feel grateful,' he said warmly, 'for the intention of the advice, and for the great kindness which has accompanied it. Whether or not I succeed in Australia, I shall always have one pleasant remembrance to look back upon.'

'My father, and I also, will be glad if you feel thus,' she said, with the ordinary calm kindness of her tone; 'and now, I must go to town. You leave to-morrow?'

'Yes; I am sorry, in one way, to say so.'

'Then papa will be able to give you his final counsels to-night. I know he wishes to have some last words with you.'

Dinner over and the night being fine, as usual, an adjournment to the sea-balcony was carried unanimously. When the first cigar was half through, Mr. Frankston thus addressed his guest—

'So you are off to-morrow, Antonia tells me, and can't be persuaded to wait for the grand picnic. I don't say you're wrong. When the ship's ready and the wind's fair, it's better to wait for no repairs. You're going to walk, too. It's a long way; but you're young and strong, and you'll find out all I can tell you for yourself; if you don't, all the telling in the world won't help you. Now, see here, we'll arrange everything for the first twelve months, or two years, if you don't care to change.'

'You're most kind and generous, my dear sir, and I don't know what I should have done without you,' said Ernest.

'Thank you,' said Mr. Frankston; 'we'll see about that in about five or six years, if we all live so long—we can't tell just yet. I may be persuading you not to buy in with a rising market, which would double your money in three years, or I may be saving you from losing all but what you stand upright in in about the same time. I think it's the last, but we can't tell. This is an uncertain country, particularly about rain. And rain means fat stock, cheap money, and general prosperity.'

'But can't one provide against the want of rain?' inquired Mr. Neuchamp, who was prone to array himself against Providence, holding that all things might be met or conquered by energy and foresight. 'Irrigation, for instance.'

'There is *no* provision that can be made,' said the man of experience, 'except on a small scale, and irrigation means labour; and paying for labour in Australia, except to a very limited extent, means ruin. A great drought is like a heavy gale at sea; you may be saved, or you may go down with all hands. One visitation is as easy to stop or to calculate about as the other.'

'And is it a drought now?'

'Yes; and one of the worst ever known.'

'Then what will happen?'

'Stock,' said the old man, 'will keep on falling in price. Many stockholders will be ruined, including Selmore, if he does not clear out Gammon Downs to a—'

'A black hat,' laughed Ernest. 'I shall remember that joke. It came near, as our American fellow-passenger would say, costing me five thousand pounds.'

'But they won't be all ruined,' continued Mr. Frankston; 'and what I strongly advise you to do is this—you've left your money, for a year certain, in the Bank of New Holland, for which you'll get tidy interest, and it's as safe as the Bank of England—you go, where I give you this letter of introduction, to Forrester, who is a good fellow and knows me, and it's a good station, Garrandilla; that's a great matter, as you will find. There you will be treated like a gentleman. It will cost you nothing but your clothes. There you'll learn all that can be learnt about stock. In a couple of years, say (here Mr. Neuchamp winced), or perhaps eighteen months, you'll be fit to look after a station, and able to buy one for yourself.'

'Don't you think a year's experience,' pleaded Mr. Neuchamp, 'might—'

'No, I don't,' stoutly asserted the senior; 'and in two years it's my belief that your five thousand pounds will buy as large a station as ten thousand would now.'

The following morning saw Mr. Neuchamp, who had risen early and made all his arrangements, fully prepared for the momentous plunge into real life. He had attired himself in an old tourist's suit of rough serviceable tweed, and donned a pair of thick-soled lace-up boots fitted for climbing mountain sides, and the roughest pedestrian work that might occur. He had filled his knapsack with the requisites that a gentleman cannot dispense with, even in the lightest marching order, and had adopted a brown wide-awake hat, which he trusted would relieve him henceforward from any injurious sobriquet. Thus armed at all points, he awaited breakfast and the arrival of Antonia Frankston, to whom he felt inclined to bid a more heartfelt farewell than he had thought any young lady in the southern hemisphere would have earned the right to receive.

Let me not be understood to assume for a moment that Mr. Neuchamp was wholly insensible to the tender passion. But he was fully possessed and occupied for the present by the 'enterprise of great pith and moment' which he contemplated. And the boy-god found the tenement of his heart for the time so thoroughly filled by busy, unsympathetic ideas, that he was fain to hover like a bird round a populous dovecote, vainly seeking a single unoccupied pigeon-hole.

'Friendship, indeed,' Mr. Neuchamp confessed to himself, 'had sprung up of an intellectual and truly fraternal nature between himself and this girl, who had but few companions, and fewer intimates of her own age.' But he told himself that it was a prosaic alliance of intelligence, natural, and almost inevitable between two people not very different in age, whose temperaments were rather widely apart, but whose tastes and feelings assimilated closely. Just the kind of feeling he might have had for his lady cousins in England, but that they showed no respect for his opinions and openly jeered at his aspirations.

Now Antonia Frankston paid the compliment of respect to all the principles and opinions which he enunciated, even while doing battle unyieldingly against their practical application.

'It is a great matter to be thoroughly comprehended,' he had said to himself. 'One may be right or one may be wrong. I am the last person to deny free exercise of opinion, and the healthful effect of free antagonism. But I must own to a preference of being understood by my critics.'

Under this stimulus he had poured forth, in the leisure time which he had abundantly enjoyed with Miss Frankston, his plans for the regeneration of society, and of Australian life in particular. He had foretold the reign of abstract justice, and the coming dethronement of shams. He saw afar a general refinement in manners, pervading culture, which was harmoniously to fuse classes, now so unhappily divided; the co-operation of labour with capital, and the equal partition of the public lands. In a word, all the fair visions of the higher life, the splendid possibilities of the race which commend themselves to ardent youth and generous manhood, in that springtime of the heart when beautiful emanations are evolved in multiform glory, to be chilled and withered by colder age and hard experience.

To the record of these and similar aspirations, as they poured forth from the enthusiastic soul of Ernest Neuchamp, tinged with poetic thoughts and dignified by a pure 'enthusiasm of humanity,' had Antonia listened, by no means without interest. It was new to her to hear projects free from the taint of selfish gain or personal advantage. And though she entered her protests, gently but firmly, against many of his conclusions, there was to him a deep interest in dialogues in which he secured so patient, so fair a listener, gifted with a high and cultured intelligence.

Thus Mr. Neuchamp made all necessary adieux, and having received his credentials, in the shape of a letter of introduction to the owner of Garrandilla, where he was to abide during his novitiate, and a letter of credit in case he should have unexpected need of money, departed from the hospitable gates of Morahmee.

With his knapsack on his back he paced through the city. Being not sufficiently philosophical, I must confess, to avail himself of the George Street pavement, he crossed Hyde Park, and turning round to take one last look at the blue waters and the grand headland, it may be that his eyes rested lingeringly upon the nearest point which he could recognise to Morahmee.

Then he turned his back upon nature's loveliness and fond regrets, and strode resolutely onward towards the far untried Waste—to him the land of hope and of endeavour.

Taking a somewhat diagonal course adown and across the old-fashioned dingy streets, where the aged, decrepit, but in some instances picturesque dwellings tell a tale of the earliest colonial days, Mr. Neuchamp presently debouched upon the great arterial thoroughfare which, before the advent of the steam king, led to that somewhat mysterious domain, vaguely designated as 'the bush.'

Here he began to put on his tourist pace, and no longer trammelled by fear of the fashionable world, exerted those powers of progression which had won him fame in Scottish Highlands, by Killarney's fair lake, and on the cols and passes which, amid eternal snow, girdle the monarch of the Alps.

Mile after mile, at a rattling pace, went he, pleased to find himself once more upon a highroad, though comparatively disused, as the Dover and Calais route, where the great empty posting-houses tell of 'ruin,' and the 'ruthless king,' which has driven coach and guard, ostler and landlord, boots and barmaid, all off the road together. Such had been the doom of this once inevitable and crowded highway; and Mr. Neuchamp noted with interest the remains of a former state, long passed away.

'Really!' soliloquised he, 'I have come upon a locality adapted for antiquarian research. I did not expect that in Australia. As I perceive, those old buildings are massive and imposing, with walls of solidity far from common. What fine trees are in the orchards! I must see what o'clock it is. This venerable mansion seems inhabited; I wonder if I could get a glass of beer?'

This latter outcome of the inner consciousness, not particularly germane to antiquarian research, was the result of a discovery by Mr. Neuchamp that he was uncommonly heated. The truth was that he had, in the ardour of his feelings, been pelting along at the rate of four miles and a half an hour, forgetting that the thermometer stood at 85 in the shade; hence his complexion was much heightened; his shirt-collar limp to a degree whence hope was fled for ever; 'his brow was wet with honest whatsyname,' while a general and unpleasant saturation of his whole clothing told the tale of a temperature unknown to his European experiences. To his great contentment, the hostelry was inhabited and still offered entertainment to man and that fellow-creature, whose good example had the more highly organised vertebrate followed what romances of crime had remained unwritten; what occupations, literary and sensational, had been gone; what reputations, even of Ouida, Miss Braddon, and that 'bright particular star,' of the firmament of fiction, the great George Eliot herself, had been faint and prosaically mediocre! The surviving of the past favourites of the 'shouting multitude' owed its spirituous existence to the fact of a byroad from certain farms, here reaching the old highway. By dint of an early start, and a little night-work, the farmers and dealers were able to reach and return from the metropolis within the day, thus dispensing with the swift and, to provincial ideas, somewhat costly train. But the long hours and late and early travelling necessitated beer; hence this relic of past bibulousness with ancient porch hard by a real milestone, the twelfth, which our wayfarer hailed with joy, eagerly scanning the deeply-graven numerals.

He found the outer room presided over by an excessively clean old woman, whose starched cap and general get-up reminded him of a well-known Cambridge landlady. Espying a pewter, he demanded a pint of ale, and sitting down upon a bench, disposed of the cool draught with the deep enjoyment which the pedestrian or the worker alone knows. This duty completed, he consulted his watch, and finding that mid-day was passed, decided upon a slight refection of bread and cheese, and a halt.

'So you still keep the house open?' he observed to his hostess. 'I see a good many of those along the road are closed.'

'So should we 'a been closed too,' said the ancient dame, 'but this road, as the fruit-carts and firewood and small farming loads comes in by, keeps a little trade up, and we've not a big family; there's my husband, as is out, and my son, as works in the garden, and does most of the work about the place, and Carry.'

'And you have lived here a long time, I suppose?'

'Over forty years, since my husband, John Walton, got a grant of land, and we came here just after we married. We built the house after we'd made a bit of money, and planted the orchard, and did every mortal thing as is done.'

'And you lost all the traffic when the train commenced to run.'

'All the paying business; everything but this small line as we used to despise. Father, he was for clearing out, but I couldn't bear to leave the old place; we'd saved a bit o' money, and says I: "Well, father, suppose we live on here comfortable and steady, and don't change. There's Jem and Carry fit to do all the work; we don't need no servants, you can potter about the garden, and the pigs and poultry, and bee-hives, and they all makes a bit of money, or saves it, and we'll, maybe, do as well as those that goes up into the bush, and goodness knows where." But you'll have some lunch, sir—please to walk this way.'

Mr. Neuchamp was forthwith inducted into an old-fashioned room, the size and pretensions of which showed the different style of the entertainment once supplied. Leading from this were several bedrooms, to the open door of one of which the old dame pointed. Here, with the help of a sufficiency of cold water and the cleanest towels, he restored himself to a condition favourable to the proper appreciation of lunch.

When he returned he found the table being laid by a neatly-dressed, modest-looking young woman of five or six and twenty.

'I suppose you are Carry?' he said, mentally comparing her with an English country girl of the same rank and condition, and concluding that the damsel before him did not show to any great disadvantage.

'Mother's been telling you, sir, I suppose,' said the girl, smiling; 'she's glad to talk about old times with any one, it's nearly all she has to do now.'

'Well, we had a chat about the state of the roads,' affably rejoined Mr. Neuchamp; 'you have a very nice old place here, and I think you were very wise to stay.'

'I don't mind it,' said the girl, 'though it is awfully dull sometimes. I'm used to a quiet life; but it's rather hard upon Jem, my brother that is, sir, for he might have bettered himself in many ways.'

'How do you think he might?'

'Why, ever so many times he's had offers of employment, but he won't leave the old people; and then, he might go into the bush.'

'The bush! and is every one who goes into the bush certain to do well?'

'Oh no, sir; but every young man of spirit in the colony likes to have a turn, and run his chance there some time or other. Excuse me, sir, but you haven't been very long out, have you?'

'How the deuce does she know that?' inquired Mr. Neuchamp of himself. 'Is there anything written on this brow, and so on? However, I have catechised her sufficiently, and cannot object to a little cross-examination in return.'

'Well, Carry, the truth is that I have *not* been very long out from home, as you very wisely have discovered; that's the reason I am a little inquisitive about your country. But how did you know?'

'By lots of things,' said Carry, rather mischievously; 'by your having such a fresh complexion, and so many mosquito-bites,—they don't bite us natives that way; and by your clothes, and your shirt-collar, and your boots, and your pack, or whatever it is—and by your being on foot.'

'What a long list, Carry! and the worst of it is, that if I was asked how I should know whether you are a native, as you call yourself, and not an English girl, I should not have half as many things to swear by.'

'And what would they be, sir?'

'Let me see. I think you are a little paler, for one thing—but that's the heat, I suppose—and rather taller—and a little, only a very little slighter—and your hands are smaller; just let me look, for I can't be sure; and, on the whole, rather prettier than most English girls are.'

'Oh, nonsense!' interrupted Carry at this point, with a not wholly displeased expression. 'I don't believe half of it. I'm sure everybody says English girls have such lovely complexions and figures, and cut out us poor "currency lasses" altogether.'

'That's not true, Carry, my dear,' protested Mr. Neuchamp with warmth. 'I can assure you that no one would think to look at you that you had lived all your life in a climate something like a greenhouse, with the door shut. It can't be such a very had one after all, if it turns out such very nice specimens of—'

Here Miss Carry pretended to hear her mother calling, and discreetly departed.

Ernest was too experienced a pedestrian to overwork himself, and blister his feet the first day, thereby converting the remaining portion of the journey into a penance; so finding himself in pleasant quarters, he determined to wait till the cool of the evening, and go on as far as the ancient and venerable town of Parramatta, which he was led to believe reared its double spires about eight miles farther on.

After enjoying the home-baked bread, the well-cured bacon, the fresh butter, and another tankard, he occupied himself with observing the pictures, which in rather grand gilt frames adorned the room. They smacked of the good old days. There was 'The Tally-ho Coach leaving the

Post-office, Sydney.' A true English four-insider, with a team of highly improbable grays, proceeding at an impossible pace, from a pillared edifice with an enormous clock. The celebrated racehorse 'Jorrocks,' as he appeared winning his forty-fifth race, the majority of the cheering crowd depicted as wearing cabbage-tree hats. There was also the terrific finish at the Five Dock Steeplechase between Fergus and Slasher, with a sketch of the astonishing struggle, when Traveller beat Chester for the Sydney Cup after the fifth heat, on the old Sandy Course. This turf triumph had occurred about forty-five years since.

Much meditating upon the comparative antiquity and hoary age of incidents, even in a colony, Mr. Neuchamp paid his modest bill, shouldered his knapsack, and prepared to depart from this beer fountain in the desert. Meeting the pleasant glance of Carry as he was passing the door, he turned and said, 'I must come down to Sydney next year, and I'll be sure to pay you a visit, Carry.'

'Oh, do!' she said; 'mother will be so pleased. But you haven't told me your name; how shall we hear of you?'

'If any one talks about Ernest Neuchamp to you, it will be of me.'

'Ernest is a pretty name,' said the girl, 'but "Newchum!" that is not your real name, is it? of course you are a new chum, though it would be rude to say so.'

'And what is "a new chum," Carry? That is not my name, though the pronunciation is not so far unlike.'

'Why, a new chum is a new arrival—a gentleman that—'

'A black hat?' suggested he.

'Well, it's all the same, I believe,' she answered; 'it means somebody who has just come and doesn't know anything about the country.'

'And a most extraordinary country it is,' muttered he; 'it appears that it is not to be known very readily, even after a short stay. Well, here is my card, Carry; you can spell it at your leisure. Good-bye, my dear, and take care of yourself till I come back next year.'

'Good-bye, sir; be sure you stop at the "Red Cow," at Parramatta.'

This badinage over, Mr. Neuchamp pursued his journey, much refreshed in body, but exercised in mind by the similarity of his name to the accusation of newness and cockneyism, so to speak, which the colonial appellation conveyed. 'Most vexatious!' said he to himself; 'I thought I saw Antonia look warningly more than once at her father, when he seemed disposed to dwell on the pronunciation of my name. That must have been the *mot* she forbade.'

The sun was low as he strolled into the quiet, old-fashioned, rather hot town of Parramatta. Here he beheld, within a dozen miles of the thronged and eager metropolis, a population for the most part more incurious and unenterprising than if their habitation had been five hundred miles inland. Every one walked or sauntered down the streets with that thoroughly provincial absence of hurry which is so refreshing to the wearied mental labourer.

Among the lower classes, generation after generation had been born and grown, and aged, since the first occupation of the wonderful land, which has made such haste to become a nation. There seemed a large population of well-to-do retired capitalists, something under the millionaire class, who, having built cottages and planted orangeries (the export of oranges is the great trade feature of the locality), felt a calm confidence that here they could wear out life with less than the usual friction.

He was much surprised and pleased to observe the unusually large number of oaks, elms, and ash trees which had by the pious founders been planted in and around the town. Many of these were of great age, speaking in an Australian sense, and had grown to be ornamental and dignified of aspect, besides being useful in point of shade.

As he walked slowly down the principal street he was pleased to see wide stretches of grass, a river, gardens, and a considerable exemption from the brick-and-mortar tyranny of latter days. The air was becoming pleasantly cool; a certain amount of loitering and musing, dear to Mr. Neuchamp's artistic mind, was observable. A few schoolboys passed, one pair with arms round one another's neck, sworn friends and tellers evidently of some mutually thrilling tale. The cabs were delightfully old-fashioned. The very air had a Rip Van Winkle flavour about it, so utterly foreign to the genius of a new country, that Mr. Neuchamp lamented to himself, as he captured a barefooted urchin and ordered him to show him to the Red Cow Inn, that he could not prolong his stay.

# CHAPTER V

He commenced his next day's journey at an early hour, in full vigour of mind and body and in charity with all men. He had fed and rested with keen relish, and all slight fatigue consequent on unaccustomed exercise had disappeared. The morning air was fresh and cool. The indescribable charm of the unworn day rested upon the rural landscape, where farmhouses, maize fields, orangeries, and orchards alternated with primeval woodlands and wide-stretching pastures. The houses were often old, the farming indifferent, the fences decayed; but with all faults it was the country—the blessed country—and the heart of Ernest Neuchamp, a born and bred land worshipper, went out to the dew-bespangled champaign.

He halted no more until the great valley of the Hawkesbury lay before him, with again comparatively ancient settlement, composed of massively constructed houses, and even boasting—wonder of wonders—in this strange new land, of—ruins! Yes; memorials of the past were there! of an epoch when the easily acquired fortunes of the military, or other notables of the day, had been devoted to the erection of mansions more in accordance with their British recollections than with the circumstances of the colony, or indeed with their regular incomes. Studding the wide fertile meadows were farmhouses of all grades of architecture and pretension. Enormous fields of maize, in spite of the untoward rainless season, told of the unsurpassed richness of a region which, after more than half a century's ceaseless cropping, maintained its fertility.

It so happened that the first two or three individuals who encountered Mr. Neuchamp as he pursued his way along the uniform high road, which led through the flat, somewhat Flemish-looking district, were men of unusual height, breadth, and solidity. Beyond the quick but observant glance habitual to him, our traveller exhibited no surprise at what he took to be exceptional individuals accidentally met. But after several miles' travelling and a repetition of inhabitants of the same vast stature, he commenced to realise the fact that he had come upon a human family of near relationship to the Anakim.

He then remembered some jesting remarks of Mr. Frankston, in which, for the purpose of pointing to some anecdote of entertaining, if not wholly instructive tendency, he had said 'as big and as slow as a Hawkesbury man,' or words to that effect.

'Here, then,' mused Ernest, after finally possessing himself of the fact, 'you have the result of an agricultural population, located upon rich level country, with ample means of subsistence and an absence of anxiety about the morrow almost absolute. Nearly eighty years have passed since the parent-farmers of this community were settled upon these levels. In their descendants you have the true New Hollander, like his prototype, large, phlegmatic, slow-moving, unenterprising, but bearing within him the germs of valiant resistance to tyranny at need, of steadfast labour, of mighty engineering, of deathless struggles for political freedom!'

Having traversed this land of Goshen—evergreen and fertile oasis of the eucalyptus wilderness, not excepting its Platt Deutsch habit of periodical total immersion, Ernest halted upon an eminence which bore traces of having been artificially cleared. He gazed upon the broad winding river at his feet, the wide expanse of river, sharply contrasted with the savage heights and rugged ravines of the great mountain-chain which apparently barred all onward path.

He moved a short distance forward, attracted by the appearance of the remains of an edifice placed exactly upon the brow of the hill, and found himself among the ruins of a mansion of far more than ordinary pretensions.

Fire had destroyed much of the main building, but neglect and abandonment were visible in the dislodged pillars, broken steps, grass-grown courtyard, and roofless hall.

'This has been no ordinary home-wreck,' thought he; 'it needs but little imagination to picture to oneself the overflowing hospitality, the wild revelry, the old-world courtesy, that these crumbling walls have witnessed. Mark the great range of stabling! For no ordinary carriage and pair, with couple of hacks only, were they needed, I trow. There you can still trace the shape and sweep of the avenue leading from the outer gate to the front entrance, and see where the broken bridge spanned the little brook! A few glorious irregular orange-trees mark the place "where once a garden smiled." This was doubtless one of the great houses in the period which corresponded with the palmy days of the West Indian planters, with the old slave-holding times of the Sunny South, when money was plentiful and (compulsory) labour cheap; when the magnates of the land held high festival, not periodically but as the rule of their daily life, and drank and danced and drove and diced and fought and feasted, all heedless of the morrow, whether in South Carolina, Jamaica, or in Sydney. The morrow *had* come during the lives of some proprietors. In other cases, not until their heirs were fitted to realise the misery of a lost inheritance. And was this the end, the moral, of that *bon vieux temps*? The broken arch, the down-trodden shrubberies, the ghostly portals?'

By the time Mr. Neuchamp had brought his musings to a reluctant conclusion, the sun lay goldenly in the clear autumn eve, athwart the dark blue many-shadowed mountain-chain which rose with abrupt sternness from the broad green fertile levels. A wondrous clearness of atmosphere was manifest to the wayfarer from the misty mother-lands, now irradiated with the glories of a southern sunset. Tints of all hues and gradations of colour, clear unflecked amber, burning gold, purple, and orange, cast themselves in softly blending masses upon the fast darkening, solemn, unrelieved mountain-chain.

He was aware, from guide-book lore, that at this point the early progress of civilisation and prosperity of the struggling colony of New South Wales had come to an abrupt conclusion. All things which he saw around explained so much. Careful cultivation of land now disused and restored to grazing. A multiplication of small well-improved farms. Expensive and thorough clearing of timber from great tracts of indifferent soil, only explicable on the hypothesis of cheap labour and artificially heightened prices for all kinds of farm produce.

Then the end had come. The pent-up flocks and herds, the fall of the protection prices, dearth of employment for labour, the vigorous manhood of the colony native to the soil clamouring for remuneration and adventurous employment—all the causes, in fact, which lead to the decay of a weak or the development of a strong race.

One people, one 'happy breed of men,' in such straits and urgency, has ever found chiefs of its own blood capable of guiding it to death or victory. The time was come—the men were at hand—Wentworth, Lawson, and Blaxland, hereditary leaders, as belonging to the military aristocracy, and to the squircarchy of the land, stood forward and fronted the supreme crisis. Taking with them a scant equipment, they cast themselves into the interminable wilderness of barren rock and mountain, frowning precipice and barren heath, endlessly alternating with 'horrible hopeless sultry dells' for leagues, which no white man had hitherto measured or traversed.

The problem, upon the favourable solution of which hung the life of the infant settlement, was, whether a region lay beyond this pathless natural barrier, which in pasture alone should prove sufficiently extensive to sustain the flocks and herds so rapidly increasing in numbers and value.

It was a task difficult and dangerous beyond what, in this day of feather-bed travel, the imagination can easily reach. But the reward was splendid; and they, with hunger-sharpened features, barefooted and almost naked from contact with bush and brier, with the unshaken courage and dogged obstinacy to the death, proper to their race, reached forth the strong right hand, seized, and held it fast.

For, after untold weary wanderings, with loss of burdened beasts, famine, doubt, and every hardship but that of divided counsels, they stood one day upon a mountain-top and saw stretched out before them the glory of the great unknown, untrodden, Austral interior, fated to be the pasture ground of millions of sheep and beeves and horses, the home of millions of Anglo-Saxons. A portion of this they saw when they sighted the first tract of richly grassed park-like forest, the first rippling river, the first prairie-like meadow.

The yet unfolded treasures of the boundless waste were doubtless seen in the spirit by the poet soul, the statesmanlike intellect, the patriotic heart of William Charles Wentworth.

Thus far the guide-book narrative, which perhaps Mr. Neuchamp partially recalled and revolved as he betook himself to the last of the older country towns of the land, which lay amid gardens and church spires on the nether side of the broad river, under the shadow of the ancient mountain superstition, now with 'hull riddled' by broadsides of steam, like other fallacies exploded by modern determination and the remorseless logic of the age.

On the morrow the pilgrim girded himself for the long ascent which plainly lay before him when he should cross the bridge and leave the cleared fertile vale.

Rising at an earlier hour than usual, he quitted the village inn before the sun had more than cleared the eastern horizon.

Ernest enjoyed in silent ecstasy the calm fresh beauty of the morn, as following the old road,—now winding round the spur of a mountain; now scarped from the hillside with a sheer fall of a thousand feet ere the tops of the trees could be beheld, which looked like brierbushes at the bottom of the glen; now running with comparatively level measure along the plateau from which an endless vision of mountain, valley, and woodland was visible,—he gradually ascended to an elevation from which he was able to take a last glance at the rich lowlands through which the course of the river gleamed in long bright curves.

Mr. Neuchamp was a tolerable botanist, a rather more advanced geologist. He therefore possessed the unfading interest which he can ever ensure who reads with heaven-cleared eyes the book of nature. He was able to gratify both tastes without departing from the beaten track. Around, before, above him he beheld shrubs, forest trees, flowers, grasses, utterly unknown previously, but which from early reading he was enabled to recognise and classify. Every step along the sandstone slopes or heath-covered mountain-top was to him a joy, a surprise, an overflowing feast of new and pleasurable sensations.

Descending again from an elevation where the mountain wind blew keenly, and the eagle soared from thunder-blasted giant eucalyptus adown the stupendous glen, at the sunless base of which lay an ever-gurgling rivulet of purest spring-fed water, he shouted aloud at the rare ferns which grew in unnoticed tender beauty where 'rivulets dance their wayward round.' He saw the deserted and rude appliances where the wandering miner had essayed to 'wash out' a modest deposit of the great conqueror, gold!

Then would he happen upon some long-disused, half-forgotten 'camp,' a half military station, where a subaltern had been stationed with some hundred convicts, whose forced labour made the road upon which he now so peaceably travelled.

There were the huts, here the great blocks of stone which they had hewn and raised from the quarry; there had been the triangles where, pah! the contumacious or luckless convict had the flesh cut from his back or much bemarked at least by that high official the government flogger. How wondrous grand the view, at morn and eve, before the eye of hopeless God-forsaken men, who in deliberate wrath and unendurable misery, cursed therefrom the day and the night, the moon and stars, the country, and every official from the gaoler to the governor. He gazed at the glorious cataract where the lonely water gathers its stray threads to fall like the lace tracery of a veil over the sullen spur. He saw the rock battlements and pinnacles, bright in the morning sun, against the rifted water-washed bases of which in long past ages the billows of an ancient sea had rolled and dashed. He saw the huge promontories which frowningly reared themselves on the verge of measureless abysses or obtruded their vast proportions and dizzy height into the boundless ocean of pale foliage which stretched, alternating but with sandstone peaks and masses, to the farthest horizon. From time to time he encountered men in charge of droves of horses and of cattle. These of necessity pursued the old and rugged road, not caring to use the swifter, costlier trainage. At first Mr. Neuchamp used to stand in the middle of the road, until he was warned by the fierce eyes and glancing horns of the cattle, and the extremely unreserved language of the accompanying stockmen, that he was violating etiquette and incurring danger.

Ever and anon he would halt as the warning steam-whistle heralded the approach of a locomotive, and marvel and muse as he saw the long train wind swiftly and securely adown or up the graded mountain side. He saw the half-advancing, half-receding series of approaches which at length land the travellers and the merchandise of the coast upon the pinnacles of the Australian Mont Cenis, and he thanked God, who had made him of one kindred with the men who had conquered nature, both in the land of his fathers which he had left and in the new land, a void and voiceless primeval forest but yesterday.

Much reflecting upon the overflowing *pabulum mentis* which had been spread before him on that day, Ernest was as grateful as a philosopher could be when he saw at the rather chilly approach of eve the outline of a building, faulty as a work of primitive art, as a specimen of any known order of architecture beneath contempt. It was the humble abode of one of the innkeepers of a former *régime*, who had retained his lodgment upon the keen mountain plateau, and still smoked his pipe beside the roaring log fire in frosty winter nights. He now gathered russet pippins in his orchard, with an increasing sense of solvency, long after the last of the coaches had rattled away from his door to face the awful grades of the midnight mountain stage.

When, therefore, after a glorious day of intellectual exercise and frank bodily toil this most praiseworthy hostelry was reached, Mr. Neuchamp felt that fate had but small chance of doing him an injury on that particular night, had her intention been ever so unkind. He walked briskly up to the house, and was then and there taken in charge by a fresh-coloured, broad-shouldered, cheery individual, evidently the landlord, or a gross personal forgery of that functionary. He was promptly relieved of his knapsack, and lodged in the cleanest of bedrooms, with spoken and definite assurance of dinner.

'I see you a-comin' up the hill, with my glass, a good two miles off,' said Boniface. 'You see, sir, there ain't no other place but mine for twenty mile good. So I made the old woman have everything handy for a spatchcock. *He* always liked a spatchcock. Many a time he's been a furragin' and a rummagin' over every nook and cranny of these here mountains till he must have walked them blessed iron legs of his very near off. Ha, ha, ha! You'll excuse me, sir; but when I see the knapsack, I took you for the Rev. Mr. Marke, the heminent-geehol-holler.'

'Geologist, I suppose you mean,' asserted Ernest. 'Well, I hope you are not deeply disappointed; I am glad to find that there's a man in Australia besides myself who is fond of using his legs.'

'Bless your heart, sir, you'll find when you've a been in the country a few years more' (here Ernest contracted his brow) 'that there's a many gentlemen likes a goodish long walk when they can get a bit of a holiday. There's Counsellor Burley, he thinks nothing of a twenty-mile walk out and in, nor his brother neither. They all comes up to me when they want to stretch their legs a bit. But I must see to your tea, sir.'

Mr. Neuchamp was partly interested in this record of pedestrianism other than his own. Nevertheless, he experienced a shade of disappointment at finding that he was not in such a glorious monopoly of tourist life as he had imagined. However, as he stretched his slipper-encased feet on either side of the great fireplace, in which burned a fire, which the keen, almost frosty mountain air made pleasant and necessary, he came to the conclusion that 'none but the brave,' etc.; or, in other words, that no man who has not done a fair day's journey, upon his own legs, if possible, can thoroughly, intensely, comprehensively enjoy a well-cooked, well-served evening meal, like unto the spatchcock which immediately followed, and put a period to these reflections.

# CHAPTER VI

It may be doubted whether a large proportion of what man is prone to call happiness is secured by any mortal, in so compressed and complete a form, as by the reasonably weary wayfarer during an evening spent in a cheery old-fashioned inn. The conditions of enjoyment are superbly complete. The body, healthily tired, craves utter repose, supplemented by the creature-comforts so plentifully accorded to a solvent lodger. The mind, ever a comparative reflex of the organic register of the body, is so far dominated as to lie luxuriously and ruminatively quiescent. The great ocean of the future, with possible armadas, Columbus discoveries, whirlpools, and typhoons, lies mist-shrouded and peaceful-murmurous. The mild lustre of fairly-purchased present enjoyment is shed lamp-like over the whole being. The difficult past, the uncertain future, are shut out from the mental view as completely as are the dark streets and stranger groups of a city, by shrouding curtains, when the interior life is alone visible. Care, save by improbable hazard, is thrust out till the morn. Till then the joys of unpalled appetite. Slumber, soft-touched, silent nurse, points with warning finger to the couch. Reverie may be fondled, darling nymph, without the rebuke of cold-eyed prudence. The wayfarer is a monarch for that evening only. His subjects haste to do his bidding. His purse contains a compressible coronet, investing him with regal dignity and absolute power, while the talisman coin is potent. Burly Sam Johnson loved 'to take his ease at an inn.' Was there an added luxury in the uncounted cups of tea therein possible, dissevered from the fear of accidents to Mrs. Thrale's table-cloth?

The supper had come and gone, and Mr. Neuchamp was sleepily watching the glowing embers in the fireplace with a strong mental deflection towards bed, when the pistol-crack of stock-whips, the lowing of cattle, and a faint echo of the far pervading British oath prepared him for a new and probably interesting arrival. His first impulse was to rush wildly into the road, in order to see a drove of cattle by moonlight, but having accidentally observed that the stockyard was very near the house, he restrained himself and awaited the landlord's irrepressible report.

In a quarter of an hour that sympathetic personage, evidently the bearer of important news, entered the sitting-room.

'Hear the whip, sir? that was Ironbark Ike, with a couple o' hundred head of fat cattle of the () and Bar brand. Splendid lot. Bum character, old Ike; been a stockman and drover this fifty year. Like to see him, sir? he's a-smoking his pipe in the kitchen.'

Like to see him? Of course Mr. Neuchamp would like to see him, though he mildly assented, and did not betray the tremulous eagerness with which he mentally grasped the chance of beholding a stockman of half a century's experience, in his eyes little less than a sheik of the Bedaween.

Following his trusty host to the large smoke-blackened, old-fashioned kitchen, he saw a sinewy, grizzled old man, smoking an extremely black pipe by the fire, who turned a pair of spectral gleaming eyes upon him, and then resumed his position.

'Ike, this is a gentleman going up the country; he ain't been out long' (Ike nodded expressively), 'and he wants your advice about buying a cattle station. He'd rather them nor sheep.'

'Sheep be blanked,' said the old man savagely. 'I should think not. Who the blank would walk at the tails of a lot of blank crawling sheep, when he could ride a good horse after a mob of thousand-weight bullocks, like I've got here to-night?'

'Mr. Landlord,' said Ernest, 'I should like a glass of grog. Won't Mr.—a—Ike, here, and yourself join me?'

The refreshment was not declined, and having been produced, Ike abandoned his pipe and proceeded to expound the law as regarded cattle—wild, tame, fat, store, branded and unbranded, broken-in, or 'all over the country'—in an oracular tone, suggestive of experiences and adventure far beyond the reach of ordinary men.

'Travelled this line? ah! You remember me a fairish time, Joe; but I've been along these ranges and gullies with stock long before the old road was finished, when you were sure to meet more than *one* bushranger, and had to carry your grub and camp for weeks together. Many a queer drive I've had on this very track. They had no steamers fizzin' up and down the rocks then, takin' sheep and cattle behind 'em, all mashed up together in boxes like so many herrin's. It took a *man* to bring a mob of fat bullocks from the Lower Castlereagh or the Macquarie, let alone the Narran, in them days.'

'I suppose you had some roughish trips them days,' suggested the host.

'You may swear that, Joe,' affirmed the war-worn stockman, with a grim contortion of his facial muscles; 'take the book in your right hand, as they say, when you are in the "jump-up." Here,' added he, as he swallowed his brandy at a gulp, and made a sign to the landlord, 'fetch in another round, if this gentleman here ain't too proud, and I'll tell you a yarn about drivin' cattle—one you don't hear every day.'

The replenished glasses reappeared, and the veteran of the 'spur, the bridle, and the well-worn *brand,*' having filled his pipe and partly emptied his glass, made a commencement.

'It was a matter of thirty years ago, or more; I was a young chap then and pretty flash, knowed my work, and wasn't afraid of man, beast, or devil. Well, I'd got a biggish mob of fat stock for them days—there was no ten thousand head on any man's run then—and a rough time we'd had of it. It had rained every day since we started. We'd had to swim every river and every creek as we come to, and watch for the first fortnight, all night long, with the horses' bridles in our hands.'

'I suppose they were rather wild cattle?' inquired Mr. Neuchamp, sipping his brandy and water distrustfully.

Ironbark Ike bent a searching look upon his interrogator before he answered.

'Wild? Well, I suppose you might call 'em that, and make no mistake. They'd come off a very far outrun, where they'd been, as one might say, neglected. Never see a yard for years, some on 'em. They was that wild, that as we drove along, if they came to the fresh track of a "footman," they'd stop and smell it and paw the ground and roar for ever so long. We'd hard work to get 'em by it. As to seein' people on foot, there wasn't much of that; and any travellers they kept clear enough of us, if they'd ever heard of the DD cattle.

'Well, we'd dodged them along pretty fair, that is me and a Narran black boy and a young Fish River native chap, that was pretty nigh as unbroken as the black boy; he could ride the best, but the black boy had twice as much savey.'

'Some o' them darkies is pretty smart,' interposed the host, gradually becoming less respectful to his ancient guest, of whom he apparently stood in considerable awe.

'Smartest chaps ever I had on the road was blackfellows when they're wild; as long as they can ride a bit, the wilder the better, and get 'em off their own ground, then they're afraid to bolt.'

'I should have supposed when they have had the benefit of education they would have been more valuable assistants,' mildly asserted Mr. Neuchamp.

'Ruins 'em, bodily and teetotally,' asserted Ike, with iron decision. 'No educated blackfellow was ever worth a curse. But tame or wild they've all one fault, and it drops 'em in the end.'

'Indeed, how singular!' said Ernest, 'how strange that this sub-variety of the human race should have one pronounced weakness! And what may it be?'

'Drink!' shouted the veteran, draining his glass. 'We can do another round, Joe. Never knew one of 'em that didn't take to drink, sooner or later; and, in course, that cooked 'em,' he added, with an impressive moral air.

'Sure to do,' echoed the landlord, appearing with fresh rummers.

'I have no doubt,' assented Mr. Neuchamp blandly, but much in the dark as to the real nature of the culinary process described.

'Well,' proceeded Mr. Isaac, settling himself calmly down to his fourth tumbler, 'where was I? with those blank cattle, oh! at the top of the road where it used to make in, at the top of Mount Victoria. By gum! it makes me feel as if there was no rheumatism in these blessed old bones of mine when I think how we rode all that blessed day. All the night before we'd been on our horses, round and round the cattle, in a scrub full of rocks; it rained in buckets and tubs, thundering and lightning, and pitch dark; and I, knowing that if the cattle broke loose, we'd never see half of 'em again.'

'Why, bless my soul!' ejaculated Mr. Neuchamp, completely dislodged from his previous conviction that cattle were a more pleasing and interesting description of stock than sheep, 'how did you ever succeed in keeping them?'

'We did keep 'em, and that's about all I know,' responded the fierce drover of other days. '*How* we did it the devil only knows. I swore enough that night for him to lend a hand, if he's on for such fakes, as some says. I rode slap into Tin Pot, the black boy, once, taking him for an old cow, and Tommy Toke, the white lad, ran against a tree and knocked one of his horse's eyes clean out. Well, daylight came at last, and we had the cattle at our own price, blast 'em. All day they was very sulky and slinged along, and wouldn't feed. Well, we was sulky too, for we'd no time to stop and cook a bite, it was so thick.'

'What started 'em so?' inquired the landlord; 'they'd had a deal of camping before they came so far.'

'God knows!—a kangaroo or a bear, or they saw a ghost or a blackfellow—something we couldn't see; and once they were fairly up, the devil himself wouldn't get them to settle again. Now I knew a first-rate camp two or three miles from the bottom of this here hill, almost as good as a yard, but with a bit of feed and water in, a regular wall of rock all round; one man, with a fire, could keep 'em first-rate. So my dart was to get to this place, and I was looking forward to a bit of hot damper and a warm quart or two of tea, with a quiet smoke.

'Just as I thinks of this we turned the corner, and there, in the narrowest part of the road, was a road gang, as they call it, a goodish crowd of chained convicts makin' believe to mend the road, with a party of soldiers to look after 'em, and a young officer to look after the soldiers, and a white-whiskered, hard-hearted old rascal of a corporal to look after *him*.

'The corporal was a-walking up and down, on guard, backwards and forwards, very stiff and solemn. There'd been a chap bolted (and shot dead, too) the night afore, so he had on a bit of extra pipeclay.

'Our mob propped, dead—the cattle and Tin Pot and Tommy Toke—at what they'd never seen afore. Now we couldn't give the party the go-by anyhow, unless they went into their huts.'

'Why not?' asked Mr. Neuchamp, deeply interested.

'Because the mountain was like the side of a house above the road, and fell straight down below five hundred feet, like a sea-cliff. There was just that chain or two of level track, and that was all. I goes up to the corporal, "I say, mate," says I, "can't you get your canaries off the track here for about a quarter of an hour, and let my mob of cattle pass?"

'He looks at me, turning his eyes, but not his head, and keeps on marching up and down like a blessed image; all he says was, "Make an application to the officer in command," says he.

'So I looks about, and presently I sees a slight-built young fellow, in a shell jacket, lounging about a tent.

'"'Scuse me, captain," says I, "will you order your men to leave off their work (work, thinks I) and keep the road clear while I get my cattle past? They're awful wild, and won't face the track with all these chaps in yellow and black and leg-irons. They never see a road gang before."

'"What extraordinary cattle for New South Wales!" said the young fellow; "I should say there was plenty of room between the men and the hill. Can't move her Majesty's troops nor the industrious gang before six o'clock."

'By—, I *was* mad. If we couldn't get the cattle by with the light, we ran the risk of their breaking before we got to camp and having another night like last night over again. It *was* hard! I ground my teeth as I went back and passed the corporal, walking up and down with his confounded musket.

'When I got past him I saw the cattle staring and looking hard, drawn up a good deal closer. The two boys were very sulky at the notion of another night watching and riding, with scarce anything to eat for twenty-four hours. So was I, when I thought of the long cold hours if we didn't make our camp.

'Suddenly an idea came into my head; I see something as give me a notion. "Tommy Toke," says I, "you look out to back up and keep the tail of the mob going, if they make a rush. Tin Pot, you keep on the upper side, and look out they don't break back. They're a-going to make a — charge."

'What started me on this plan all of a sudden, was this wise. We had an old blue half-bred buffalo cow and her son, a four-year-old black bullock, in the mob; he followed his mother, as they will do sometimes. He was a regular pebble, and the old cow hadn't been in a yard since he was branded. She was the biggest tigress ever I see; that's sayin' something. Well, I see the old Roosian paw the ground now and then, and keep drawing towards the corporal, as was marchin' up and down same as he was in Buckingham Palace.

'I keep watching the old cow drawin' and drawin', and pawin' and pawin'. He thought she might be a milker. Suddenly she gives a short bellow, makes for the corporal at the rate of forty miles an hour, followed by the black bullock, and the mob behind him.

'The first thing I saw was the corporal a-flyin' in the air one way, his musket another, and the cow, the black bullock, and the whole of the mob charging through the soldiers and the road gang.

'"Back up, boys," I roared, "keep them going!" as we swept through the party; soldiers running one way, the convicts, poor beggars, making their chains rattle again in their hurry to get safe away. That was a time! I saw the young soldier-officer capsized on to one of his men. Such a smash I never see; it was all downhill luckily. Away we went at the tail of the mob, galloping for our lives, and soon left red coats and yellow trousers, muskets and leg-irons, far behind us. Luckily the mob was too wild to break, and before sundown we were miles from the bottom of the hill, and had the cattle safe inside of the rock-wall camp, where we had a good feed and a night's sleep, both of which we wanted bad enough.'

'I'll be bound you did,' assented the landlord; 'it's a hard life, is a stockman's—out in all weathers, and risking your life, as one might say.'

'Life?' said the saturnine, grizzled old land-pirate, who had apparently relapsed into a different train of thought; 'what's a man's life in this country; leastways used to be. Here!' roared he, dashing his hand upon the table, 'bring in a bottle of brandy, Joe, and a kettle of water, and I'll tell you a yarn about old days as'll make your hair curl, unless this here gentleman's ashamed to drink with old Ike?'

Mr. Neuchamp had by this period of the evening made the discovery that he had invoked a fiend that he was unable to lay; as the old stockman glared at him with half-infuriate, half-imploring eyes, while putting his last observation into the form of a question, he felt much inclined to defy and refuse his uncomfortable boon companion. But having evaded the implied obligation to drink so far he thought it expedient to comply, partly from the novelty of the experience, partly from his dislike to a possible quarrel.

'Ha!' said the strange old man, as he half filled his tumbler with the powerful spirit, and stirred the heavy red glowing logs in the stone fireplace till they shot up a shower of sparks, and threw out a fierce heat like the mouth of a furnace; 'fine thing is a fire! that put me in mind of it. Fill up, curse ye! Joe, ye old, half-baked Jimmy. It was over on the Dervent side, afore I came here at all, that two chaps as did a good deal on the cross, that's how it was told me, was a-skinnin' a bullock in a gully, as had only one end to it.'

'What do you mean by that?' inquired Mr. Neuchamp. 'Surely—'

'I mean,' impatiently broke in the narrator, 'as you could run stock in at one end, and if they got high up they found a wall of rock at the far end, and they couldn't well get back, it was so tarnation narrow. Now do you savey? They were the only coves as knew the secret of it in that part, and many a beast, and many a colt and filly—horses was horses then—they branded or put away there. Well, as I was saying, they wasn't two very particular chaps, and they was a-skinnin' of a bullock, having previously killed him; there warn't no doubt of that, as the head was on the ground close by with a bullet hole not very far off the curl. Similarly it was a "cross" beast. No mistake about that either. The hide, three-parts off, showed the RX brand; one that belonged to H., one of the largest stockholders in the island, and a man who would prosecute any man as dared touch his property, to the gallows, if he could get him there. No hope of mercy from *him*. They had no right to take the bullock, of course it was felony, and now they were caught red-handed by this chap—Pretty Jack; he was the ugliest man in the island, and he was going to turn informer. He grinned when he came up. "There's my liberty," says he, pointing to the beast; "I'm sorry for you, boys," says he, "but every man for himself." The men looks at one another, then at him; he had 'em in his hand; they saw the courthouse crammed, and heard the judge pass the sentence, a heavy one of course, for a second colonial conviction. They heard the gaol door clang as they were shut in for the long infernal years which would bring 'em nearly, if not quite, to the end of a man's life. Some of this sort these two chaps *had* tasted before; they shuddered and trembled when they thought of it, and the man who was to do all this by his own willing informing was their own friend and fellow-prisoner; an accomplice, too, in a goodish lot of undiscovered crimes. He sat looking at the beast with a stupid grin on his ugly face. They looked at each other. Then one man walked past him on the track, and stopped. When he saw this man's eyes, and the murder written there, he called out, "For God's sake, don't kill me, mates; it was all in joke, I never meant to inform on you." But it was too late—they were too much afraid of their own lives to trust them to him; besides their anger had been kindled against the man who had been an accomplice, and was now an informer. "All right, Jack," called out one of the men, "help us to get off this hide." He did so nervously, and anxious to curry favour. The hide was soon stripped, and as they turned to make some joking remark, one of them struck him over the head with a heavy piece of wood. The wretched fool fell on his knees, groaning bad enough.

'"O my God!—Charley," said he, in his agony, "what's this about?—you won't really hurt me? for the love of God, for the sake of my wife and the young ones, pity me; I never meant it, God above knows."

'"Nonsense, man," said one of them, "we ain't a-going to hurt ye; we're only a-goin' to stitch ye up in this here hide a bit, to keep ye from gabbin' while we're putting this bullock away. Now lie still, or by — I'll pole-axe you."

'He laid quiet, thinking he would soon be let go, and while the men laced him up in the hide, making eyelet-holes, and running thongs of hide through, which made it fit pretty close, he thought he might lie for a few hours, and then the people from the next place would find him, and let him go free.

'The men cut up the bullock. They lighted a large fire and put the head, offal, and feet upon it; they packed part of it on a wheelbarrow. Then they hung a strong green-hide rope between the two trees above the fire; one said something to the other in a low growling tone; he shook his head, but at last they came towards the bound-up wretch; he was not able to stir, in course, but it *was* pitiful—my God, so it was, to see his eyes move like an animal's in a trap, as the men went up to him.

'"For God's sake, men, spare me," he moaned out.

'"Spare you?" said the oldest of 'em; "spare a man who betrays his own pals, and sells his fellow-men for a miserable ticket-of-leave? Damn you!" he roared, "your time's up, if you had a dozen lives. Here, Ike."

'Between them they raised him, lifted him in their arms, and hung him up by the rope actually across the roaring fire. The wet hide protected him for a bit, but when the fire began to take effect his shrieks (they told me) was that horrid and unnatural that they had to stop their ears.

'There they stopped till the shrieks died away in death. How he writhed and screamed, and prayed and cursed, and wept and struggled like a maniac. But the tough hide held through everything, though he wrenched it as if he could break an iron band. It was a long while to watch the tongues of the flame dart up as inside the black sheet still writhed a shuddering, howling form. It couldn't have been much like a man's at last. Then all the noise died away, and the bag hung steady and still.'

'And did the fiends who perpetrated this awful deed escape punishment?' asked Ernest.

'Well, I don't know about 'scaping punishment,' said the ancient colonist, looking somewhat like one of Morgan's buccaneers, questioned as to the retribution, moral or otherwise, that followed the sack of Panama, 'but they got clear off, and it was years afterwards that a half-burnt hide with a skeleton inside was found near the old camp.'

'And did the principal criminal never suffer remorse?' still inquired Ernest, with horror in every tone; 'are such men suffered by God to live?'

At that moment the fire blazed up; a change, wonderful and dread, came over the face of the old stockman. He started up; his eyeballs glared like those of a maniac; every muscle, every feature was convulsed. 'Who talks of murderers? They? He? *I* did it. I, Bill Murdock, and the devil. *He* was there; I see him grinning by the fire now. Ha, ha! I can hear *his* screams, my God, my God! as I've heard 'em every day since. I hear 'em now. I shall hear 'em in hell! Look!'

So speaking, with eyes protruding, with every facial nerve and muscle quivering with horror and unspeakable dread, he pointed towards the fireplace, as one who sees the approach of a form, horrible, unavoidable, unearthly. Then, gasping and shuddering, he fell prone and heavily to the floor, without an effort to save himself.

The landlord approached and loosened his handkerchief. 'It's partly the grog,' he whispered to Ernest. 'Nobody can say how much brandy and how much truth's mixed up in this here yarn; but he's seen some rough work in his day, has Ike—though I never see him like this before. Thank you, sir; I can get him to bed now.'

Mr. Neuchamp promptly sought *his* couch, deciding that he had come in for a much larger dose of the sensational element than he had counted upon, and doubting whether he should repeat the experiment.

When he awoke, after a heavy but perturbed slumber, the sun was up, and his first question was of the welfare of the strange old stockman.

'Gone, hours ago, sir. He just slept till nigh hand daylight, and then he roused out his men, lets the cattle out of the yard, and off he goes.'

'And was he able to sit on his horse,' was Mr. Neuchamp's very natural question, 'after drinking a bottle of brandy and having a fit?'

'A deal better nor we could, I expect, sir. He's iron-bark right through, that old Ike. Takes a deal to kill the likes of him.'

'Apparently so,' assented Ernest. 'What wonderful energy, what indomitable resolution must he possess! Used in a better cause, what results might such a man not have reached! "'Tis pity of him," as the Douglas said of Marmion, who in this century, instead of that in which Flodden was fought, might have adorned a colony too, if there had been any one to lay the information, "for that he did feloniously and unlawfully obtain the custody of one young lady," etc. etc., anent that forged letter. Heigh ho! I don't feel quite as much in the humour for walking to-day as I did yesterday. Still, it's a case of Excelsior, I suppose. *En avant*, Neuchamp! St. Newbold inspire thy son and servant.'

# CHAPTER VII

When Mr. Neuchamp looked around, after completing his toilette, the scene strongly stirred his imaginative mind; it was unique, unfamiliar, and majestic. At his feet, down the long incline of the mountain, lay the vast foreign-foliaged, primeval forests, the silver-threaded, winding rivulets, the hoary crag-ramparts of yesterday's travel shrouded in billowing, rolling mists, or rich in combination of light and shade, colour and effect, and at the bidding of the morning sunbeam. As far as vision extended, nought but these characteristic features of the mountain wilderness was visible. Immediately around him, however, were decisive though humble evidences of the domination of art over nature. The inn orchard, with its autumn-blushing apples, stables, barn-yard, the cheerful smoking chimneys in the 'eager air'—all these told of the limited but absolute sway of civilised man. Ernest's ideas gradually shaped themselves into the concrete fact of breakfast.

After this luxurious meal Mr. Neuchamp felt his ardour for travel and exploration rekindled. He inquired the road from the landlord and boldly pushed on. Much the same fortune attended him, sometimes traversing rugged and barren country, and at other times finding cottages, farms, and orchards upon his route. When, however, he reached the more open forest lands, he found that a portion of the carefully graded highway was in process of being metalled. Here were many parties of stonebreakers at work by contract, apparently preferring such labour to the more monotonous daily wage.

Asking for water at one small camp, he found in the cook a well-mannered youngster, doubtless a gentleman. Ernest was pressed to take more substantial refreshment, but he declined the offer.

'How far do you think of going to-day?' inquired the affable stone-compeller.

'About half a dozen miles,' replied Mr. Neuchamp, who by this time had completed the chief portion of a fair day's trudge.

'My reason for asking,' continued the basaltic one, 'is, that we are going to have a little dinner at an inn just so far distant. The party consists of my mates—very decent fellows—and our superintendent, who is a regular brick. We shall be glad if you will join us.'

'Most happy indeed,' answered Ernest, especially gratified to enter upon a new phase of life utterly outside of his previous experiences, and perhaps more typically Australian than anything he could have stumbled upon except by the merest accident. He had dined in many queer places and met with strange company in his day, being always ready to extend his observations in the interest of philosophical inquiry, but a dinner of persons who broke stones upon a highroad for their subsistence, and who were presumably gentlemen, he had never yet been so fortunate as to hear of, much less to partake of.

'If you don't mind waiting half an hour,' pursued the Amphitryon, 'while I change my clothes, we can walk down comfortably together.'

'Are you in the habit of having these little dinners to solace your rather austere labours?' inquired Ernest.

'Well, not exactly; though we have not been so very uncomfortable here for the last six months. We are all gentlemen, in our party, out of luck; and a man might do worse, who is young and strong, than earn six shillings a day by fair downright labour, in a cool climate. All we have to do is to pile up so many yards of metal for the road superintendent to measure. When he "passes it" our money is safe, and we are as independent as le Roi d'Yvelôt. We live comfortably, smoke our pipes in the evening, sleep unusually well, and enjoy real rest on Sundays. But "little dinners" are expensive, and there would be a slight probability of some of the party going "on the burst," after three or four months' teetotalism.'

'On the burst? I do not quite follow.'

'On the burst,' explained the colonist, 'vernacular signifying a protracted and utterly reckless debauch. It's an Australian malady. Hope you'll never be in the way of infection. But as good men as either of us have got inoculated and never wholly recovered. Now, the occasion of this entertainment, which is given by me,' continued the metallician, 'is, like Mr. Weller's new suit of clothes, a "wery partic'ler and uncommon ewent." Fact is, I've been left a few thousand pounds by a good-for-nothing old uncle of mine in England, who never gave me so much as a shilling knife all his life, and is now gone to glory, and with all his earthly goods me endowed, much against the grain. And so I'm going to Sydney by the coach to-morrow, and home by mail steamer on Monday after. What do you think of that for a lark?' inquired he, giving a leap, and shying his hat into the air with a schoolboy joyousness much at variance with his previously imperturbable demeanour.

'I think it's a very pleasant story, with a capital ending,' said Ernest, 'and that's a great matter. I don't suppose the stonebreaking has done you any harm, except roughening your hands a little.'

'Not a bit in the world—a good deal the other way. I was a lazy young scamp while my money lasted. Now I can do a man's work, know personally what a day's labour actually is, and shall respect (and be able slightly to check) the task of the born labourer all my life after. Here we are at the inn.'

Thus talking, they arrived at the inn, a roomy and respectable hotel, where the up coach and the down daily met and deposited hungry passengers, who were accommodated with hasty but highly-priced meals. Here they were met by the landlord, a civil and capable personage, who inducted them into bedrooms, and shortly after into a snug private parlour, where, with considerable splendour of glass, flowers, and table-linen, preparation for the dinner was partially made.

Here Mr. Neuchamp found several gentlemen-like men, in tweed morning costume. Before long the superintendent appeared. Ernest was introduced by his new friend. The conversation became general, and within a reasonable time dinner was announced.

This repast was exceedingly well served, cooked, and, it may be added, appreciated. The wines were fair, and so was the drinking, though within the bounds of discretion.

Subjects of general interest and of political bearing were discussed in a manner which showed that the *pabulum mentis* had not been lost sight of, toils notwithstanding. The health of their friend, 'who by an unexpected but by no means unkind freak of Fortune—a divinity of whom they all had previous experience—was about to be translated to a happier hemisphere,' was suitably proposed and responded to; as was the health of their excellent superintendent, who, a father to them in counsel and admonition, had always treated them as gentlemen, though temporarily filling unpretending positions.

Lastly was toasted the health of the gentleman who had done them the honour to join the entertainment, at the invitation of their old friend and comrade. The speaker trusted that 'their honoured guest, not very long since a resident in dear old Ireland, or England—sure it was all one—would not immediately be reduced, he meant impelled, to make choice of their healthy, manly, but somewhat monotonous occupation. It was well enough in its way. He, Brian O'Loghlan, was not there to find fault with an honourable means of subsistence. But he trusted that his young friend would make trial of other colonial avocations, before betaking himself to the geological experiments in which they had been lately engaged. Of course he had it to fall back upon. And if ever necessity compelled him, he spoke the sentiments, he felt sure, of every man at the table when he said that they would be charmed to welcome their esteemed though but lately acquainted friend to their independent, industrious, and ancient order of free and accepted stonebreakers.' (Continued applause.)

This toast, to which Ernest 'briefly but feelingly' responded, expressing his 'admiration of the institutions of a country which permitted access to industrial occupations generally esteemed as close guilds and corporations in Europe, to gentlemen of culture and refinement, such as his host and his friends whom he saw around him that day, without detriment to their social position and prospects,' closed the entertainment.

The fortunate legatee and his comrades departed to seek their tent, while Ernest and the superintendent remained and smoked a pipe together (the latter gentleman, at least, indulging in the narcotic), while they talked over the somewhat exceptional circumstances of the entertainment, and the accidental stroke of luck which had occasioned it.

On the following morning they breakfasted together in much comfort, and then separated, as so many pleasant chance comrades are compelled to do in this life. The Government official drove off in his buggy to visit another line of road, while Mr. Neuchamp, full of hope and rich with the gathered spoils of his late adventure, paced cheerily along the high road to fortune and the mystical desert interior.

Halting at mid-day by a watercourse favourably situated for temporary rest and refreshment, he heard the half-forgotten words of a favourite operatic air trolled forth by a rich voice with unusual effect and precision. Looking round for the performer, he descried, lying under a noble casuarina tree, the roots of which spread halfway across the little creek, a tall man, whose worn and somewhat shabby habiliments were strongly at variance with the distinction of his air and the aristocratic cast of his features. Beside him was a small black camp kettle, from which he had been preparing the usual traveller's refreshment of 'quartpot tea.' He was smoking, of course, and as he half raised himself and saluted Ernest, that observer of human nature thought he had rarely seen a more striking countenance.

'In which direction are you travelling?' inquired Mr. Neuchamp.

'Towards Nubba,' said the unknown, 'and a devilish dull track it is. Do you happen, by any chance, to be going there?'

'My route lies past that place, I believe. As we are both apparently on a walking tour we may as well be fellow-travellers, if you have no objection.'

'Most happy, I am sure,' assented the stranger, with the ease of a man of the world; 'one so rarely has the pleasure of having a gentleman for a comrade in this part of the creation. May I offer you some tea? Sorry to say my flask is empty.'

'Many thanks—I prefer the tea. Perhaps, on the other hand, you will make trial of part of my provender?'

Here Mr. Neuchamp exhibited an ample store of solids, which he had had the foresight to bring with him, and the stranger, after observing that the brisk air gave one a most surprising appetite, made so respectable a meal that he would almost have fancied that tea and tobacco had alone composed that repast which he had just finished.

The mid-day halt over, the newly-made acquaintances took the road with great cheerfulness, and, on Ernest's part, a considerable accession of spirits.

'Here,' thought he, 'is one of those happy contretemps that so rarely occur—out of books—in an old country. There, if you did meet a man, under these circumstances, you would be afraid to speak to him until you had actually gauged his social position and standing. Here, now, is a gentleman evidently of culture, travel, refinement, who, like me, prefers from time to time to lead this half-gipsy, half-hunter life entirely for the pleasure of unconventional sensations.'

For the first hour or two Mr. Neuchamp kept up a sustained cross-fire of conversation with this fortunately found travelling companion. Whether formerly in the army or not he did not definitely state, but from certain of his reminiscences and stray sentences, such as 'when we took Acre,' Mr. Neuchamp thought he was not far wrong in assigning him a military rank. Certainly his experiences were extensive. Had been everywhere, had seen everything, knew all the colonies from Northern Queensland to South Australia, the gold-fields, the stations, the cities, the law courts. How lightly and airily did he touch upon these different localities and institutions! Knew London, Paris, Vienna, Florence, Rome, St. Petersburg. The *haute volée* of many cities knew him well evidently. His whole tone and bearing denoted so much; and with an air half of philosophical unconcern, half of humorous complaint against fate, he confessed that he had not been lucky.

'No!' he said, 'they used to say in the old 108th I was too deuced lucky in everything else to hold honours where the stakes were golden; and so it has been with me ever since. The boy who ran up the whole score of social success before his beard was grown, the man whom princesses fought for, and world-famed diplomates, soldiers, and savants flattered, has ended thus: to find himself growing old in a colony where talent and social rank are mocked at if unassociated with vulgar success; and here stands John Lulworth Broughton, without a friend, a coin, or a home wherein to lay his head.'

'You shall never need repeat that indictment against fate,' cried Ernest enthusiastically; 'I, at least, can discriminate between the talents and the qualities which should have controlled success and the temporary obscurity which ill-fortune has accorded. Trust to me in the future. Is there no enterprise which we could engage in jointly, where, with my capital and your experience, we might work with mutual advantage?'

The stranger's haughty features assumed a different expression at the mention of the word capital, and his melancholy dark eye brightened as he said promptly—

'I know a splendid run, not very far from where we stand, large enough and good enough to make any man's fortune. I have been prevented from occupying it hitherto by want of funds, but a hundred pounds would pay all expenses at present. We could then take it up from Government, and it would bring in, half-stocked, two or three thousand a year almost at once.'

'Not far from here—the very thing!' exclaimed Mr. Neuchamp, who had had nearly enough walking. 'But I thought that all the good land was taken up except what was a long way off.'

The stranger explained that by a lucky accident he had been trusted with the secret of this magnificent country, which you entered by a narrow and well-concealed gorge; that the old stockman was dead who discovered it, and that a beautiful, open, park-like country, whenever you got through the gorge, was waiting to reward the first fortunate occupants who were liberal enough to meet the small but indispensable preliminary disbursement.

Mr. Neuchamp thought he could see here a splendid opportunity of at once making a rapid fortune, of demonstrating a rare perception of local opportunity and judicious speculation, and of proving to Mr. Frankston and to Antonia his ability to control colonial circumstances without a novitiate.

He could imagine old Paul saying, 'Well, Antonia, my pet, you see this young friend of ours has shown us all the way. Here it is, in the *Herald*: "Splendid discovery of new country, by E. Neuchamp, Esq. Large area taken up by the explorer and partner. We must congratulate Mr. Neuchamp, who has not been, we believe we are correct in stating, many months in Australia, upon developing a masterly grasp of judicious pastoral enterprise, which has left the majority of our older colonists in the shade."'

After this and other intoxicating presentiments, it was finally agreed that they were to proceed to Nubba, where Ernest was to hand Mr. Broughton his cheque for a hundred pounds for outfit and preliminary expenses, upon which that gentleman would at once proceed to point out and put him in possession of this long-concealed but none the less virgin and glorious Eldorado.

With head erect and flashing eye, in which sparkled the ideal lustre of imminent wealth and distinction, Ernest walked on towards the small village which Mr. Broughton had indicated as their probable destination for the night. That accomplished individual indeed, pedestrian feats in the Oberland, South America, Norway, and Novogorod notwithstanding, found it difficult to keep up with his future partner—his boots, possibly, which were neither new nor apparently calculated to withstand the wear and tear of rough country work, prevented his attaining a high rate of speed. But had Ernest been less preoccupied he might have marked a sour expression upon the aristocratic features, heard a savage oath, vernacularly vulgar, issue from under the silken moustache.

Soon, however, in a break of his fairy tale, while he was deciding whether he should send his brother Courtenay a cheque for ten thousand pounds, or surprise him with a personal proffer of that amount as a Christmas box, he became aware that he was outpacing his companion from whom this golden tide of fortune was to date and issue. He stopped and permitted him to come up. At the same instant a horseman, in the plain but unmistakable uniform of a police trooper, rode at speed from the angle of the forest track, and overtook them.

Pulling up his well-bred horse rather suddenly, he fixed a keen and searching glance upon the pair. His features gradually relaxed into a familiar and disrespectful expression as he addressed Mr. Broughton.

'Why, Captain! what's come to you? Here's the whole force in a state of mobilisation from Hartly to the Bogan about the last little plant of yours—and now here you are, a-walking into our very arms, like a blessed 'possum into a blessed trap—- why, I'm ashamed of you; hold up your hands.'

Mr. Neuchamp gazed upon the face of his illustrious friend as this vulgar exordium was rattled off by the flippant but practical man-at-arms, in wonder, consternation, sorrow, and expectancy.

Could it be anything but the most annoying and inexplicable of mistakes, and would not this noble-minded victim of blind fortune repudiate the shameful accusation with scorn in every line of the stern sad features?

He gazed long and fixedly into that face; a deeply graven expression *was* there. But it was an alien, unsatisfactory expression. It showed slight contempt, but habitual deference to that branch of the civil power mingled with a sardonic, half-stoical, half despairing resignation to ignoble circumstance.

Puzzled, doubtful, but by no means dismayed, Mr. Neuchamp indignantly asked the trooper what he meant by speaking insolently to his friend, Mr. Broughton—in stopping him without a warrant upon the highway?

'Mr. Howard, alias Captain, alias the Knight of Malta, alias the Aide-de-Camp, alias John Lulworth Broughton, is as much my friend as yours; leastwise we know one another better; don't we, Captain?'

Mr. Broughton, upon whose wrists the handcuffs were safely adjusted, merely nodded, upon which the trooper requested Mr. Neuchamp to permit his hands to be similarly fettered.

'What?' said Ernest, flushing so suddenly, at the same time making a stride forward, that the wary official backed his horse, and taking out his revolver, presented it full at his head.

'What for?' said the trooper; 'why, on suspicion, of course, of being concerned with the Captain here, in the Barrabri Bank robbery the other night, that all the country is going mad about.'

Here the Captain found his tongue.

'You're going mad yourself, Taylor; the reward and the mobilisation, as you call it, have been too much for you. There's no evidence against me this time, nothing that you could call evidence worth a rap; and don't you see that this is a gentleman just out from home, and green as grass; or he wouldn't go on foot with a thundering big knapsack on his back, picking up with—ahem—shady characters like me.'

'That's all very well, Captain,' assented the trooper; 'but the cove's hair and complexion, and height, and age, as was with you in the plant, and *Police Gazette*, corresponds with the other prisoner's.'

Ernest's face, at this description of himself, was a study; so sharply engraved were the lines which indicated wrath, disgust, and horror.

'Very sorry, my man, and all that,' continued Senior-Constable Taylor, who had not got the stripes for nothing, 'in case your turn don't square, but you must come before the police magistrate of Boonamarran and see what *he* thinks about it. I won't put the darbies on ye, if you'll promise to come quietly, but by — if you leave the track for a moment I'll send a bullet through you before you can say knife.'

Under this proclamation of martial law, there was nothing to be done by any sane man but to submit; so Ernest made answer that he had no objection to walking as far as Boonamarran, where no doubt his innocence would be made clear.

In a kind of procession, therefore, was Ernest Neuchamp forced, as the Captain would have said, 'by circumstances' to make his appearance in the small but not wholly unimportant town of Boonamarran. As they passed up the principal street, a very large proportion of the available inhabitants must have assembled to mark their arrival at the lock-up.

Behind them rode the trooper with a mingled air of inflexible determination and successful daring. The Captain marched in front with his manacled hands almost disguised by his careless walk, remarking calmly on the appearance of the town, which he criticised freely, also the leading inhabitants. By his side, burning with rage and mortification, walked Ernest, feeling very like a galley slave, and wondering whether there was any possibility, in this strange land, of being sentenced mistakenly to a term of imprisonment. Thus feeling for the first time a keen sensation of distrust for his own obstinate predilections, coupled with an awakening respect for the opinion of others, the time passed in varieties of mental torture, till they arrived at the lock-up, a strong wooden building, into a small room of which they were unceremoniously bundled, while a heavy bolt closed behind them.

'I really am extremely sorry, sir,' quoth the Captain, after they were left to themselves, 'to have brought you into this highly unpleasant position. But circumstances, my lifelong enemies, were too strong for me; and for you, too,' he added reflectively.

Mr. Neuchamp was not a vain man, though proud; above everything he was a philosophical experimentalist. Under any given position he could soon have ceased to struggle and rage, and have commenced to analyse, theorise, and deduce.

'I ought to be so justly enraged with you,' he replied, 'that any apologies would only arouse contempt. You have deceived me, it appears, with a view to rob me of my money, and you have been instrumental in causing, for the first time in my life, the loss of my liberty. But I will confine myself for the present to asking, in all seriousness, why you, a man of culture and mental endowments, having enjoyed the advantages of travel and refined society, should voluntarily have lowered yourself to your present surroundings by a course of vulgar and short-sighted criminality?'

'Well, I'll tell you the real naked truth, as far as I know it when I see it,' said the Captain, cutting off a solid piece of negrohead tobacco and putting it into his mouth. 'I have had an immense quantity of what the world calls advantages, there's no denying, and yet they would have been all well exchanged for one simple bit of luck, which I did *not* happen to possess—that of being born honest! That, I distinctly state and affirm, I was not. Whatever the reason is, I was always an infernal rogue from the time I could write myself man, and long before. Whether the faculty of passionate and sensuous enjoyment was intensified in my idiosyncracy, while at the same time my reasoning powers were feeble and my conscientiousness absolutely nil—I can't say. The fact, *unde derivata*, remained (and a *fait générateur*, as the French say, it was), when I wanted anything it always occurred to me with restless force, that the shortest, most natural, and obvious way to possession was to steal, take, and unlawfully carry away the same. I should have made a famous king; in him annexation is a virtue of the highest order. As a general, could I have overleaped the earlier grades, I should have gone amid shouting thousands to an honoured grave, for I am cool and cheerful in danger, and a demon when my slow blood is fairly up. But as the son of an eminent clergyman, as a mere unit in refined society, my sphere was wretchedly circumscribed. Society became my foe, my fatal foe. Young man, if you hurl yourself upon society, she laughs at the superincumbent hostile weight. If she merely reclines upon you, moral asphyxia results. I have, mind, cast away home, friends, love, honour, position. If I hadn't such an infernally good constitution, death would have long ago squared the account. I am sorry when I think of it. But present troubles once over— *"Libem, libem!"'*

Here he broke forth into the great drinking song, which he trolled out until the massive timbers of the building echoed.

'And your intention, as far as I was concerned?' asked Ernest, unable to refrain a certain toleration for the 'larcenous epicurean.'

'Well, I couldn't resist trying to appropriate your hundred pounds. You threw it at a fellow's head, as it were. It was partly your own fault.'

'My own fault,' echoed Ernest, in astonishment, 'and why, may I ask?'

'When people are very *very* imprudent, they, as the Methodists phrase it, "put temptation in the way" of other folks, not afflicted, let us say, with severe morals. Now why don't you ride a decent horse when you're travelling, like a gentleman?'

'But surely a man may walk in a new country, if he likes?' pleaded Ernest, half amused at his arguing the question so seriously with a swindler and convicted felon.

'Excuse me,' answered the man of experience, with the readiness of a practical advocate; 'you might drive a tax-cart down Rotten Row, or wear a wideawake and a tourist suit at a flower-show, as far as the power to do so is concerned. But you wouldn't do it, because it would be unfashionable, therefore incorrect. It's unfashionable for a gentleman to walk in this country, therefore nobody does walk on a journey, except labourers, drunkards, persons of bad character like me, or inexperienced young gentlemen like you.'

'Many thanks for your neat explanation and wholesome advice,' said Ernest. 'I don't know whether I shall not act upon it.'

'And may you better rede the advice than ever did the adviser,' quoted the Captain gravely, sonorously, and in final conclusion.

Next morning, after experiencing what fully justified Clarence's exclamation, Mr. Neuchamp and his fellow-traveller were 'haled' before the stipendiary magistrate, who looked at Mr. Neuchamp in a manner so unsympathising that it hurt his feelings.

'John Lulworth Broughton,' said the trooper, in a loud matter-of-fact voice, 'alias Captain Spinks, alias the Knight of Malta, and Ernest Neuchum appears before this court, in custody, your worship, charged with robbery under arms. How do you plead?'

'Not guilty, of course,' replied the Captain, with a shocked expression.

'Not guilty,' said Ernest, in an anxious and horrified tone; 'I wish to explain, I am travelling to the station of—'

'Any statement that you or the other prisoner may wish to make, *after* the evidence is complete, I shall be happy to hear. Until then,' said the police magistrate, with mild but icy intonation, 'I must request you to keep silence, except when cross-examining the witnesses for the Crown.'

Ernest felt outraged and choked. The evidence then being 'gone into,' showed how a certain bank manager at a lonely branch had been awakened at midnight by two men masked and armed; one tall, dark, spoke with a fashionable drawl; the other middle-sized, active, fair-haired, with blue eyes, about twenty-four, spoke rather slowly. Here the police magistrate, the clerk of the bench, the spectators, and the other police constable turned their heads towards Mr. Neuchamp. 'Speaks like a native. Ah! very strong point.'

Witness after witness being examined piled up the evidence that a tall dark man and a middle-sized fair one had been seen at the scene of the robbery, near the place, the day before, the day after. Every sort of circumstantial evidence was forthcoming, except a link or two which the jury might or might not consider necessary. The magistrate thought a *primâ-facie* case for committal had been made out. He was commencing the impressive formula—'Having heard the evidence, do you wish to make any statement, etc. etc.,' when a telegram was put into the hand of the senior constable of police.

Reading it rapidly, and handing it to the police magistrate, that official said: 'In consequence of the information just received from my superior officer, by telegram, I beg to apply for the discharge of the younger prisoner.' The police magistrate acceded. Thereupon the door or the gate of the dock was opened and Mr. Neuchamp, permitted egress through the same, much like a rabbit from a hutch, was formally discharged.

'It would appear,' said the stipendiary magistrate, 'from the latest information in the hands of the police, that an instance of mistaken identity has in your case occurred, leading to your—a—apprehension and detention, which, under the circumstances, I regret. Senior-Constable Taylor was fully justified in arresting you as the companion of a notoriously bad and desperate character' (here the Captain smiled serenely, and stroked his moustache)—'in arresting you on suspicion of felony. It appears that the person described in the *Police Gazette*, and whom you unfortunately appear to resemble, has been arrested, and is now in custody at Warren. You are therefore discharged, and as you are a young man of respectable appearance, I trust that it will be a warning to you; a—that is to say, as to the choice of your associates. John Lulworth Broughton, you stand committed to take your trial at the next Quarter Sessions,' etc. etc.

The telegram which had so suddenly and effectually changed the current of Ernest's destiny ran as follows: 'From Sub-Inspector Hawker, Warren, to the officer in charge of police, Boonamarran. The right man, Captain Spinks's mate, arrested here, 4 A.M. Discharge fair prisoner forthwith.'

Ernest left the court certainly a sadder and a presumably wiser man, and sought a private room in the chief inn, having some difficulty in evading the invitations to liquor pressed upon him by the chief inhabitants, who, having fully agreed that if ever a man looked guilty he did, were anxious now, in reactionary regret, to make him amends for their unfounded and evil thoughts.

Among the persons firmly, perhaps unceremoniously, repelled, was a pale young man with longish hair and an intelligent countenance. This personage sat down and hastily wrote a report of the proceedings, in the course of which he dilated upon the hardship of an untried man suffering the degrading and mental torture to which, if innocent, he is perforce subjected, in the present state of the law. This was at once forwarded to a leading metropolitan journal. A telegram of a sensational nature was also despatched for the evening paper: 'Arrest of a gentleman newly arrived, for robbery under arms. The case broke down. He is now at liberty.'

# CHAPTER VIII

When a man has suffered the indignity of actual incarceration, a savour of irrevocable dishonour is apt to cling to the sensation, however innocent the victim may subsequently be proved. Some robes once soiled cannot be washed white. The bloom cannot be replaced upon the blushing fruit. And Ernest sorrowfully reflected that, for all future time, if one of those ruthless vivisectors, a cross-examining barrister, chose to ask him, as a witness before a crowded court, whether or not he had ever been in gaol charged with highway robbery, he would be compelled to answer 'yes,' with the privilege of explanation after that categorical answer, of course. Much regretful and indignant thought passed through his mind before lunch. The last Neuchamp that had heard a prison door barred behind him was enclosed by a troop of Ironside dragoons in the donjon at Neuchampstead, while they merrily revelled above, and praised the malignant's ale and serving-maids. That was honourable captivity. But to be boxed up in 'the logs' of a bush township, side by side with a confessed robber and swindler! It was hard! The star of the Neuchamps was for a time under an evil influence. However, after a remarkably good lunch and a bottle of Bass (dear to England's subalterns in every land of exile) a more cheerful and philosophical frame of mind succeeded. After all, anybody might be arrested by mistake. No one would ever hear of it, any more than of the detention of Livingstone for a day by King Unilury on the Moombitonja. His friends at Morahmee would *never* discover it, that was as certain as anything could be.

He 'had a great mind,' as the phrase runs, to buy a horse, and so relieve himself, for the future, from all risk of evil communications, and other misfortune, which society seemed, with one accord, to trace directly to his using his own proper legs for purposes of locomotion. But he was a true reformer in this one particular. He was not less obstinate than enthusiastic, and he told himself, as he had commenced his journey on foot, that he would so end it, and complete the distance to Garrandilla in spite of all the strange people in this very strange country. He had his own secret doubts as to whether he would need much persuasion to ride or drive whenever he returned to Sydney. But in the meanwhile, and until he was fairly landed at Garrandilla—

Having plentifully refreshed himself, and even provided something edible in case of accidents, he accordingly left town very early next morning, shouldering his knapsack, as usual, and cleared off about ten miles of his journey in the comparative coolness of early morn.

Here he discovered a friendly creek, possessing shade and water, so flinging himself on the sward, he addressed himself to some corned beef with a vigour unabated by previous misfortunes.

Preoccupied with these minute but necessary details, he did not observe that another man had, like him, selected the spot as appropriate to rest, if not to refreshment. The personage whom he so suddenly descried was not pedestrianising, like him, as two serviceable roadsters grazed within a few yards, their fore legs confined by the short chain attached to two leather straps, which had more than once attracted his attention in his travels. In one respect the new traveller differed from any other wayfarer whom Mr. Neuchamp had as yet encountered; for, in spite of the inconveniences to which his late incautious acceptance of companionship had subjected him, he could not refrain from a close examination of the stranger. The unknown was apparently not about to make or to drink a pot of tea. Neither was he smoking, preparing to smoke, nor obviously having just finished smoking.

'Good-morning,' said this person, bending a pair of exceedingly keen gray eyes upon Ernest. 'Travelling early, like myself. Bound for Nubba?'

'Yes!' answered Ernest.

'Going any farther?'

'As far as Garrandilla,' he replied.

'Humph!' said the new acquaintance. 'I suppose you were at Boonamarran last night. I left Boree station early, and am going on as soon as my horses have had another half-hour's picking at this patch of good feed.'

'Have you breakfasted yet?' inquired Ernest.

'Well, I'm not particular about a meal or two,' cheerfully replied the stranger. 'I can always find a salad, and with a crust of bread I can manage to get along.'

'Salad in the bush?' asked Ernest, with astonishment. 'I never heard of any before.'

'There's always plenty, if you know where to look for it,' gravely answered the stranger; 'only men in this country are a deal more fond of making for the nearest public-house than of studying the book of nature, and learning what it teaches them. No man need fast in this country if he knows anything about the herbage and the plants he's always riding and trampling over.'

'You amaze me!' said Ernest; 'I always thought people ate nothing but meat in this country.'

'When you've been longer in Australia' (Ernest groaned) 'you'll find out, by degrees, that there's a deal of difference in people here, much as, I suppose, there is in other countries. See here,' he continued, taking up and cropping with great relish a succulent-looking bunch of greens, 'here's a real good wholesome cabbage—warrigal cabbage, the shepherds call it. Here's another,' uprooting a long dark-green fibrous-looking wild endive. 'As long as you've these two and marshmallow sprout, you can't starve. Many a pound it's saved me, and you may take my word for it there's more money made in this country by saving than by profits. I suppose you're going to learn colonial experience at Garrandilla.'

'How can he know that?' thought Mr. Neuchamp. 'These people seem to guess correctly about everything concerning *me*, while I am continually deceived about them.'

'I am just bound on that errand,' he answered, 'though I cannot tell how you arrived at the fact.'

'Well, I didn't suppose you were going as a shepherd, or a stockman, or a knock-about man,' said the stranger carelessly, 'so you must have been going to learn the ways of the country.'

'Do you know Mr. Jedwood?' inquired Ernest.

'Yes; heard of him. That's a good manager; sharp hand; teach you all about stock; make you work while you're there, I expect.'

'I don't mind that; I didn't come up into the bush for anything else. It's not exactly the place one would pick for choice for lounging in, is it?'

'I don't know about that. I'm never contented anywhere else,' said the unknown.

'And I suppose you're looking out for an overseer's situation,' inquired Ernest, exercising his right of cross-examination in turn. He thought by the stranger's economical ideas that he could only be upon his promotion, and not yet arrived at the enviable and lucrative position of 'super,' as he had heard the appointment called.

The stranger smiled faintly in his own grave and reflective fashion, and then, leaning on one elbow and pulling up a tuft of *Anthistiria australis*, which he chewed meditatively, said, 'Well, I have jobs of overseeing now and then.'

'And you expect to save enough money some day,' demanded Ernest, rather elated by the success of his hit, 'I shouldn't wonder, to go into a small station, or leave off work altogether?'

'Some of these days—some of these days,' repeated the stranger, staring absently before him, 'I expect to have what I call enough. But you can't be sure of anything.'

'In the meanwhile you save all you can,' laughed Ernest.

'It's no laughing matter,' said the stranger; 'if you don't save you waste your money, if you waste your money you get into debt, if you get into debt you get so close to ruin that any day he may put his paw down and crush you or lame you for life.'

'That's a solemn view to take of a little debt,' said Ernest, 'but you are right on the whole; and when I come into a station of my own I will be awfully saving.'

'That's right; you can't go wrong if you act up to that. Now, see here, we're about fifteen miles from Nubba.'

Here the stranger raised himself from his recumbent position, exhibiting to Ernest a tall, well-made, sinewy frame, with a keen handsome visage half covered with a bushy brown beard. The eyes were perhaps the most remarkable feature in the face; they were moderate in size, but wonderfully clear and piercing. There was the rare look of absolute unbroken health about the man's whole figure which one sees chiefly in children and very young persons.

'I've a second horse and saddle,' continued the tall stranger; 'I generally take a couple when I'm travelling, they're company for one another, and for me too. So if you are going by Nubba, just you ride this roan horse, and we'll jog on together.'

Ernest considered for a moment. He had paid *de sa personne* for over-hasty acquaintanceship. But he could not for a moment distrust the steady eye and truthful visage of the man who made this friendly offer. He was interested, too, in his talk, and deeming him to be of a rank and condition that he could in some way repay for the obligation, he accepted it frankly.

'Very well,' he said, 'I shall be glad to go with you as far as Nubba. I suppose your horse won't be anything the worse for me and my knapsack.'

'Not he. We'll saddle up. I have a good way to go before sundown.'

'May I ask to whom I am indebted for the accommodation?' inquired Ernest. 'My name is Ernest Neuchamp.'

'Well, Mr.—a—Smith,' said the stranger, with a slight appearance of hesitation. 'It don't much matter about names, except you have to write a cheque or pay a bill. Now then, here's your horse; he's quiet, and an out-and-out ambler.'

After walking for several days, it was a pleasant sensation enough when Ernest, a fair horseman and respectable performer in the hunting-field, found himself on the back of a free easy-paced hackney again. The roan horse paced along at a rate which he was obliged to moderate, to avoid shaking his benefactor, whose horse did not walk very brilliantly, into a jelly.

'This is my morning horse,' said Mr. Smith, slightly out of breath—though he sat his horse with a peculiar instinctive ease, not alone as if he had been accustomed to a horse all his days, but as if he had been born upon one. 'When you are going a longish journey, you generally have one clever hack and one not quite so good. Well, what you ought to do is to ride the roughest one in the morning, while *you're* fresh, and in the afternoon take the fast or easy one, and you finish the day comfortably.'

'Indeed,' said Ernest, 'that never struck me before; but in England we don't ride far, and never more than one horse at a time.'

'Fine country, England,' said Mr. Smith musingly. 'I was reading in Hallam's *Middle Ages* the other day about these Barons making war upon one another. They must have been a good deal like the squatters here, only they didn't get fined for assaults at the courts of petty sessions, and they had their own lock-ups, and could put a chap in the logs or in their own cellar, and keep him there. I should like to see England.'

'Then you never have seen the old country?' said Ernest. 'How strange it seems to see a grown Englishman like you, for you are one, and very like a Yorkshireman too, who has never seen the chalk cliffs and green meadows. When do you intend to go?'

'Some day, when I can afford it,' answered Mr. Smith.

They were now going at a good journeying pace, not far from five miles an hour, through an open, thinly-timbered, well-grassed country. The grass was long, rather dry looking, and of a grayish green. The road was perfectly smooth, without stone, rut, or inequality of any kind. The day had become insensibly warmer, but the air was wonderfully clear, pure, and dry. Mr. Neuchamp felt sensibly exhilarated by the atmospheric tone.

'What a grand climate,' he thought, as Mr. Smith had subsided into rather an abstracted silence. 'Here we have a combination of sufficient warmth for comfort and high spirits, with that bracing cold of night and early morning necessary to ensure appetite and energy. And there are months upon months of this weather. Once bring a man or woman here, with a sound and unworn constitution, and they might live for ever. No wonder the general tendency of the features of the country-born people is towards the Greek type. The vales and groves of Hellas had no brighter sky than this deep azure, no purer air, no softer whispering breeze.'

After this slight æsthetical reverie Mr. Neuchamp fell a wondering as to the precise social status of his preoccupied but accommodating companion. Rendered wary by previous mistakes, he bestowed great care and caution upon his analysis, and after a most judicial summing-up, decided in his own mind that Mr. Smith was a working overseer, with aspirations superior to his present position, which, from his economical habits and self-denying principles, he would at some distant period realise. 'Yes,' said Mr. Neuchamp to himself, 'I shall see him some day with a nice little station of his own and four or five thousand sheep. He will of course be able to work up from that. But how pleasant it will be to visit him some day and behold his honest pride at having successfully surmounted all his difficulties and triumphantly landed himself upon his own property! How we shall laugh over to-day's salads and wise saws.' Here Ernest woke up from his Alnaschar musings by which the deserved greatness was to be bestowed upon Mr. Smith. That individual, all unconscious apparently of his imminent and triumphant pastoral profits, called out—

'Do you see that rise with the plain beyond? Well, Nubba's about a mile the other side. I'm going forty miles farther, so I must have something to eat before we start. Come and have dinner, or whatever you call it, with me.'

They rode into the bush town together. The usual wide street or two; the straggling shops and cottages; at each corner a large pretentious store or hotel, a bullock dray, a buggy, a horseman or two, a score of foot-passengers, the incoming mail with four horses and five lamps, made up the visible traffic and population. Forest land had been monotonously prevalent before they reached the town; a vast, apparently endless plain, the first Mr. Neuchamp had ever seen, stretched beyond it to the horizon. As they rode up to a balconied and two-storied brick hotel he noticed a new ecclesiastical building, the architecture of which contrasted strangely with that of the majority. His educated eye was attracted.

'What a nice church—Early English too; I never expected to see such a building here.'

'Yes,' said Mr. Smith uninterestedly, 'looks neat and strong; see they've finished it since I passed this way last.'

'It has a decidedly Anglican look, now one examines it. Quite a treat to see such a building in the wilderness. Do you happen to belong to the Church of England, Mr. Smith?'

'Well, I may say—that is, I believe I'm a Protestant; I don't know about any denomination in particular. There's good men in all of them. I respect a man who does the work well that he believes in, and is paid for doing. That's my view of the matter.'

'But the glorious tenets of the Reformation to which the English Church has ever held firmly ought to commend its teachings to every open-minded intelligent man,' said Ernest, a little moved.

'I can't say,' said Mr. Smith slowly; 'I don't know if we should believe in old Harry the Eighth much in the present day. He wouldn't quite do for us out here, though I reckon him a grand Englishman in many ways. Here's the inn, and I'm not above owning I'm ready for a chop.'

The horses were put into the stable; Mr. Neuchamp conveyed his knapsack into a bedroom, and in a comparatively short time joined Mr. Smith at one of the most tempting meals he had lately encountered.

It was past mid-day, and nothing in the way of disparagement could have been fairly said against the appetite of either gentleman. 'What will you take, beer or wine?' asked Mr. Smith, ringing the bell as they sat down.

Ernest thought pale ale not inappropriate, though he wondered at his theoretically economical friend being so luxurious in practice. 'Just the way with all these bushmen,' he thought. 'This poor fellow will have to go without something for this; but I won't hurt his feelings by refusing to join him.'

'Bring in some bottled beer, then,' said Mr. Smith. The waiter flew to execute his command.

'Here,' thought Ernest, 'is another example of the superior sympathy of colonial manners. Here is the poor overseer, working his way up in the world, and he is treated with as much deference as if he were a wealthy man. There is nothing like a colony for the repression of vulgar servility to mere wealth.'

Here the waiter, bearing beer, reappeared.

'I don't take anything but tea myself,' said Mr. Smith, 'but to those who are used to it cool bitter beer goes well in any kind of weather. Anything is better than the confounded hard stuff.'

Mr. Neuchamp did not comprehend whether the latter deleterious compound was a solid or a liquid, but he was annoyed at drinking at the expense of a man unable to bear the cost, and who did not keep him company in the consumption of the liquor.

'I wouldn't have had anything but tea if I had known that was your tipple too,' he said. 'I'm not averse to Good Templarism in the desert, and can live on coffee as well as a Bedouin Arab. You must come to my place some day when I have one, and we'll drink tea till all's blue.'

'Very well,' said Smith. 'I'm passing Garrandilla—shall I say you're coming along by degrees, and will be there some day?'

'Just so,' said Ernest; 'there's no necessity for hurry. Tell Mr. Jedwood that, picking up colonial experience as I go along, I shall be there within a month.'

'Well, good-bye,' said Mr. Smith; 'I daresay we shall see each other again. Don't you go and waste your money, mind that, and you'll be a big squatter some day.'

'I don't know about that,' said Ernest; 'I don't so much want to make money, you know, as to do some good in the land.'

'That's quite right,' said Mr. Smith, grasping his hand with the hearty grip of the man of whole heart and strong will, 'but you try and make some money first. People won't believe in your opinions unless you show them that you can make money to begin with; after that you can say anything, and teach and preach as much as you like; and if you want to hold your own in any line you fancy, don't you go and waste your money, as I said before. Good-bye.'

The horses had been brought round; Mr. Smith, rather inconsistently, gave the highly respectful groom half a crown after this economical homily, and mounting the roan horse touched the other with the bridle rein, and ambled off at the rate of six miles an hour.

'Good-hearted fellow, Smith,' said Mr. Neuchamp expressively to the landlord, who with a select part of the townspeople had paid Mr. Smith the compliment of assembling to see him off; 'hope he'll get on in the world; I feel sure he deserves it.'

'Get on in the world, sir!' echoed the landlord, in tones of wild amaze; 'who do you mean, sir?'

'Why, Mr. Smith, of course, the gentleman who has just ridden away,' said Ernest, rather tartly. 'He is a most economical but estimable and intelligent person, and I feel convinced that he will get on, and have a station of his own before many years.'

'Mr. Smith! a station of his own!' said the landlord in faint tones, as of one preparing to swoon. 'Do you know who you're a-talkin' of, sir? why, that's Habstinens Levison, Hesquire, the richest man in Australia. Station of his own! Good lor—('scuse me, sir, you ain't long from 'ome, sir?); why, he's got *thirty stations*, sir, with more than a hundred thousand head of cattle, and half a million of sheep! So I've heard tell, leastwise.'

Mr. Neuchamp thought it would not be inappropriate if *he* fainted after this astounding revelation. He had heard Mr. Frankston tell a story or two of the wealthy and eccentric Abstinens Levison, and here he had met him in the flesh, and had been rather proud of his penetration in summing him up as an overseer on his promotion, who had saved a few hundred pounds and would be a squatter before he died.

'Mr. Levison was here one day, sir,' continued the landlord, 'callin' hisself Smith, or Jones, or something; he don't want to be worrited by charity-agents and such; when the clergyman spotted him and asks him for something towards the Church of Hengland there—'andsome building, ain't it, sir?—what I call respectable and substantial—he writes him out a cheque very quiet and crumples it up and gives it 'im; when he looks at it outside, blest if it warn't for five hundred pounds!'

'I suppose the reverend gentleman was contented with that,' said Ernest, thinking of the stranger's non-committal remarks as they passed the same building.

'Not he—parsons ain't never contented, 'specially those as has a turn for begging for a good object—they say. Next time he passes through, our reverend thought he'd touch him a bit more. "Mr. Levison," says he, "this here beauteous structure as you've so magnificently contributed to, ain't got no lightning-conductor, and it's a pity such a pooty building should be hinjured by the hangry helements," says he. "Look here," says Levison, "I've helped you to build the church, and given my share; if God Almighty chooses to knock it down again, He can do so, it's no business of mine any further," he says.'

Ernest thought this very like one of Levison's reflective, unprejudiced speeches, and could imagine his saying it without any feeling of irreverence. Five hundred pounds without a word, unobtrusively, hardly caring to use his own well-known name for fear of the drawbacks and disabilities of proverbial wealth. 'A most extraordinary man truly,' thought Ernest—'simple, strong, manifestly of the true hunter type; a man given to lone journeyings through the wilderness; fond of preserving his incognito, and of the small, wellnigh incredible economies which speak to him of his earlier life.' Now, Mr. Neuchamp saw the secret of the ultra-respectful bearing of the servants and landlord of the inn to the owner of a couple of millions of acres, leasehold, and of more sheep than Esterhazy, and more cattle than a score of Mexican rancheros. 'He certainly is a man of unpretentious demeanour,' thought Ernest. 'Whoever would have guessed that he was so tremendous a proprietor! "Don't you go for to waste your money." Was that the way he had made the nucleus of this colossal fortune? and did the occasional saving of a meal, and the utilising of the edible plants of the plain and forest dell, go to swell the rills which joined their streams of profit into the great river of his prosperity?' Ernest Neuchamp all but resolved to give up speculating upon the character and professions of these provokingly unintelligible colonists, to believe what he saw—even that, with deduction and reason—and to 'learn and labour truly to get his own living,' without constant reference to the motives and practice of others engaged in the same necessary pursuit. All this he for the time fully believed that he would in the future carry out. But his nature, with its passionate proclivities for intellectual research, continued to whisper of regions of territory and character yet unexplored, and to beckon the ardent champion of light and truth forward even yet, though clouds of distrust and disappointment clustered round his path.

Mr. Neuchamp decided to stay where he was that evening, and to take a strictly impartial and prosaic survey of the town and environs.

# CHAPTER IX

The town of Nubba was a fair specimen of Australian settlement that gradually grows and bourgeons on a favourable spot, where highroads pass and converge. Here there had been, primarily, a ford of the occasionally flooded river. The teams, bound from or for the far interior, camped upon the broad flat made by the semicircular sweep of the river, and so established it as a stage and a resting-place. Then a reflective mail-driver built a public-house, doubtful but inevitable precursor in all colonial communities of civilisation, even of the organised teaching of Christianity. Then a blacksmith's shop, a butcher's, a baker's, followed; in due course a second inn, a pound, appeared; finally a bridge was built; and Nubba represented an established fact, named, inhabited, and fairly started in the competitive race with other Anglo-Saxon cities, walled and unwalled.

Still further progress. Anon it boasted a full-blown municipality, with a mayor, aldermen, a town clerk, ratepayers, all the ordinary British machinery for self-government. The streets were aligned, metalled, and culverted; the approaches to the town cleared and levelled; several stores, two flour mills, three banks, four churches, ten hotels, and scores of intermediate edifices, including a massive gaol, all built of stone, arose. A resident police magistrate reigned, having jurisdiction over three hundred square miles, assisted by neighbouring country justices. Strict, not stern, they were a terror to evildoers, and no particular laxity of legal obligation was permitted the lieges on account of their distance from the metropolis. Let but so much as a Chinaman or a blackfellow be slain by chance, medley, or otherwise, or a calf stolen, at the extreme limit of this far-stretching territory, and all actors and participators were tried, committed, or discharged, as the case might be. The costly and august machinery of the law was put in motion with the same impassive exactitude as if the offenders resided in Middlesex or Devonshire.

'There,' said Mr. Neuchamp, possessed of these facts, and indeed having experienced in his own person the unrelaxing grip of the law, 'is the precise point of difference between the state of society in English and other communities. In other lands, notably in America, the vast distances and what are superficially called the rude circumstances of early settlement, are permitted to condone infringements upon the social rights. When these become too flagrant Judge Lynch interferes, and rude justice, or injustice, is done. In the meantime, right has often suffered irrevocably at the hands of might. But an Englishman, in what far land soever under the flag of his country, suffers under no such policy of expediency. He carries his law with him. He relies for protection of life and property upon the Queen's Government, to which he has for his life long appealed in his hour of need, and never in vain; and he generally receives justice, whether he be in the heart of a continent or in a populous and accessible seaport.'

Southward of the future city, Mr. Neuchamp observed farms, orchards, enclosed pasture-lands—all the signs of a thriving agricultural district,—great stacks of grain and hay, fields of maize, pigs, and poultry in profusion; while the steam flour mills, whose mechanical whirr and throb ceased not, night or day, showed that the supply of the staff of life was large and continuous. Every farm had been but recently occupied, and yet on all sides fencing, building, girdling trees, the manifold acts of agriculture combined with pasture, were proceeding energetically. The land was richer, the timber more dense, and possibly the climate more temperate and humid than the northerly division following the downward course of the river exhibited.

In this direction the metalled road after a couple of miles abruptly terminated, the way thenceforth continuing by a broad Indian-like trail, which led towards the fervid north. Few trees were seen after this immediate vicinity of the town was quitted, and the immense plain lost itself in a soft and silvery haze which enveloped the far distance and spread to the horizon.

'Well,' soliloquised Ernest, 'this is perhaps not exactly the place a half-pay officer would come to or a reduced merchant's family, anxious to discover cheap living, good society, efficient teaching, musical tuition, and an agreeable climate, in perfect combination. But even they might do worse. The great secret of steady, inevitable prosperity here is the wonderful cheapness of land combined with its abundance.

'What a rush would there be in Buckinghamshire, if "persons about to marry," or others, could "take up," that is merely mark out and occupy, as much land as they pleased up to a square mile in extent, previously paying down "five shillings the acre"—save the mark!

'And the land is as good here, if you except the choicest meadow farms. The climate is benign and healthful—say it is hot during the summer, fewer clothes are wanted; the water is pure and plentiful; firewood costs nothing. The forest is clear of underwood, and park-like; you do not need to hew yourself an opening out of an impenetrable wood, as in Canada. The climate and natural advantages of the land constitute an income in themselves. When I think of the severely tasked lives, the scanty, often dismal, outlook of our labouring classes, I am filled with wonder that they do not emigrate in a body. "To the northward all is" plain.'

Here therefore Mr. Neuchamp observed but faint signs of civilisation. The pastoral age had returned. Great droves of cattle, vast flocks of sheep, alone travelled this endless trail. The mail, of course, dusty and of weather-beaten aspect, occasionally rattled in with sunburned and desert-worn passengers from the inner deserts. But few stock were visible on the plain, 'grassy and wild and bare' within sight of the town. Still, by all classes, Ernest heard this apparently wild and trackless region spoken of as a rich pastoral district, equal in profitable trade to the agricultural division, and indeed perhaps superior in the average of returns for investment.

'I am a great believer in the plough myself,' he thought, 'but I suppose these people know something about their own affairs.'

Mr. Neuchamp was beginning to derive practical benefit from his experiences. This was a great concession for him.

Next morning, having ascertained his line of route, and that Garrandilla was about two hundred and fifty miles distant, Ernest shouldered his knapsack and prepared to finish his little walk.

'It's a lucky thing that there are no Red Indians or wild beasts on this particular war-path,' thought he, as he left the town behind him and was conscious of becoming a speck upon the vast and lonely plain. 'I feel horribly unprotected. Even an old shepherd might rob me, if he had a rusty gun. I might as well have carried my revolver, but the weight was a consideration. How grand this sandy turf is to walk upon. I feel as if I could walk all day. Not a hill in sight either, or, apparently, a stone. I can imagine some people thinking the scene monotonous.'

Such a thought would have occurred to many minds; but there was no likelihood of such a feeling possessing Ernest Neuchamp. To him the strange salsolaceous plants, so succulent and nutritive, were of constant interest and admiration. The new flowers of the waste were freshly springing marvels. The salt lake, strewn with snowy crystals and with a floor like an untrodden ice-field, was a magical transformation. The crimson flags of the mesembryanthemum cast on the sand, the gorgeous desert flower, the strutting bustard, the tiny scampering kangaroo, were all dramatic novelties. As he strode on, mile after mile, at a telling elastic pace, he thought that never in his whole life had he traversed a land so interesting and delightful. All the day across the unending plains, sometimes intersected by small watercourses. Towards nightfall, however, this very unrelieved landscape became questionable. Ernest began to speculate upon the chance of finding a night's lodging. Not that there was any great hardship in sleeping out in the mild autumnal season, but the not having even a tree to sleep under was a condition of things altogether unaccustomed, unnatural, and weird in his eyes.

Just as the sun was sinking behind the far, clear, delicately drawn sky line, a deep fissure was visible in the plain, at the bottom of which lay *planté la,* a rough but not uninviting hostelry. There he succeeded in bestowing himself for the night. He was perhaps more fatigued than at any previous time. He had been excited by the prairie-like nature of the landscape, and had covered more ground than on any day since he started.

The food was coarse and not well cooked, but hunger and partial fatigue are unrivalled condiments. Bread, meat, and the wherewithal to quench thirst are amply sufficient for the real toiler, not overborne, like the luxurious children of civilisation, by multifarious half-digested meals. Mr. Neuchamp, therefore, on the following morning, having slept magnificently and eaten a truly respectable breakfast, surveyed the endless plain from the back of the ravine with undiminished courage.

He amused himself by considering what sort of mental existence the family who kept this wayside caravanserai could possibly lead. 'They must feel a good deal like Tartars,' decided he. 'Here they are deposited, as if dropped from the sky upon this featureless waste. They have no garden, not even a cabbage or a climbing rose; no cows, no sheep; of course they have half a dozen horses. I saw no books. They do not take a newspaper. The landlady and her two daughters occupy themselves in doing the housework, certainly, in a very perfunctory manner. The man of the house moves in and out of the bar, smokes continually, and sleeps on the bench in the afternoons. When travellers come, occupation, profit, society, and information are provided for the whole household till the next invasion. What are their hopes—what their social aims? Some day to sell out and live in Nubba, the landlord informed me. How little of life suffices for the millions who possess it in this curiously fashioned world of ours!'

Mr. Neuchamp took his departure from this uninteresting lodge in the wilderness, and commenced another day's travel, not altogether dissatisfied with the idea that the end of another week would bring his pilgrimage to a close.

Mid-day found him still tramping onward over ground so accurately resembling that he crossed during his previous day's journey, that if he had been carried back he could not have detected the difference. A feeling of great loneliness came over him, and despite the doubtful success of his chance acquaintanceship, he began to wish for another travelling companion, of whatever character or condition in life. He had not shaped this desire definitely for many minutes before, as if the attendant friend was watchful, a man debouched from a shallow watercourse, and walked towards him.

The new-comer carried, like himself, a species of pack strapped to his shoulders, but it was rolled up after the country fashion, in a form commonly known as a 'swag,' containing apparently a pair of blankets and a few articles of necessity.

Ernest saw in the traveller a good-looking, powerful young man, patently of the ordinary type of bush natives of the lower rank—a stockman, station hand, horsebreaker or what not. Then his expression of countenance was determined, almost stern. When Ernest accosted him, and asked him if he were travelling 'down the river,' like himself, his features relaxed and his soft low voice, a very general characteristic of Australian youth, sounded respectful and friendly in answer.

He was therefore considerably astonished when the young man promptly produced a revolver, and presenting it full at Mr. Neuchamp's person, called upon him in an altered voice, rounded off with a ruffianly oath, to give up his watch and money.

The watch was easily seen, as part of the chain was visible, but much marvelled Ernest Neuchamp that the robber, or any other man, should know that he had money with him. It was indeed a chance shot. The young marauder, having judged him to be a gentleman not long in the country, who was fool enough to travel on foot when he had plenty of money to buy a good hack, also decided that he must have a five-pound note or two wherewith to negotiate in time of need.

Ernest Neuchamp was brave. The action of his heart was unaltered. His pulse quickened not as he stood before an armed and lawless man. He did not, of course, particularly care to lose a valuable family gold watch, or ten pounds sterling. But far more deeply than by personal loss or danger was he impressed by the melancholy fact that here was a fine intelligent young fellow, physically speaking, one of the grandest specimens of Caucasian type anywhere procurable, dooming himself, merely by this silly act, with, perhaps, another, to long years of lonely, degrading, maddening prison life. He did not look like a hardened criminal. It may be that a single act of sullen despair, derived from others' guilt, had driven him to this course, which, once entered upon, held no retreat.

There were few cooler men than Ernest. He became so entirely possessed with a new idea, that circumjacent circumstances, however material to him personally, rarely affected him.

'My good fellow,' he commenced, sitting down deliberately, 'of course you can have my watch and a tenner, that I happen to have about me. I don't say you are welcome to them, either. But what principally strikes me is, that you are an awful fool to exchange your liberty, your youth, your good name, your very life, for trifles like these. Did this ever occur to you?' asked Ernest with much gravity, handing out the watch and one five-pound note, and feeling anxiously for the other, as if he hoped he hadn't lost it. 'Why, hang it all, man, you put me in mind of a savage, who sells himself for a few glass beads, a tomahawk, and a Brummagem gun. Surely you *can't* have considered this view of the subject, so deeply important to you?'

'It's devilish important to you too,' said the bushranger grimly, though he looked uneasy. 'You're a rum cove to go talking and preaching to a chap with a revolver at your head.'

'I don't suppose that you would shoot a man in cold blood for giving you good advice! A watch and a few pounds are no great loss to me, but the taking of them means death and destruction to *you*—a living death, worse a hundredfold than if you were lying there with a bullet through your heart. That's what I really feel at this moment. You are taking *your own life with your own hand*! Think, do think, like a good fellow, before it is too late!'

'That you may go straight back to the Nubba police station as soon as I slope,' said the robber. 'I could stop that, you know.'

'I never intended it—not that your threat prevents me. But once entered on the trade of bushranger, I am not the only man you will rob. Others, of course, will inform, and in a week your description—age, height, hair, scar on the forehead and all—will be at every police station in the four colonies. You may have a month's run, or two, and then you are—'

'Shot like a dog, or walled up for life, and driven about like brutes that are called men.'

'Perfectly right. I am glad you agree with my view,' said Ernest eagerly; 'then *why* don't you retreat while you have time, and the chance is open? Look at this blue sky; think of a good horse between your legs on this broad plain, of a day's shooting, of waking full of life and vigour and going cheerfully to work on your own farm. Such a deuced good-looking, upstanding fellow as you are—what devil put it into your head to give every enemy you have in the world such a chance to laugh at you?'

'Perhaps the devil did. Anyhow, I have been hunted about and falsely accused by the police, about horses and cattle that I never saw a head of; so I turned out.'

'Just to put them thoroughly in the right,' said Ernest. 'They will thank you for that, and say they always knew it from the first. For God's sake, if you have a grain of sense in your composition, if you have the least wish to live a man's life and stand erect like a man before your fellows, for the sake of the mother that bore you' (here the robber ground his teeth), 'give up this stupid, stale trick of highway robbery, and you will cheat Old Nick yet.'

'Well, I begin to think I *was* an infernal fool to turn out. It seems a trifle now to be vexed at, but what can I do? I've gone too far to turn back.'

'Have you attempted to stop any one but me?' asked Ernest.

'No! I was waiting for the coach, which ought to have been here by this time, when I met you. Ha! there it comes.'

'Take your resolution now,' said Ernest solemnly, springing to his feet and standing before him. 'Your fate for life or death is in your own hand: the life of a hunted, half-starved wolf, with perhaps a dog's death, on one side; life, health, youth, liberty, perhaps a happy home, on the other. Are you mad, that you hesitate? or does God suffer the enemy to deceive and destroy in the dark hour a lost soul?'

As Ernest spoke, he fixed his clear blue eyes upon the face of the robber, now working as if torn by strong emotion.

Suddenly the latter strode a pace forward, and casting the revolver away as far as he could throw it in the dull green grass, said, 'Damn the — squirt! I wish I had never seen it. Here's your two fives, sir, and my best thanks, for I ain't much of a talker, but I feel it. Good-bye.'

'Stop!' cried Ernest, 'where are you going, and what do you intend to do, and have you any money?'

'I don't know. I haven't a copper; it was being chaffed about that by a girl I was fond of that made me think of this. I suppose I'll drop across work before long. God knows! it's never hard to get in the bush.'

'The deeper shame on him who takes to evil courses in such a country,' said Ernest; 'but I don't intend to preach to you. You have acted like a man, and I will stand to you as far as I can. I can perhaps get you work on a station I am bound for. So come along with me, and we shall be fellow-travellers after all.'

The coach passed just then, filled with passengers, who looked with idle curiosity at the wayfarers.

'Those chaps would have had a different look in their eyes about this time, only for you,' said the ex-brigand grimly. 'A little thing makes all the difference. I might have shed blood or got hit before this. However, all that's past and gone, I hope. I can work, as you'll see, and I'll keep square for the future if I haven't a shirt to my back.'

The armistice completed, the two curiously-met comrades recommenced their march. When Mr. Neuchamp, once more in possession of his timekeeper and cash, had sufficient leisure to return to his usual observing habit, he could not but be struck with the fine form and splendid proportions of Mr. 'First robber,' who went singing and whistling along the road with an elastic step, as if care and he had parted company for ever and a day. He was a brown-haired, bright-eyed, good-natured-looking fellow of five or six and twenty. His natural expression seemed to be that of mischievous, unrestrained fun, though the lower part of his face in moments of gravity showed firmness and even obstinacy of purpose. He stood nearly six feet in height, with the build of an athletic man of five feet eight. His broad shoulders, deep chest, and muscular arms showed to considerable advantage in contrast with his light, pliant, and unusually active lower limbs.

'A dangerous outlaw,' thought Mr. Neuchamp; 'roused by resistance, whetted with the taste of blood, and desperate from a foreknowledge of heavy punishment, he would have ended his life on the scaffold, with perhaps on his head the blood of better men; and it looks as if I, Ernest Neuchamp, have this day been the instrument of turning this man's destiny, at the point of amendment or ruin. "So mote it be."'

The day was spent, and Mr. Neuchamp had begun to entertain transient thoughts of moderate roadside comforts and the like, when his companion stopped and pointed to a cloud of dust almost at right angles to the road.

'Travelling sheep,' he said, 'and coming this way—a big lot, too.'

'Are they?' inquired Mr. Neuchamp. 'What are they doing out there?'

'Travelling for grass, most likely; or for sale. Perhaps short of feed or water, or both; they're "out on the wallaby" until the rain comes.'

'What is the meaning of "out on the wallaby"?' asked Ernest.

'Well, it's bush slang, sir, for men just as you or I might be now, looking for work or something to eat; if we can't get work, living on the country, till things turn round a little.'

'Oh! that's it—well, don't be afraid, things are sure to turn round a little, if we wait long enough. Who's this, coming galloping at such a rate?'

'Looks like the overseer. He's coming to see if there's any water in the creek. They'll camp here most likely. He's in a hurry.'

The individual thus criticised was a stout man, past middle age, who bore himself with an air of great responsibility and anxiety.

'Hallo!' he said, pointing to the creek, 'is there any water there?'

'Lots,' said the pene-felonious traveller—'good place to camp.'

'How do you know?' cautiously inquired the overseer.

'Because I've been this road often, and know every water-hole and camping-place and feeding-ground from this to Wentworth.'

'All right, you're the very man I want; that is, I want two men for one of the flocks. I've just sacked a couple of idle rascals, and run short—will you and your mate come?'

'He's not used to droving work,' pleaded the experienced one, doubtful of Ernest's wish for occupation of that sort.

'Oh, never mind; any fool can drive travelling sheep; you're sharp enough, at any rate. I'll give you five-and-twenty shillings a week each. You can join when they come into camp. What do you say?'

'Very well,' said Ernest, 'I will engage for a month—not longer, as I have to go to a station called Garrandilla then.'

'All right,' said the overseer, 'we pass it; it will be something to get hands so far;' and away the man of many troubles galloped.

'What do you say now? Here we are provided with easy, honest, and well-paid employment for as long as we please, with high wages, unlimited food, and sleeping accommodation. I shall rather take them in at Garrandilla.'

The army of sheep—about thirty thousand, in fifteen flocks—at length reached the valley before dark, and the overseer, pointing to a flock of two thousand more or less, said, 'There's your mob—if either of you want to go, you must give me a week's notice. If I sack either of you, I shall pay him one week in advance.'

As the sheep approached, feeding in a leisurely manner, and gradually converging towards the flat, the two men walked towards the leading flock.

'Hallo!' said the ex-brigand to one of the shepherds, 'are you the two chaps that the cove has sacked, because we are to take your flock?'

'All right—you're welcome, mates, to my share,' said an elderly colonist; 'that super's a growlin', ignorant beggar as runs a feller from daylight to dark for nothing at all. If all the other men was of my mind we'd leave him to drive his — sheep himself.'

'That's the talk!' said the highwayman cautiously, 'but we're hard up, and that makes the difference; we go on till we pick up something better. What will you take for that dog of yours? I suppose he can hunt 'em along.'

'Best dog from here to Bourke. I'll take two pounds for him.'

'No you won't. I'll chance a note for him, and that's about our last shilling, isn't it?' added he, looking at Ernest.

'Well, the dog's worth a couple of notes, young feller,' said the shepherd reflectively, 'but as you're a-goin' to take the sheep, and down on your luck, why, you can have him.'

Ernest nodded assent as purse-bearer.

'Will you give us chain and collar in the camp to-night? I'll pay you there,' said the negotiator. 'I suppose you won't clear out till to-morrow?'

'No fear—it's a good way to Nubba, and Bill and I are going back to the timber country; we've had enough of these blasted plains, ha'n't we, Bill?

Enough to burn a blessed man's blessed eyes out. Five-and-twenty bob a week don't pay a cove for that. I mean to stick to the green grass country for a spell now.'

At nightfall the fifteen flocks of sheep were all brought in, and 'boxed,' or mixed together, to Ernest's astonishment. 'How in the world do they ever get them into the same flocks again?' he asked.

'They don't try,' it was explained. 'They just cut them up into fifteen equal lots in the morning, as near as they can, a hundred or two more or less makes no great difference, and away they go along the road stealing as much grass as the squatters are soft enough to let them.'

'And will they stay quietly here all night?'

'Safe as houses. Sheep ain't like cattle; they don't like skirmishing about in the dark. So after tea a man can light his pipe, roll his blanket round him, and make believe to watch till daylight. It's a very off chance if e'er a sheep stirs any more than himself.'

'It doesn't seem a hard life,' said Ernest, as they sat on a log and ate chops fried in a pan, using a large flat piece of damper partly as plate, partly as *entrée,* while the pint of quart-pot tea tasted better and was more refreshing than the highest priced Souchong in the daintiest china.

'Well, it's a long way from hard work, but six months of it at a time, as I've had now and then, makes you feel you've had enough for a while; besides, it's Sunday and workday; not an hour's change week in, week out.'

'I daresay that makes a difference,' admitted Ernest, 'but I wonder what a Buckinghamshire field labourer would think if he were suddenly offered twenty-five shillings a week, with all the bread and mutton he could eat, and a small bag of tea.'

'And half rations for the dawg,' put in the Australian, throwing their new purchase about half a pound of mutton.

'By the way,' said Ernest, 'what is his name? and yours too, for I don't know yet? I suppose he will be very useful. I'm glad you bought him.'

'My name's Jack Windsor; his name's Watch; he's that useful that three men with two pairs of legs each couldn't do the work that he'll do for us with these crawling sheep. He's a cheap pound's worth, and that you'll find before we go far.'

When the evening meal was finished Mr. Neuchamp and his henchman went over to one of four fires which had been lighted at opposite sides of the woolly multitude. Jack Windsor lighted his pipe and lay down upon his blanket, where he smoked luxuriously and dozed by turns. Ernest reclined in the same fashion, and after a short struggle with his very natural drowsiness fell fast asleep.

At daylight next morning Mr. Neuchamp awoke without it being necessary for any one to call him. The bosom of great mother Hertha was harder than any resting-place which he had hitherto tried; but youth and an adventurous disposition being on his side, he found when dressed that the mental thermometer registered an altitude fully above the average. The sheep were still lying down and appeared by no means to be anxious to crop the dewy grass, or whatever somewhat wiry and infrequent herbage did duty for that traditional description.

'Yonder's the cook's fire,' explained Mr. Windsor, pointing to a rising smoke; 'we'd better get our breakfast to begin with.'

Round a blazing fire, the warmth of which, in the sharp autumn morning, was decidedly pleasant, were grouped thirty or forty men engaged in talking, warming themselves, and in a leisurely way partaking of a substantial breakfast. From a pyramid of chops, replenished from an immense frying-pan, with a handle like a marlin-spike, each man abstracted whatever he chose. Wedges of damper (or bread baked in hot ashes) were cut from time to time from great circular flat loaves of that palatable and wholesome but somewhat compressed-looking bread, while gallons of hot tea were procurable from buckets full of the universal bush beverage.

The overseer and some of the horse drivers were absent, as the hacks and cart-horses had wandered during the night rather farther than usual. Ernest and his companion applied themselves to the serious business of the hour, the former conscious that he was being subjected to a searching inspection from his fellow-employees. His rough tweed suit was sufficiently different from the blue serge shirts and peajackets of the others to mark his different social position, had not his hands, fresh complexion, and general appearance denoted him to be a 'new arrival,' and more or less a swell. Swells out of luck are unfortunately by no means rare as ordinary bush hands in Australia, and such a phenomenon would not ordinarily have excited curiosity or hostile criticism. Still a little rough jesting is not to be avoided sometimes when an obviously raw comrade joins a bush brigade.

It was natural enough then that a tall, dissipated-looking fellow with a whiskerless face and long hair, a leader and wit of the community, should step forward and address Mr. Neuchamp.

'Well, Johnny, and what do you think of travelling with store sheep in this blessed country? You didn't do none o' that in the blessed old country as you've just come from, did ye now?'

'My name is not Johnny,' replied Ernest, arresting mastication and looking calmly at his interlocutor. 'As for driving sheep, it would be pleasant enough if people didn't ask impudent questions.'

There was a shout of laughter from the crowd at this retort, which was held to have rather turned the tables upon the provincial humorist.

'Come, come, Johnny! don't cut up rusty,' he continued; 'you may as well tell us what sort of work you bolted from to turn knock-about-man; counter-jumping, or something in the figs line, by the look of your 'ands, eh?'

Mr. Neuchamp had a reasonably good temper, but he had not as yet been accustomed to aught but extreme civility from the lower classes. He had not slipped on too recently the skin of a knock-about-man to realise how it felt to be chaffed as an equal by a fellow-servant.

'You're an insolent scoundrel,' said he, dashing down the remainder of his breakfast, 'whom I will soon teach to mind his own business. Put up your hands.'

Ernest, though not above the middle size, was strongly knit, and had received the ordinary fisti-culture which enables the average English gentleman to hold his own so creditably against all comers. He was a hard hitter when roused, and doubtless would have come out of the encounter with honour. But his antagonist was three inches taller, longer in the reach, a couple of stones heavier, and being in top wind and condition after six months' road-work, and withal a sort of second-rate bruiser, might have inconvenienced and would certainly have marked Mr. Neuchamp in any case.

Just as his late tormentor had lounged forward into a careless guard and an insolent oath, Ernest felt himself quickly but firmly pushed aside, while Jack Windsor stood like a lion in the path.

'Take it out of me, ye cursed infernal bully; what the devil is it to you if a gentleman likes to have his colonial experience this way? You're a deal too fond of showin' off and taking the change out of men that isn't your match. Now you've dropped in for it lucky. Mind yourself.'

The crowd closed in with great though unspoken delight at this prospect of a real good fight. They intended to interfere directly the new chum, as they called him, and 'Bouncing Bob' had had the first flutter. But here was a 'dark horse,' evidently good for a close heat. What a glorious relief from the monotony of their daily dodging along the road with stubborn and impoverished sheep!

'Bouncing Bob,' though a smart fellow enough with his hands, liked a small allowance of weight, science, or pluck; he was better at a winning than an uphill fight. He now distinctly felt that the chances in the contest would be likely to be the other way.

Mr. John Windsor did not leave him long in doubt. Quick as lightning his left was in, and though by a rapid counter Bob managed to score a smack that counted for first blood, it was apparent that he was no match for the stranger, who was at once stronger, more active, and more scientific.

A couple of inches shorter, Jack Windsor was the heavier man. Bob's activity gave him the chance of escape from two falls, one of which nearly finished the fray; but he failed to come so well away from a right-handed feint, which occasioned his catching finally a terrific left-hander, sending him down so decisively that he saw no particular use in coming to time.

'I suppose I may as well give you best,' he said, rising with some difficulty and showing an apparently fatally ensanguined countenance; 'I didn't begin except for a bit of chaff. It's making a darned fuss about a — new chum.'

With this Parthian shaft he departed, to be in readiness for the flock when cut off; while Jack Windsor amused himself whistling softly. Before he replaced his shirt he said, 'Now, look here, boys; we don't want to interfere with anybody, but this gentleman here is my master for the time, and any one who wants to take the change out of him will have to come to me first.'

'All right,' said one of the crowd; 'it won't do Bouncing Bob any harm to get a floorer or two, he's only being paid for many a dab he's given himself.'

Just at this moment a great clatter of bells was heard, and the overseer rode in at a gallop on a barebacked steed, with all the camp horses before him.

'Now, look alive, men, and get your sheep out. Don't be sticking in this camp all day. Hallo! What's the row about?'

'Nothing much, sir,' returned Windsor respectfully; 'me and that long chap they call Bob had a bit of an argument; he began it, and he's got a black eye or two. I don't suppose there'll be any more of it.'

'Well, take care there is not, or I shall have to sack the pair of you. Quite enough to do without fighting now. Get away with your sheep, like good fellows. The carts can follow.'

A section of about the required number having been made at the time by a line of men getting behind the leading sheep and driving them forcibly forward, at the same time preventing them (if possible) from running back to the still larger lot, Jack signed to Mr. Neuchamp, and putting the dog Watch at their heels, who aided them vociferously, they found themselves in possession of eighteen or nineteen hundred sheep, which they drove for some distance at right angles to the road.

'Now what we've got to do, sir,' said Jack, 'is to keep quietly behind these sheep all day. We must not go more than half a mile away from the road, or we'll be 'pounded. We can't follow the flock in front very close or let the one behind get too near us, or we shall get boxed.'

'What do you mean by boxed?' demanded Ernest.

'Well, mixed up. You see, sir, sheep's very fond of keeping all together. It's their nature. If they get any way close they begin to run, the front to the back and the back to the front, and all the men and dogs in the world wouldn't keep 'em apart.'

'And what harm would that be?'

'Well, we should have four thousand sheep to manage instead of two, and they wouldn't drive so well or feed so well, and as these sheep are as poor as crows already, that wouldn't suit.'

'I see,' replied Ernest. 'I think I understand the principle of the thing.'

'All right, sir,' assented Jack. 'Now, we've got the day before us, and nothing to think about till dinner-time but the sheep. Did you bring any grub with you?'

'Not I—don't we stop?'

'Not a stop till sundown. You see, sir, the days are short now, and it's more fair and straightforward like to the sheep to let 'em go nibbling and feeding all day, just keeping their right distance from one another, till camping time, then they draw in together, and they can camp till further orders.'

To keep slowly walking up and down, back and forward, behind a flock of sheep, from 7 or 8 A.M. till 5 P.M., the rate of speed and progress being considerably under a mile an hour, did not seem likely to turn out a cheerful occupation for three weeks. Mr. Neuchamp's heart sank under the contemplation for a moment. But after all he considered that he was doing a good deed in the conversion of a weak brother (morally) from a criminal career to honesty and a good reputation. This was a result which would have overpaid him for considerably more inconvenience than he was liable to suffer now. Besides, he was picking up colonial experience practically with greater speed and thoroughness than he was likely to do at any station; therefore he stifled all unworthy feelings of impatience, and trudged steadily behind his sheep, at the opposite side from Windsor, as if he had been born and bred for the task, like the dog Watch.

That sagacious animal excited his astonishment and respectful admiration. The livelong day he kept trotting backward and forward behind the flock, always keeping at a certain distance, and merely intimidating the lingerers and weakly ones without harshness or violence. If a sufficiently lively crawl was not pursued, he occasionally, by a gentle make-believe bite, gave a hint as to what he could do if necessary. His half-human instinct had plainly convinced him that loudness of bark and general assertion were amply sufficient in the woolly as in the human world to produce the most gratifying submission and acknowledgment of superiority.

About noon the fresh air, the continuous though not violent exercise and healthy appetite of youth, combined to produce a feeling of deep regret that he had not been more provident about lunch. However, Mr. Jack Windsor, drawing over, produced a large parcel containing corned mutton and bread enough for an English labourer's family for a week.

'I thought, sir, as you'd like a snack, so I muzzled enough grub for two; I've got some cold tea in the billy.'

Ernest noticed that his retainer had commenced to carry a small camp kettle containing probably two quarts, which he nothing doubted held water. This repast was now complete. The friends munched away at the very substantial luncheon as they strolled along behind the ever-nibbling sheep, and after giving Watch a very ample supply, washed it down with nectar in the shape of cold tea.

'Well,' quoth Mr. Neuchamp, with a deep sigh of contentment, 'how comparative are all things! I never remember to have enjoyed a mid-day meal more in my life. This fresh day air must be a wonderful tonic; or is it the early rising and Arcadian simplicity of life? I believe that they insist upon a lot of virtuous behaviour at a cold-water establishment such as the people would never stand in their ordinary lives. But because it's an "establishment" they let the doctor bully them to bed at nine, get up at six, eat early dinners of mutton chops and rice puddings (how I laughed at a guardsman's face at Ben Rhydding once when the bell rang at 1 P.M. and he was marshalled to such a repast), and unexpectedly find themselves placed in possession of an appetite and health again.

'It's something of the same sort of thing here. If I had gone a trip with a drover from Tillyfour to London with West Highland cattle, I daresay I should have doubled my appetite and general vitality. There, however, it is not "the thing" to do. Here it is not the best form apparently—but you may carry it off without any accusation of insanity. One thing is certain, I shall never respect good cooking so much again. The cook to cultivate is *yourself* unquestionably. Guard your appetite, keep it in a state of nature, and the rudest materials, if wholesome, provide us with a daily feast, and a measure of enjoyment of which over-civilised, latter-day men are wholly ignorant and incapable.'

# CHAPTER X

The days, after all, passed not so funereally by. The weather was utterly lovely. The wide plain was fanned by delicious wandering breezes. Mr. Neuchamp had ample time for philosophical contemplation, as long as he 'kept up his side' of the flock. If he became temporarily abstracted while musing upon the fact that the ancients travelled their stock for change of feed, probably doing a little grass stealing, when the season was dry—

'Pecusve Calabris ante sidus fervidum

Lucana mutet pascua'—

the dog, Watch, would be sent round by his alert comrade to sweep in the spreading outsiders and warn him of his laches. Just before sundown one day the flocks were converging towards a line of timber suspiciously like a creek. The overseer rode up. He looked with approval upon the well-filled flock, now quietly feeding, and thus addressed Ernest—

'Well, youngster, and how do you like shepherding?'

'Pretty well,' he answered; 'it's better than I expected.'

'You and your mate seem to get on very well; the sheep look first-rate.'

'Glad you think so. My mate is a person of experience, so is the dog. It isn't hard to drive a flock of sheep, I find, with two good assistants.'

'Well, I don't suppose you'd have made much hand of them by yourself. However, a man's a man when you're travelling with sheep on a road like this. Don't you listen to those other vagabonds, and you'll make a smart chap by and by.'

'Thank you,' said Ernest; 'I'll try and keep as innocent as I can under the circumstances.'

The overseer rode off, puzzled as to whether the new hand was laughing at him or was 'a shingle short.' Slightly damaged people, whether from drink, disappointment, a lonely life, or the heat of the climate, were, unfortunately, not particularly scarce in the locality.

'Whatever he is, he and that rowdy-looking card can keep their sheep and feed them first-rate,' he said to himself, 'and that's all I've got to look out for. Perhaps the young one's going jackerooing at Jedwood; if so, he has more sense than he looks to have.' The month wore on with dreaminess and peace, so that Mr. Neuchamp began to think he would not be so unreasonably delighted to get to Garrandilla. Each day, soon after sunrise, they moved from camp at a pace extremely suitable to the thick coming fancies which filled the mind of Ernest Neuchamp during the first hours of the untarnished day. There was the glorious undisturbed sun, with autumnal tempered beams. On such endless plains Chaldean and Israelitish shepherds, in the world's youth, had travelled or held vigil. No vast awe-striking ruins lay on these great solitudes. No temple eloquent of the elder races of the earth. But the stars burned by night in the all-cloudless dark blue dome as they sat in nominal watch, and Ernest mused of the silent kings of this mysterious human life, changeless destiny, till the morning star seemed to approach his solitary couch, as did that lonely orb which held converse with Morven, the son of Ossian.

In the daily round of guiding and pasturing he learned much of the complex nature of the under-rated intelligence of the sheep. His companion, Mr. Jack Windsor, had cultivated a habit of observation, and knew, as gradually appeared, something, not always a little, of everything rural.

'Rum things sheep, sir,' he would remark, as he commanded Watch to abstain from troubling and signalled Mr. Neuchamp to come on to his side; 'I always see a deal of likeness to the women about 'em. If they don't want to do a thing you can't drive 'em to it. No, not all the men and dogs in the country. If you want 'em to do anything particular, pretend you don't wish 'em to do nothin' of the sort. Give 'em lots of fair play, that's another good rule, same as women. When it comes to anything out-and-out serious, act determined, and let them have it, right down heeling, and all the fight you're master of.'

As it was from time to time pointed out, when principles and admonitions came into play, Ernest was enabled to comprehend the many ways in which stock can be benefited when travelling by discreet and careful feeding, halting, watering, and humouring. So that he actually possessed himself of an amount of practical knowledge with which a year's ordinary station life might not have provided him. As for the rest of the men, his easy, unassuming equality of manner had rendered him personally a favourite with them. They held that a fair fight settled everything, without appeal, and having come to the conclusion that Mr. Neuchamp was a swell, presumably with money, travelling with sheep for his amusement—incomprehensible as was that idea to them—they felt that he was in a kind of way Jack Windsor's property, who was likely to be pecuniarily benefited during the stage of Mr. Neuchamp's softness and inexperience. Hence he was in his right to do battle for him. They would have done the same had they similar golden hopes. And now the matter being over, and 'Bouncing

Bob' relegated to a 'back seat' as wit and occasional bully of the camp, they held, after the English fashion, that the discussion could not be reopened. So all was peace and harmony.

One day, as they were sleepily voyaging over the grass ocean, Jack Windsor, who had gone out of his way to look at a man leading a horse, returned with exciting news. The horse aforesaid was young, and in his opinion a great beauty—'a regular out-and-outer,' was the expression—and, by great chance, for sale. 'Would Mr. Neuchamp like to buy him? If he wanted a horse at Garrandilla, he could not do a better thing.'

'When you get there, sir, of course you'll want a hack. There'll be no more walking, I'll be bound. You'll have messages to carry, boundary riding to do, cattle-driving, getting in the horses—all sorts of fast work. Well, either they'll give you a stiff-legged old screw, that'll fall down and break your neck some day, or a green half-broken young one that'll half kill you another road. I know the sort of horses the young gentlemen get at a station where a man like Mr. Jedwood's the boss.'

'Very well, what does he want for the colt? Is he a very good one?'

'I haven't seen his equal for years; don't know as I ever saw a better. Why he's fool enough to sell him I can't tell. But it's all square. I know the man, and where his run is; you'd better go over and see him.'

'So I will; but how can he be kept or broken in?'

'I'll break him; I can rough-ride a bit, and will put him among the other horses and short-hobble him.'

Accordingly Ernest went over and saw a noble, good-tempered-looking dark gray colt. He had a large full eye, black mane, legs, and tail, with a shoulder noticeable even amid the rounded proportions of colthood.

'So this young horse is for sale?' he said inquiringly of a middle-aged stout man, like enough to be a brother to their own overseer.

'Yes!' said the man, pulling at the halter, which had galled the colt's under jaw. 'I started to take him down to the lower station, and he's such a brute to lead that he has nearly pulled me off more than once. I won't lead him a step farther if we can deal.'

'What will you take for him?' asked Ernest.

'Well,' said the stranger, 'I believe he's a real good 'un, though he's never been backed yet. I don't know or care much about horses myself; they're useless brutes, and eat more grass than they are worth. I'll take ten pounds for him.'

'Very well,' said Ernest, 'he's mine at that price, and I will send a man over with the money, if you will deliver the horse to him.'

Jack Windsor was overjoyed to hear that the colt was actually bought.

'I can break him easy enough,' he said, with all the eagerness of a schoolboy. 'He is half handled now, and it will be easy for me to back him.'

'But how shall we keep him till we get to Garrandilla?'

'Oh! I'll square it with the chap that looks after the spare horses; there's a mare with them as he'll likely take to. He can't get away far in hobbles anyhow.'

So Jack being sent off with the whole of Mr. Neuchamp's remaining capital, in half an hour returned with the colt at the end of a long halter, and a properly witnessed receipt from John Williams of Boro, which he handed to Ernest.

'I made him draw out a receipt, all regular, and get the nearest man I could cooey to, to sign it. There's no knowing but somebody might claim the colt without this—say you'd worked him on the cross. There's nothing like being safe with a good horse like this.'

Mr. Neuchamp was pleased with his purchase, which he immediately christened 'Osmund,' after an old hunter with a favourite family name at Neuchampstead.

'I'll do nothing but handle him to-day,' said Windsor; 'to-morrow I'll get a spare saddle and bridle, and will tackle him.'

'Good gracious!' said Ernest, 'is that the way you break horses in this country? Have you no cavesson, or breaking-bit, or web surcingle?'

'All them's very well when you've got 'em,' said Mr. Windsor; 'but they don't have saddlers' shops on the plains, and if a man can ride he can do without 'em, and do justice to his horse too.'

So next day Jack procured an old bridle and saddle, the bit belonging to which he carefully wrapped round with rag, thinly increasing its bulk and rendering it fit for 'mouthing' or slightly bruising, *without cutting*, the corners of the lips of a young horse. This and the saddle, by means of patience and persuasion, he managed to get fairly placed and buckled upon Osmund, who objected a little, but finally marched along not very much alarmed by his novel accoutrements. All this time the sheep-driving was efficiently conducted by Mr. Neuchamp and the dog Watch, who amply justified the anticipations indulged in by Mr. Windsor at the time of his purchase.

In about another week they expected to arrive at Garrandilla, when the curtain would rise on the first act of the drama of Colonial Experience, with Mr. E. Neuchamp in the *rôle* of first gentleman.

Two or three days only had passed when Jack Windsor announced to Mr. Neuchamp that the colt was quite quiet enough to back, and that he would perform the ceremony that very morning, as soon as the sheep were steadied to their first feed.

'Back him, now!' exclaimed Ernest in tones of horror, 'why, he cannot be nearly mouthed.'

'Oh yes, he is,' assented Mr. Windsor, playfully pressing against the bit and causing Osmund to retrograde; 'he's got mouth enough for anything, and between leading and hobbling he's steady enough to make a wheeler in a coach. When I have finished you won't find fault with him for not being steady, I'll be bound. Just you stand close to his shoulder, and hold him while I get up.'

Ernest, though much mistrusting the preliminary instruction of a week's leading, and the simple addition of a bridle and saddle as being sufficient to take the place of all the two months' lunging, belting, cavessoning, driving, dressing, which had been the invariable curriculum of the colts at Neuchampstead, deferred to his follower's opinion.

'I don't think he's got any bucking in him,' he said; 'he carries his head too high for that, and his mouth's that tight, I could pull him on to his tail if he tried any tricks. He's a bit frightened, and when he's got over that he'll go like an old horse.'

'I should say that buckjumping was produced in this country by bad breaking,' said Mr. Neuchamp oracularly. 'It all depends upon how a horse is treated.'

'Don't you believe it, sir. Bucking is like other vices. Runs in the blood. I've seen horses that had twice and three times the time taken over 'em that this colt has, and by good grooms too, in good stables, and they'd buck, and buck too till they'd half kill themselves, or you. And as for a stranger, they'd eat him.'

'And how do you account for that?' asked Mr. Neuchamp. 'Why should one horse be free from that particular vice, and another with the same amount, or even more handling, be unmanageable from it?'

'Why do boys at the same school turn out different? It depends upon the families they come off. So it is with the horses. One strain will be reg'lar cannibals, no matter how steady you are with 'em; the others you can catch and ride away, and they'll be as quiet as lambs, and yet game all the time, as I believe this one of ours is.'

As he spoke he touched the colt's side, and he moved off after the sheep in a steady and confident manner, more like an old horse than a young one. He occasionally stopped and sidled, or indulged in a playful plunge or kick. Of course these little irregularities were only amusing to Mr. Windsor, who was in truth a matchless rough-rider, and wellnigh impossible to be thrown by horses of good family or bad. By the end of the day Osmund was apparently as quiet as a trooper, and when unsaddled and turned out seemed quite at home with the cart-horses.

'Now,' said Mr. Windsor, as they sat at their evening meal, 'you've got, sir, what everybody is always a-talkin' about and never seems to get, an out-and-out good hack, fast and easy and well bred, and a stunner to look at. I'll forfeit my month's wages if he ain't a sticker, as well. These quiet ones are just as game as the savages, and indeed more so, in my opinion, because they can eat and rest themselves better. And I wouldn't sell him, if I was you, if I was offered double what you gave for him.'

'I don't think I will,' said Ernest; 'but surely good horses are easily picked up in this country, if one is a fair judge. There must be such thousands upon thousands.'

'So there are,' replied the Australian, 'but we might be gray before you dropped on another nag like this, 'specially for ten notes. Look at his shoulder, how it goes back; see what loins he has; good ribs; with out-and-out legs and feet. He's more than three-parts bred; and if he don't gallop and jump a bit I'm much deceived. He's a bottler, that's what he is; and if you ever go for to sell him, you'll be sorry for it.'

'Well, I don't think I will, Jack,' asserted Mr. Neuchamp. 'I shall always want a horse while I'm in the country, and I think I shall make a pet of this one.'

For the remaining days, before the 'reporter' entered the Garrandilla gate, to give legal notice of the invading army of fleece-bearing locusts, Osmund was ridden daily, and became more docile and obedient to the *manège* day by day.

As the long lines of sheep, flock after flock, fed up and finally mingled at the Garrandilla gate, a big man, with a distinctly northern face, rode up on a powerful horse and looked keenly at the array of sheep, horses, men, and dogs.

'Where's the person in charge?' he asked of one of the shepherds.

'I believe he has gone to the township,' said the man; 'he'll be here to-night.'

'Have you seen anything of a young gentleman coming up to my station? I am Mr. Jedwood.'

'Not that I know of. There's two chaps with that last flock, one of 'em's a "new chum."'

Mr. Jedwood rode down to the flock indicated, and there discovered Mr. Neuchamp in the act of eating a piece of boiled corned mutton, and looking around in an unsatisfied manner, as if anxious for more.

'You are Mr. Neuchamp, I think, a gentleman introduced by letter to me by my old friend Paul Frankston?'

'The same,' said Ernest, putting down his damper and mutton carefully and standing up. 'I intended to present myself to-morrow morning, after being settled with.'

'Settled with?' said Jedwood, in a tone of astonishment. 'You don't mean to say you've really hired yourself to drive travelling sheep! Not but it's a sensible thing enough to do; still you're the first "colonial experience" young fellow that it ever occurred to within my knowledge.'

'I had reasons for it, which can be better explained by and by,' answered Ernest. 'In the meantime, there is a travelling companion of mine whom I should feel obliged if you could employ at Garrandilla. Jack, come here!'

Mr. Jedwood looked keenly at the ingenuous countenance of Mr. Jack Windsor, and then, after suffering his eye to fall approvingly upon his athletic frame, said—

'There's always employment at Garrandilla for men that know how to work, and are not afraid to put out their strength. What can you do, young man?'

'Well, most things,' answered the Australian, with quiet confidence; 'fence, split, milk, drive bullocks, stock-keep, plough, make dams, build huts; I'm not particular, till August, then I'm a shearer.'

'Can you break horses?' asked the squatter, 'for I have a lot of colts I want badly to put to work, and I can't get a decent man to handle them.'

'I can break horses with here and there one,' responded this accomplished new-world labourer. 'Mr. Neuchamp and I finished one as we come along, didn't we, sir?'

'*You* did, and wonderfully well and quickly, too,' assented Ernest. 'I had nothing to do but to hold him. I think I can give my personal guarantee, Mr. Jedwood, if you think it of any value, that Jack can tame any horse in the land.'

'Then you can come up to-morrow with Mr. Neuchamp,' said the squatter, 'and I'll hire you till shearing. Shall I send a horse for you?' he added, addressing Ernest.

'No, thanks, I have my own here; I'll ride him up.'

'You seem to be pretty well provided for a new arrival,' said the proprietor good-humouredly. 'What with your wages in hand, a horse, a man, and a month's character as a travelling drover, you have not wasted your time much, though old Paul seemed quite anxious about you, and wrote several letters.'

On the following morning Mr. Neuchamp had a short interview with his master, the overseer, who was in high good humour, having secured two hands in their place at the township aforesaid, one of them a shepherd, most fortunately, at the right (*i.e.* the concluding) end of his cheque.

'Well, you're going to leave us, I suppose, just as you're getting used to the sheep; but I can't complain, as you gave me fair notice. You've been a month, that makes five pounds each. Here's your money, lads,' with which he tendered a five-pound cheque to each of them. 'Good-day to you, and good luck.'

'Good-morning. You have my best wishes,' said Ernest, making a bow which quite overwhelmed the overseer.

'Here you are, Jack,' said Mr. Neuchamp, as soon as the man of sheep had departed; 'I always intended you to have my share of the profits of this droving transaction.'

'That be hanged for a yarn! I beg your pardon. I mean, I couldn't think of taking it, sir.' And Jack's face really assumed a most unwonted expression—that of genuine diffidence and modesty.

'But you must,' said Ernest imperatively; 'you must take it, in payment for the discovery and breaking of Osmund, besides you will want a fit-out in clothing and other things.' So he cast the cheque at his feet.

'Well, if I must, I must,' said Mr. Windsor reluctantly. 'It's a good while since I was as rich as this, and all on the square, too; that's what gets me. Never mind, sir, if we both live you'll get over-value for this bit o' paper some day.'

It was now time to make tracks for Garrandilla. Ernest did not see any road, or know the precise line of country, but Mr. Windsor taking the matter in hand, they soon found themselves in front of a very small slab cottage, standing solemnly alone, at the rear of which, however, were huts, sheds, farm buildings, and haystacks, in such number and abundance that Ernest thought they must have fallen upon the township by mistake.

Mr. Jedwood, however, appeared at the door, and walking out to meet them, told Windsor to betake himself to the stables, and to remain there until he came out to see him, to feed the horse, and to inquire of the groom, who would inform him where he could feed himself. He then invited Ernest to follow him into the house.

'I am glad to find that you have turned up at last,' said his host; 'not that, of course, never having seen you, I should have grieved overmuch myself if you hadn't, but poor old Paul seemed so anxious that, for his sake, I began to feel an interest in you. If you will walk this way I will show you your room in the barracks—there is a pile of letters for you.'

Ernest felt really pleased to be placed in possession once more of any sort of bedroom, and proceeded to render himself presentable to general society. After these necessary changes had been accomplished, he commenced to look over his letters, of which there were—*Americanicé*—'quite a number.'

First of all he opened one in the bluff characters of Mr. Frankston, bold, and easily read, as the true heart of the writer. It ran thus:—

> My dear Boy—What, in the name of all the rocks and shoals between the Sow and Pigs and Maafu Reef, are you cruising about so long before turning up at Garrandilla? Is the reason masculine, feminine, or neuter? By the bye, Charley Carryall was here the other day. Told me some first-rate yarns—sorry you weren't at Morahmee to hear 'em. Well, but why haven't you fetched your whaling-ground—I mean your run—yet?
>
> Antonia was in a great way when she saw the telegram, in the *Evening Times*, that you had been apprehended and locked up for keeping company with 'another prisoner.' Ha, ha, ha! Can't help it, couldn't really! She kept picturing you in a dungeon, and all the rest of it. I said that you would enjoy it for a day or two, during the hot weather. What do you think about walking? Have you got a horse yet? We are all very middling. Couldn't you square it with Jedwood to come down at Christmas? There's not much work doing then anywhere. The verandah at Morahmee won't be half a bad place about that time, if it's as hot as it was last year. I saw Hartley Selmore the other day. He sold Gammon Downs to a young fellow, just out. My head clerk is rather a queer old character.
>
> 'Ah! sir,' he said, 'don't you think Mr. Selmore will go to hell for selling such a place to that poor young gentleman?'
>
> 'Really I don't know,' I answered; 'there always seems a sufficient supply of young fellows with a little money and no brains. If they were not gobbled up by the Selmores, some other big fish would be sure to have them.'

However, Antonia said Hartley was a cold-blooded rascal, and I was nearly as bad for making light of his villainy. So I did not take much by my joke.

Stock has fallen since you left town, and will fall more yet if the war does not come to an end, and this very dry season. So your money is all the safer in the bank. Don't on any account invest without consulting me. Work as hard as you like, but don't get sunstroke. Avoid brandy and water; and when you're very tired of wool and bullocks, see if you can't find the road to Morahmee again. Remember me to our Jedwood. He'll keep you up to the mark, unless he's altered.—Your old friend,

Paul Frankston.

# CHAPTER XI

He who embarks upon an enterprise or commences a course of life involving absolute departure from every early habit and association will invariably be assailed at some stage or period by distrust, even by despondency. It is not in man to complete all the multifarious acts and volitions pertaining to any momentous change without experiencing the strongest reactionary impulses to halt, to doubt, to waver, to retreat.

That Ernest Neuchamp possessed these, among other weaknesses of our nature, we are by no means prepared to deny. But he had one counterbalancing quality which oftentimes stood him in good stead, when on the dangerous declivities of indecision. This compensating element was a habit of reasoning out his proceedings logically before the day of battle. He formed his opinions, arranged his movements, with Prussian deliberation and purpose aforethought. Having decided upon his order of action, he vowed mentally that no infringement upon his plan should be suffered, whatever might be his own ephemeral impulses, even convictions.

Thus he often carried out programmes involving foregone conclusions, with ruthless exactitude against every feeling, taste, and sentiment then and there animating his rebellious mind. 'No!' he would repeat to himself. 'I made my calculations, carried out my reasoning to its legitimate demonstration, when no disturbing element was present. Shall I veer with every shift of wind, consult every sudden instinct or every emotional sensation? No—onward by the true and proved course!'

Steadfastly adhering, therefore, to his sketch-map, on the following morning Mr. Neuchamp accompanied his host on a tour of inspection, and gathered some approximate notion of the character of the stock and station, together with the duties which as an aspirant to the comprehensive study of 'colonial experience' he might be expected to perform.

The somewhat extensive property known as Garrandilla was divided by a river, on one side of which natural boundary the stock consisted of sheep—on the other of cattle. The northern subdivision comprised four 'blocks,' having each five miles' frontage to the Wandabyne, a permanent and occasionally turbulently flowing stream. As far back as thirty miles, the lands were held upon the usual lease from the Crown. Through all this great tract of country no man was legally entitled to travel, save on the road which passed along the course of the river, avoiding only the sinuosities of its course. North Garrandilla consisted wholly of saltbush plains, diversified only by 'belts' of myall and eucalyptus forest. It was therefore held to be appropriate for sheep, to the highly successful production of which it had always been devoted.

On the south side, the 'lay of the country,' as Jack Windsor would have called it, was different. Marshy flats, interspersed with lagoons and reed-beds, extended along, and for several miles back from the river. With this exception the greater part of the area was covered with more or less open forest, while at 'the back,' or the extreme limit of the unwatered region away from the river, were ranges of hills precipitous and heavily timbered, among which the cattle roved at will during the winter season, returning to the low grounds as the fierce sun of the Australian waste commenced to dry the interior watercourses.

At a short distance from 'the house,' Mr. Jedwood's cottage, or hut, as the residence of the proprietor was indifferently designated, stood a roomy, roughly finished building known as the 'barracks.' Here lived the overseer, a hard-working, hard-riding, weather-beaten personage, who appeared to exist in a chronic state of toil, anxiety, and general lack of repose.

Three of the numerous bedrooms were tenanted by young men, upon the same footing as Mr. Neuchamp, neophytes, who were gradually assimilating the lore of Bushland, and hoping to emulate the successful career of Allan Jedwood, or other pastoral magnates. One of these was a far-off kinsman, Malcolm Grahame by name, a steady, persevering, self-denying Scot; while another, Mr. Fitzgerald Barrington, erst of Castle Barrington, County Clare, sufficiently expressed his nationality and general tendencies by his patronymic and titular designation. Lastly was a brown Australian boy, of eighteen or nineteen, very sparing of his words, and prone to decry the general intelligence of his comrades, from a comparison of their woodcraft with his own, in which competition they were, for the present, let us say, manifestly inferior.

Into this society Mr. Neuchamp voluntarily and contentedly entered, holding that his education would be the sooner completed if he graduated, so to speak, before the mast, than from the captain's cabin. To the barracks also were relegated those just too exalted for the men's hut, while not eligible for the possibly distinguished company occasionally entertained at 'the cottage.' Such were cattle-dealers, sheep-buyers, overseers of neighbouring stations, and generally unaccredited travellers whose manners or appearance rendered classification hazardous.

Ernest managed to have a preliminary conversation with Mr. Jedwood, in which the latter gentleman, who was extremely plain, not to say blunt, of speech, put his position fairly before him.

'You will understand, Neuchamp,' said he, 'that, though I feel bound, on account of old Paul, who was a good friend to me in time past, to do what I can for you, you must not look for any great amount of consideration from the overseer, Mr. Doubletides, or from the other youngsters. I hope you will all be treated like gentlemen as long as you stay at Garrandilla, but you will be made useful, and set at all sorts of work, in a way perhaps that may sometimes appear strange.'

'Not at all,' replied Ernest. 'I am as anxious as any one can be to master the details of bush life, and the sooner the better. I don't think you will find any false delicacy about me, whatever may be the practical nature of my employment for the present.'

'Well, that's all right,' said Mr. Jedwood heartily. 'It's the best way, too. I had to work, and devilish hard, too, as a youngster, or I should never have been here as master, I can tell you.'

After this conversation, Ernest was put under the immediate orders of the overseer, Mr. Doubletides, who speedily made it apparent to him that bush life at a large station did not entirely consist of galloping about like Bedouin Arabs and reposing under palm or other trees of grateful shade. Galloping about there was, doubtless; but often the rides were long, weary, and unexciting, with absolutely no shade to speak of, while so continuous was the routine of carrying rations, driving sheep, bringing in working bullocks, carting water to out-stations, and generally performing no inconsiderable amount of hardish manual labour, that Mr. Neuchamp at times felt inclined to adopt the same distrustful view of it all which Mr. Weller took of the alphabet—'Whether indeed it was worth going through so much to learn so little.'

In any riding that might be ordered, Mr. Neuchamp fared sumptuously compared with the other cadets, who, confined to the ordinary station-hacks, were constantly complaining of their roughness, insecurity, or generally unamiable qualities. Osmund, now quiet, well fed, and tended in the Garrandilla stables, to use Jack Windsor's expression, 'went like a bird,' and daily demonstrated the soundness of that gentleman's choice and opinion.

Charley Banks, the Australian youngster, admired Osmund in secret very much, and at length offered Ernest five pounds to boot, if he would 'swop,' or exchange him for a chestnut mare which he, Charley, had bought out of the neighbouring pound.

'She's quite good enough for this work, Neuchamp,' he remarked, 'and you might as well have the fiver in your pocket as be wearing out your colt's legs for old Doubletides here. Jedwood will see you far enough before he gives you another one in his place, if you screw him doing his work.'

'And why would he sell or swop him at all, ye little horse-racing divil, that wants to be making a blackleg of yourself at the township races? He's the only horse fit to carry a gentleman I've seen this year past, and the very moral of a horse the whipper-in of the Barrington hounds rode.'

'You be blowed,' retorted the son of the soil; 'I don't believe you rode much to hounds in Ireland or anywhere else, or else you would stick on better.'

'Stick on!' shouted the Milesian. 'I can ride with any cornstalk that ever sat in a thing with a pillow on each flap, that you call a saddle. Sure ye'd be laughed out of any hunting-field in Britain if ye took one of them things there.'

'Well, we can stick to 'em when we are there,' sarcastically observed Mr. Banks; 'I'll bet you the fiver I was going to give Neuchamp, you don't sit for ten minutes on that chestnut colt Jack Windsor's coming up here with now, and he's ridden him, now it's the *third* day.'

Charley Banks emphasised the last number of the colt's daily experiences of man, as if no one but an elderly capitalist, with gout or asthma, could possibly decline so childishly safe a mount.

'Done with you!' shouted the roused son of Erin. 'One would think you conceited cornstalks had discovered the horse, in this sandy wilderness of a country of yours, and that no one had ever ridden or shot flying before he came here.'

'I don't know about shooting,' said the lad reflectively, 'but I'm dashed if ever I saw a new arrival that could sit a buck-jumper, even if he only propped straightforward, and didn't do any side-work. Anyway, we'll see in about five minutes.'

Here Mr. Windsor arrived upon a bright chestnut colt, with three white legs, and a blaze down the face, and a considerable predominance of the same colour into the corners of his eyes, thus giving an expression more peculiar than engaging to those organs, when used for the purpose of staring at the rider. In addition to these peculiarities, he had an uneasy tail, always moving from side to side with a feline, quietly-exasperated expression.

'Good-morning, sir,' said Jack to Ernest. 'Good-morning, gentlemen all; fine growing weather.'

'No finer,' said Barrington; 'how are you getting on with the colts?'

'Not bad,' answered the horse-tamer; 'I've backed two a week since I came, and have three in tackle, in the yard now. This one's a fine colt to go, but he's rather unsettled when the fit takes him.'

'Sorry for that, for I've a bet with Mr. Banks here that I'll mount him and stay on for ten minutes. Sure, ye knew, ye artful colonist, that he was a divil; you won't refuse me the mount, Jack, me boy, breaker to his Highness the Grand Duke of Garrandilla?'

'Not I, Mr. Barrington, if you've got a neck to spare, but you'll bear in mind yourself—he's a sour devil when his blood's up; and mayn't like a stranger. Though he's pretty fair now.'

Here Jack slid quietly to the ground and patted the colt's neck, who snorted, but when soothed was apparently quiet. Barrington gained courage, and taking out his watch, gave it to Ernest to hold.

'Ten minutes,' he said; 'and now I'll bet you all a couple of pounds each, that if I come off, not one of the lot of ye can ride him up to the stockyard and back.'

The bet was taken all round. Mr. Barrington with a confident air advanced, and getting Windsor to hold the colt closely and firmly, mounted easily and rode off. The young horse apparently took no notice of the change of riders for some time, but walked steadily off along a bank which led to the sheep-drafting yard. Barrington was charmed with himself, and with his mount, whom he immediately decided in his own mind to be an animal of fine disposition, in danger of being spoiled, as was usual in the colony, by rough breaking. As he turned back, after about five minutes' ride, he concluded to favour the company with a trot. He therefore touched the colt with his heel and slacked the rein.

Now, whether, as was very possible, though a fair and very bold horseman, he did not sit with the glove-like adherence to the pigskin's surface which characterised Mr. Windsor's every movement, we have no means of knowing; of matters of fact, however, as eye-witnesses, we can judge. The chestnut glanced nervously back with his Albino-tinged eyes, made a rapid swerve, then a diving headlong plunge, instantaneously arrested. This threw forward the incautious Barrington, while with sudden frenzy the now fully-aroused animal bounded galvanically upward with his back arched, and dropped with his mouth wrenched resistlessly from the rider's hold and almost touching the ground.

The suddenness of the act, joined with the convulsive force of the propelling power, first tended to place Mr. Barrington in a somewhat leaning position. From this he was prevented from recovering his place in the saddle by the lightning-like rapidity of the recurring headlong plunges. Strong, fearless, and elastic with the glorious activity of early manhood, he made a desperate struggle to retain his seat; but the deerlike, sidelong bounds, instantaneously reversed, gave him no chance. Failing to follow a terrific side leap, his equilibrium was disturbed, the corresponding swerve sundered him and the saddle still farther, while a concluding upward bound on all fours, 'propping,' so as to progress backward rather than otherwise, shot him forward as from a catapult, head first and clean delivered.

'Ugh! ugh! shall I ever—ugh, ugh—get my wind again? Ugh—you savage, unnatural son of a—ugh—gun—what right have you to be called a horse at all? Sure no one but a blackfellow, or Mexican, or a *native*, Banks, me boy, could expect to sit on such a baste of prey. Here's an order for five pounds, Charley, ye villain; they're good, *as yet*, and now go ride him yourself, and let me enjoy myself looking on.'

Mr. Windsor, on another horse, was by this time in pursuit of the excited animal, which kept snorting, kicking, and otherwise protesting against any other interference with his natural rights.

'He *can* buck a bit,' said Charley Banks, coolly girding himself for the fray by taking off his coat and tightening a leathern strap which he wore round the waist, 'but if you hadn't come forward, Paddy, the first time he propped, he mightn't have gone to market at all. Here goes.'

The chestnut was soon secured by the agile and deft Windsor, and held by that horse-tamer, ready for Charley Banks to bestride. Having divested himself of his coat, he advanced with perfectly unembarrassed mien towards the alarming chestnut. Staring with homicidal glare out of his white-rimmed eyes, the successful combatant was standing perfectly still, but in a constrained and unnatural position.

Before putting his foot in the stirrup, Mr. Banks examined with long-practised eye the gear and accoutrements.

'Why don't you have a surcingle, Windsor?' he said. 'What's a pair of girths to a colt like this? Call yourself a breaker? Where's the crupper?'

'I left them at home, Mr. Banks,' exclaimed the rough-rider. 'Ben Bolt (as I christened him) was getting on so nicely before you young gentlemen came in the way that I never thought of wanting the regular colts' toggery. Besides, it don't matter much.'

'Doesn't it?' demanded the unappeased critic. 'Suppose he sends the saddle over his withers? How's a fellow to sit him with one leg on each side of his neck? However, here goes.'

Mr. Banks, having enunciated his sentiments, quickly slipped into the saddle, and putting his feet well home in the stirrups, cocking up his toes, squaring his shoulders, and leaning slightly back, with easy nonchalance commanded Mr. Windsor to let him go.

Freeing the tameless one on the instant, Mr. Windsor retired a few steps, and awaited for the next act in the performance. The colt seemed in no hurry to make use of his liberty. He stood in a cramped, awkward, half-asleep position. Mr. Banks touched him quietly, but he made no response.

'Oh! hang it,' said that young gentleman, 'I did not bargain to sit here all day. I'll move you.'

Suiting the action to the word, he 'put the hooks on him,' as a jock would have said—in other words, gave him the spurs so unreservedly that nothing less than the bronze horse of San Marco or the stone charger of the Duke would have borne then unmoved. Ben Bolt did not. It was the match to the powder-barrel. With one wild plunge and a desperate rear which nearly overbalanced him, the nervous but determined animal bounded into the air. After these feats, he appeared to settle down to practical, business-like buck-jumping, impromptu, certainly, but of the highest order of excellence. He certainly *did* 'go to work,' as Mr. Windsor afterwards expressed it. Every known and unknown device which Sathanas could have devised for the benefit of a demon disguised as a horse was tried—and tried in vain. Mr. Banks, swaying easily front or rear of his saddle, never lost head or seat for an instant. Brought up in a horse-loving, horse-breeding district, he was familiar from childhood with every known form of practical or theoretical contravention of equine illegality. He could ride as soon as he could talk, and ere he wrote himself indifferently man, had backed successfully scores of unbroken horses, and ridden for wagers the cannibal Cruisers of more than one stud.

His figure, slight, but very accurately proportioned, was just above the middle height; his features were delicate and regular, with an approximation in the hardly aquiline nose and short lip to the Greek type, by no means uncommon among Australians of the second or third generation. His strength was far greater than was apparent, arising more from the toughness of his muscles than from any great breadth or solidity; and he had astonished the Garrandilla population one day by the ease with which he walked off with successive heavy bags of lour upon his back, when all hands were unloading a dray from Orange.

It was a pretty sight in its way, interesting enough to those who love contests, far from unduly safe, between men and the inferior animals, to see the ease with which the boy's figure followed each frantic movement of the infuriated animal, and with what perfect and apparently instinctive ease he retained his perilous seat. In vain the roused and desperate creature tried stopping, wheeling, sideway and forward, and indeed backward. Nearly blown was Ben Bolt, evidently relaxing the height and elasticity of his deerlike bounds. The victory was decided in favour of the imperturbable horseman, in Mr. Windsor's characteristic speech.

'By the holy poker! Mr. Banks, you've "monkeyed" him enough for one while. He won't try it on with you again in a hurry.'

The victorious athlete was awaiting with a smile of triumph on his lips for the colt to stop and recover his failing wind, when the frantic animal made a last maddened rear, trembling on the balance of falling backwards till the spectators held their breath; then dashing his head violently to the earth as he inverted his position, he stood with arched back and forelegs stretched out before him, as if he had been petrified in that position.

As he did so the saddle slid over his lowered shoulder, depressed, as in a horse jumping down a precipice, and the girths passing the 'elbows' or projecting joints of the upper leg underneath, moved, loosened and flapping downward towards the hoofs. Mr. Banks, of course, strictly associated with his saddle, could do nothing to arrest its earthward progress. As saddle and bridle approached the animal's ears, he threw up his head with tremendous force, catching the legs of Mr. Banks and casting him violently on to his back, with the saddle spread out above him. That young gentleman, however, held on to the bridle-rein with such tenacity that the throat-lash giving way, it was jerked over the horse's head, leaving the reins in the rider's hands, while Ben Bolt, with a wild snorting neigh, trotted off, free from all encumbrance, or, as Jack Windsor expressed it, 'as naked as he was born.'

Every one looked extremely grave and sympathetic as the heroic Charley sat up with the saddle in his lap, until he, in the mild monotone of his ordinary speech, said—

'That's the fruits of being too lazy to put on a crupper and surcingle, as any man that calls himself a horsebreaker ought to do. Suppose I'd hurt myself, it would have been all your fault, Windsor!'

Then he arose deliberately and shook himself, whereupon they all burst into a great fit of laughter at his rueful and injured air, as if being shot over a vicious colt's head, after ten minutes' buck-jumping, was a trifling annoyance, that the least care might have prevented.

Mr. Neuchamp walked over to the saddle, which he carefully examined.

'Why, the girths are still buckled on each side!' he exclaimed with astonishment. 'How the deuce *could* the brute have got the saddle over his head as he did—as he certainly did?'

'Bedad he did! eh, Charley, me boy? and that's a trick of rapid horsemanship *I* never saw performed before with my own two eyes,' said Mr. Barrington. 'There's many a man, now, in my country, if I were to tell this story, wouldn't believe me on my oath. They'd say it was unreasonable. You might stick them, and they'd never give in.'

'I wish one of them was on that brute's back,' said Mr. Banks, rubbing a portion of his frame. 'I thought I was as right as ninepence, and then to be slewed that way, and all for the want of a strap or two. I hate carelessness.'

'Never mind, Banks, you sat him magnificently,' said Ernest cheeringly. 'I never saw such a bit of riding in my life. It will be many a day before any of us can exhibit in the same way. I consider you fairly won your bet. But still I remain unsatisfied about the saddle coming off without breaking the girths. How *did* it?'

'Well, it's this way,' said Mr. Windsor, bracing himself for explanation. 'It's not a common thing, though I've seen young ones do it more than once or twice before. You see, first the horse sticks down his head with his nose on the ground, as if he was jumping down a well. Then he plants his feet right out before him, so as his hoofs and his nose are almost touching; his legs and his neck are all of a line. Young ones generally have a roundish, lumpy shoulder. If the saddle slips over it, and the girths over the elbows, down it must go; and when the horse draws his head backwards out of it, then you have the saddle, like this one here, popped on the ground, with never a girth or buckle broke.'

'So that's the way it's done, Jack, is it?' inquired Mr. Barrington. 'Well, if I'm forgiven for riding that divil once, I'll never tempt Providence again by crossing him as long as I stay at Garrandilla. I'd like to take him home and exhibit him. There's many a bold rider in Clare and County Roscommon, but the divil a one would stay on him for five minutes, I'll go bail.'

'Every man to his trade,' said Jack Windsor. 'Mr. Banks and me have been riding ever since we were born, and it isn't easy to get from under us, I'll allow. But I daresay there's some other games as we shouldn't be quite so smart at.'

'I tell you what,' said Malcolm Grahame, who just came on to the scene of action, 'there's Jedwood and old Doubletides up at the drafting yards, waiting for some of you to come up and help put through those hoggets that got boxed. The old man is swearing just awfu'.'

Every one hasted at this intimation to the scene of action, where the dust was ascending in a cloud, curiously reminding Ernest of a Biblical passage.

For the rest of the day, 'Keep them up, wether, hogget, ewe, weaner, slit-ear, near crop,' were the principal terms and phrases interchanged.

Ernest Neuchamp speedily discovered that he had reason to congratulate himself heartily upon the fact that, from the never-ending work at Garrandilla, he was much too tired and sleepy at night to care for conversation, or to desire congenial companionship. Had he craved for such ever so longingly, he would have found it impossible to obtain.

Allan Jedwood, a man of singular energy and indomitable persuasion, had devoted all his powers of mind and body with ceaseless, unrelaxing obstinacy to what he was pleased to consider the main end of existence.

In his case, the reaching and maintaining of an independent pastoral position had been the goal which had stood forth before his eyes, a celestial mount, but slightly obscured by mists of pleasure, extravagance, or sympathy, from his youth up.

In the pursuit of this somewhat restricted ideal, bounded by a good station, a fine herd of cattle, forty thousand sheep, and a balance at his bankers, he had spared not himself. He had strongly repressed the ordinary temptations, *desipere in loco*, to harmless dillettanteism, to amusement, or imaginative contemplation. Tendencies literary or artistic he had none. Everything in his eyes that did not lead directly to the increase or maintenance in good order and condition of his stock, he had eschewed and forsworn as unprofitable, almost immoral. Such was the rigid discipline which he had enforced over his own spirit for long years. From the days that he had been a hard-worked under-overseer, a toiling owner of a small station, a hampered purchaser of a larger one, until now, that he was sole proprietor of a magnificent unencumbered property, he had foregone nothing of this rule and regimen, and the usual effects had followed the causes. Successful labour and unwearied self-denial had created the position for which he had so longed and thirsted all his early life through.

And yet was there a side to this picture which did not call for so much gratulation. In the stern repression, the pitiless starvation to which the spiritual portion of the man had been subjected, the germs of all intellectual and speculative tendencies had first dwindled, then perished.

Unsparing vigilance, untiring concentration upon the daily routine of station work, was no longer necessary to the opulent possessor of stock and station, freehold and leasehold, town and city property. But the habits, inexorably welded into the being of the man, remained fixed and unalterable, when the circumstances which called them forth had long changed, long passed away. Still daily, as of old, Allan Jedwood rode over 'the run,' among his flocks and herds, his men and his 'improvements,' his dams, his wells, his fences, his buildings, his fields, and his teams. At nightfall, returning to the humble unchanged building which had sufficed for his wants for many a year, he spent the short evening which followed the day of hard exercise in writing business letters, or in posting up station accounts; or else, with military exactitude, he arranged with Mr. Doubletides the ensuing 'order of the day,' in which drafting of sheep, shifting of shepherds, mustering of cattle, and bargaining with dealers, took the place of marching and countermarching, sorties and retreats, embassies and diplomatic manœuvrings.

Of the progress and potentialities of the outer world—literary, artistic, social, or political—Allan Jedwood knew and cared as little as any of his Highland shepherds, frequently arriving from the paternal farm, who 'had not the English.'

In Ernest Neuchamp's zeal for mental growth, for the onward march of humanity generally, and for the particular community with which he was temporarily connected, this stage of arrested development was very painful and grievous to the soul of an enthusiast and reformer. He tried all the units of the Garrandilla world, but he found no rest, æsthetically, for the sole of his foot. Malcolm Grahame, who exhausted whatever mental vigour he possessed in trying to discover a cure for foot-rot, and in improving a natural aptitude for wool-classing, bade fair to become as complete and as prosperous a bucolic Philistine as Jedwood himself. Fitzgerald Barrington was conversational and discursive enough, in all conscience, but his mental exercise chiefly took the direction of regret for the joyous days he had spent in his father's house and among his own people—whom, not observing any near prospect of a fortune in Australia—he bitterly reproached himself for having ever quitted. Besides, he held no particular views about the destiny of the human race, or of the Australian nation, or of any other race or people but his own. He did not see the use of wasting the life that could be so much more pleasantly spent in hunting, shooting, feasting, flirting, four-in-hand driving, drinking, and dicing, as became a gentleman of long descent (if he only had the money), in bothering and interfering with a lot of low people, not worth caring about and who did not thank you the least bit.

If Mr. Charley Banks had any intellectual proclivities, they had not as yet passed a rudimentary limit. He smoked a good deal, read hardly at all except the sporting compartments of the newspapers, took more interest in the horses of the establishment than in the cattle or sheep, and was always glad of an excuse to get down to the public-house, or to gossip unprofitably in the men's huts.

As for Mr. David Doubletides, he had long since abandoned the idea that reading and writing had any other connection of importance to humanity than the accurate setting down and adding up of station accounts. He was astir at or before dawn, on horseback all day and every day, from daylight to dark, and was often sufficiently tired in the evening to fall asleep with his pipe in his mouth.

This purely objective existence, after the excitement of the first week or two, commenced to afflict Mr. Neuchamp unpleasantly.

'Good heavens!' said he to himself, 'is all the universe to be narrowed down to the number of serrations in a lock of merino wool? to the weight and tallow of a drove of bullocks destined for the market? This half wild life is pleasant enough with the open-air rambles on horseback, and the rude occasional labour. But, strictly, as a means to an end, which end is, or ought to be, the getting away from here, and the leading a worthy life in a less uniformly scorching land of monotony and privation,—fancy one doomed to linger on year after year. I see now the natural law which in desert tribes prompts the pilgrimage; without society, comfort, or companionship.'

At this period Ernest commenced to acquire, if they had been needed, additional proofs of the melancholy tendency of all human efforts to crystallise into the narrow unalterable shape of custom.

Nothing, he admitted, could be more praiseworthy and admirable than the energy, the concentrativeness, the unwearied labour which Jedwood had bestowed upon the formation of his position in early life. And now the summit had been scaled, the goal attained, the reward grasped, of what commensurate value or benefit was it, now fully realised, to himself or to others? The contracted field of labour had become a necessity of life. The means, losing their original proportions, had become the end. It was as if an animal, long compelled to a mill-horse round of unrelieved labour for the purpose of grinding a fixed quantity of meal, had, when the task was completed, voluntarily resumed the collar and gone on ceaselessly accumulating an unneeded heap.

It must be confessed that, occasionally, the unceremonious manner in which Mr. Doubletides ordered Ernest and the other young men to perform any minor task considered by him, Doubletides, necessary to be done, rather jarred upon his feelings. It was—

'Mr. Barrington, take the old roan horse and a cart, and go out to the fifteen-mile hut with a fortnight's rations for Joe Watson.'

'Mr. Grahame, see that you and Banks are up at daylight to-morrow morning, or else you won't have that weaner flock drafted before breakfast.'

'Mr. Neuchamp, you had better get away as soon as possible, and look for those five hundred wethers that old Sails dropped at the Pine Scrub yesterday; take some grub and a tether-rope with you, and don't come home till you find them.'

All this was doubtless good practice, and valuable as storing up useful knowledge against the day when he should possess a station and a Mr. Doubletides of his own. Still it occasionally chafed him to be ordered and sent about without any explanation or apology for the extreme personal inconvenience occasionally involved.

As it happened, this particular sheep-hunting trip became an adventure of much importance. Riding gaily upon the trusty Osmund, Mr. Neuchamp was fortunate enough, after a few hours' search, to come upon the 'wing' of the wether flock which had been lost by the ex-marine circumnavigator—a blasphemous old man-of-war's man, referred to by an abbreviation denoting his former work.

Full of triumph, Ernest commenced to drive them in the direction of the out-station, to which the remaining portion of the flock had been sent. For the first hour he sauntered on behind the browsing sheep, confident of his direction and not doubting but that he should reach a spot which he knew in good time. Sheep are not particularly easy animals to drive after a few miles, and it soon appeared to Ernest that the double effort of driving five hundred sheep and steering straight in a country without a landmark, was likely to bear hard upon his woodcraft.

As the sun hung low, flaunting a vast gold-red shield athwart the endless pale green waste, a sense of powerless loneliness and confused ignorance of all but the cardinal points of the compass took possession of him. He cantered from side to side of the obstinate, and perhaps puzzled, sheep, which probably had a distant impression in their woolly noddles that the line of direction lay quite another way. At length the red-gold blazonry faded out into darksome crimson, the pale green shades became dim and dullest gray—'the stars rush out, at one stride comes the dark'—and it became fully apparent to Mr. Neuchamp that he was lost.

He was sufficiently learned in the lore of the dwellers in this 'land of freedom and solitude' to know that the chief duty of man when once placed in possession of stock, sheep above all, is to 'stick by them'—to stick by them, as the captain lingers by the last plank of the breaking-up deck, in spite of danger and death, hunger, thirst, weariness, or despair. These last experiences were more likely to be the portion of Ernest Neuchamp than the former. Still it needed a slight exercise of determination to face the idea of the long lonely night, and the uncertain chance of discovering his whereabouts next day.

The night was long—unreasonably long—Ernest thought. Sufficiently lonely as well. There were no wild beasts, or robbers, likely to be 'round'; still there was an 'eerie' feeling about the still, solemn, soundless night. The rare cry of a night-bird, the occasional rustling made by the smaller denizens of the forest, the soft murmuring of the pine-tree nigh which he had elected to camp—these were all his experiences until the stars paled and the dawn wind moaned fretfully, like a dreaming infant. Having no culinary duties to delay him, Ernest saddled up his good gray steed, roused the unwilling sheep, and started forth, ready to do battle with fate in the coming day. Alas! he struck no defined trail. He hit off no leading thoroughfare. At first mid-day, and again the dewy eve, which might have been so described if the autumn rain had come—which it had not—again found Mr. Neuchamp a wanderer upon the face of the earth and no nearer home. As for the sheep, they found sustenance without difficulty, as they 'nibbled away both night and day,' all heedless of the morrow, or Mr. Neuchamp's anxious brain and empty stomach. They apparently had no objection to camp at the deserted out-station, which had so bitterly disappointed Ernest when he reached it at the close of the day.

By this time, in addition to being unmistakably and importunately hungry, Mr. Neuchamp was furiously thirsty. His satisfaction was great, therefore, when he discovered, just outside the door of the empty hut, two hogsheads filled with clean water.

He was about to plunge his head into the nearer one, like an eager horse, when a sudden thought passed through his brain, and he stopped short, with desire and dread written in every line of his face.

What was the potent thought, the word of power, that sufficed to arrest the step as if a precipice had opened suddenly below his feet to hold back the longing lips so parched and moistureless? One word, lightning-like, flashed along the wondrous telegraph of the brain. That word was 'arsenic'! Ernest looked again at the casks. The water was suspiciously clear. He could not trust it. He knew that somewhere in that direction Mr. Doubletides had been dressing the feet of lame sheep with a solution of arsenic. He had seen in the local paper an account of a thirsty shepherd and his horse similarly placed. The horse drank out of one cask, the man from the other. The horse died. Ernest was not sufficiently tired of his life to take a philosophical view of the chances. Sudden death, undignified convulsions, a visit from the coroner—an unsympathetic individual, who declined minute shades of discrimination in favour of 'three star'—'Verdict, found dead, as much arsenic internally placed as would have killed a horse.' All this was uninviting, non-heroic. Bordering on the heroic, however, was the stern resolve to pass the night without tasting one drop of the doubtfully limpid element.

# CHAPTER XII

It occasionally occurs to our unresting, unreasonable minds, prone, as we all are, to straining the mental vision and wearying our hearts with efforts to descry the form, to catch the Sibylline words, of the veiled future, that we are not so very wretched in the society of the present. After some slight intervals of sighing for the (social) fleshpots of Egypt, Mr. Neuchamp began to enjoy his life very thoroughly, and to question whether he should be so much happier after he had become a proprietor and carried out his plans of regeneration. The spring had set in, and nothing could be more lovely than the fresh warm air, the gloriously fresh mornings, the cool calm nights.

'How happily the days of Thalaba went by!' His health, spirits, and appetite were faultless. It was a time of hope and expectation for the great event of the year. The shearing was coming on, and insensibly the increase of station hands. The putting into order of the disused shearers' huts, wash-pens, machinery, and woolshed, spoke of impending transactions of importance, and told that 'the year had turned.' He had made up his mind, too, that 'after shearing he would revisit the metropolis.' There the moon-lighted, sea-washed verandah of Morahmee, with a slight and graceful form pacing thereon, musing 'in maiden meditation fancy free,' showed softly yet bright, as an occasional romance gleam through the somewhat prosaic mist of his ordinary day-dreams. It might have been the influence of the pure dry air, of the oxygenated atmosphere, which caused Ernest to become so very light of heart after this heroic resolution. If it were so, nothing that has ever been said by enthusiastic tourists in praise of the beauty and salubrity of the Australian climate can be held to be in the slightest degree exaggerated.

Another effect was noticeable about this time. Ernest commenced to be remarked, among his observing mess-mates, for a suspicious eagerness to learn and acquire all the mysteries of stock farming, some of which he might have previously overlooked. He delighted Mr. Doubletides by his alacrity, and that grim veteran remarked that in a year or two more he might be able to look after a small station himself, always provided that he had a careful overseer.

'The deuce a bit you'll see of him thin, me ould shepherd-driver, in a year or two, or next year either,' said Barrington. 'I know the signs of it.

He's going to cut Garrandilla after shearing, and he's trying to suck ye, like a marrow-bone, of all the fruits of all yer long hard life and experience, me ould warrior. And why wouldn't he? Sure I'd be off myself and invest, if my uncle would only send out the ten thousand that he promised me.'

'*Neuchamp* manage a station!' said Malcolm Grahame. 'He just knows naething whatever about foot-rot, and he disna know first-combing from pieces; it's my deleeberate opinion he'll just be insolvent within the year.'

'How do you know?' quoth Charley Banks. 'It's half luck, seems to me. I know an old cove that only branded his cattle once about every two years, and he made more money than all the district put together. Neuchamp's a good sort of notion about a horse, and he don't drink. I'll lay six to two he ain't broke next year, nor the year after.'

Garrandilla was not a fenced run. It was in the pre-wire-bearing stage, preceding that daring and wondrous economy of labour. At the period of which this veracious chronicle treats, the older pastoral tenants were wont to speak with distrust of the new-fangled idea of turning large numbers of valuable sheep 'loose—literally loose, by George—night and day' in securely fenced but unguarded enclosures.

One thing was certain, they had made their money mainly by the exercise of certain qualities, among which were numbered, beside industry and energy, a talent for organisation scarcely inferior to that required by a general of division. At Garrandilla the twenty or thirty flocks, averaging two thousand each, were marshalled, counted, gathered, dispersed, with the punctuality, exactness, and discipline of a battalion on field duty. Were all these rare endowments, these valuable habits, to be henceforth of no avail? Were the sheep to be just turned loose and seen from time to time like a lot of store cattle? Were experienced shepherds, skilled overseers, henceforth to be unnecessary? And would any young inexperienced individual who had brains enough to know a dingo from a collie, or to see a hole in a fence when such hiatus was present, do equally as well to look after five or ten thousand sheep in a paddock, as the oldest shepherd, under the orders of the smartest manager in the land? These were serious and important questions. Mr. Jedwood was not a man given to hurried outlay. The process of building up his fortune had been hard, anxious, and gradual. He had no idea of reversing the process in any possible casting down of that edifice. Therefore, with the aforesaid twenty or thirty shepherds, ration-carriers, etc., it did not admit of doubt as to there being plenty of work at Garrandilla. Of a truth the work was unceasing from daylight on Monday morning till dark, or later, on Saturday night. Indeed Sunday was often spent by Mr. Doubletides in weighing out rations, and making out a few of the men's accounts, as a species of rest from his labours not unbefitting the day.

The process of general management was somewhat in this wise. Each of the young men had certain flocks placed in his charge; these he was expected to count at least once a week. He had a small sheep-book or journal in which the name of every shepherd, with the number of his flock, was entered upon a separate page, as thus: 'John Hogan, 14th May; 4-tooth wethers; No. 2380; dead, 5; added, 14; taken out, 52—total, 2337.'

A similar account was kept of every flock upon the station, which was expected to be verified by a count at any moment. This counting it was *de rigueur* to perform early in the morning. As the shepherd usually left the yard or fold soon after sunrise, and many of the flocks were ten or fifteen miles from the head station, it followed that the young gentleman who counted a distant flock had to quit his couch at an exceedingly early hour.

Then the ration-carriers, who were always conveying provisions, water, wood, all things necessary to the shepherds, required in their turn supervision.

Nothing but the hardest bodily labours and unsleeping apprehensive vigilance kept this small army in good order and efficiency. If a shepherd lost his flock, there was mounting hot haste and terrific excitement till the sheep were found; Mr. Jedwood riding and aiding personally in the quest as if ruin was awaiting the non-arrival of the flock, to pounce down upon him and his.

There was no denying that the management of Garrandilla was very successful upon the whole. The fat sheep were eagerly competed for by dealers and others directly it was known that they were in the market. The wool brought a good though not extreme price in the home or colonial markets. The station accounts were kept by the storekeeper with the strict accuracy of those in a merchant's office. There was no waste, no untidiness, no delay, no dawdling of any kind. The men were well though not extravagantly lodged and fed, after the manner of the country. They received the ordinary wages, sometimes a shade above them. Whatever they drew from the station-store was accurately debited to them, and they received a cheque for the exact amount of the balance upon the day of their departure. What they did with the said cheque—whether they spent it in forty-eight hours at the nearest inn, whether they kept their money for the purpose of buying land, whether they put it into the savings bank, or gambled it away—was a thing unknown to Mr. Jedwood, and concerning which he never troubled himself to inquire.

When Mr. Neuchamp, in the ardour of his unquenched philanthropy, questioned him about these things, he declared that he had no great opinion of station-hands as a class, that most of them were d—d rascals, and that as long as they did his work and received the pay agreed upon he really did not care two straws what became of them.

Ernest felt this to be a very doubtful position, as between master and men, and further required to know whether, if he, Mr. Jedwood, took measures to locate a few of his best men with their families upon the frontage to the river, he would not secure an attached tenantry, and be always certain of a better and readily available class of labour.

To this Mr. Jedwood made answer that he should consider himself to be qualifying for admission to a lunatic asylum if he attempted to do any such thing. 'In the first place you would lose,' he said, 'a quantity of your best land, and your best water. In the next place, as their stock increased they would use and spoil double the quantity of land they had any legal title to. Most probably they would *not* work for you, when you needed labour, except at their own price and terms; and if you wished at any time to buy them out, they would ask and compel you to give double the price they had paid. No, no; I've kept free selectors out all these years, and, as long as I live here, I'll do so still.'

So Mr. Neuchamp had again to fall back upon his own thoughts and excogitations. He was not convinced by Mr. Jedwood, who took a narrowed, prejudiced view of the case, he contended. But he arrived at the conclusion in his own mind, that the amount of bodily and mental labour devoted to the sheep-pasturing division of Garrandilla was exhaustingly large, and that any mode of simplifying it, and reducing this great army of labourers, would be very desirable.

More and more to him was it apparent daily that there was no cessation, no leisure, no possible contemplative comfort in a life like this. It was the same thing every day. Sheep, sheep, sheep—*usque ad nauseam*.

Garrandilla was a highly unrelieved establishment. There were no ordinary bush distractions. There was no garden. There were no buildings except those positively necessary for the good guidance and government of the place. Jedwood's two rooms served him for every conceivable want here below. They really were not so much bigger than the captain's cabin in the good ship which brought Ernest to Australia. But they were large enough to eat, drink, and sleep in twenty years since, and they were so now.

At times a neighbour rode over and spent an hour or two, talking sheep, of course. Occasionally a lady, from sheer weariness or ennui, would accompany her husband or brother, and beat up the great Mr. Jedwood's quarters for a short visit.

One day Ernest was standing near the cottage in a meditative position, when a gentleman rode up, having a lady on either hand. Mr. Jedwood, with old-fashioned gallantry, promptly assisted the fair visitors to dismount, and then calling out loudly, said, 'Neuchamp, take these horses over to the stable.'

Ernest walked over, and taking the horses mechanically, was about to make for the stable, when one of the ladies exclaimed in a tone of great astonishment, 'Mr. Neuchamp!' He looked up, and to his very considerable surprise recognised one of the young ladies of the Middleton family, his fellow-voyagers.

'Why, what is the meaning of all this?' inquired Miss Middleton. 'I never thought to see you so generally useful; but I understand—you are staying at Garrandilla, and performing the "colonial experience" probation.'

'You have guessed it exactly with your usual acuteness, Miss Middleton,' said Ernest, who, slightly confused at having to act as amateur stable-boy, had now recovered his usual self-possession,—never long absent, to do him justice. 'I will come in as soon as I have stabled the horses.'

When Ernest returned he found the ladies evidently concluding a short narrative to Mr. Jedwood, in which he guessed himself to have figured. Nothing could be warmer or more pleasurable, however, than their recognition.

'And so, Mr. Neuchamp, here we meet, after all our arguments, and passages-of-arms,' said the younger sister. 'We are on our native heath, you know, so we shall take the offensive. How do you find all the new theories and schemes for improvement stand the climate?'

'Not so very badly,' assented Ernest boldly. 'I am biding my time, like the Master of Ravenswood. I intend to cause a sensation by carrying them out when I have a station of my own.'

'Oh, you must get one in this district,' affirmed the elder sister with determination; 'it would be so pleasant to have some one to talk to. We are living in utter solitude, as far as rational conversation is concerned.'

Mr. Jedwood at this juncture 'trusted that, as they did him the honour to pay him a visit now and then, they did not include Garrandilla in the conversational solitude.'

'Oh, you know, you're such an old friend. We can recollect riding to Garrandilla with papa ever since we could be trusted on horseback. It is one of our chief pleasures and resources. But really, Mr. Jedwood, you ought to build a new cottage. I used to think the old hut a splendid place once, but it looks now, you must confess, rather small.'

'Two rooms for one man, and that man an old bachelor, Miss Middleton, are not so very bad. I'm used to the old place. I can sit there and write my letters, and here, by the chimney side, I smoke my pipe and watch the embers. But I think I must put up a new place, if it's only for my young lady friends. I'll see about it after shearing, after shearing.'

But this promise of a comparatively palatial edifice after shearing had been made, to the young ladies' knowledge, for several years past, and they evidently did not place much faith in it; Miss Middleton asserting that it was lucky Mr. Jedwood had not commenced life at Garrandilla in a watch-box, as he most certainly would have continued the use of that highly compressed apartment.

They all laughed at this, and Mr. Middleton affected to reprove his merry daughter for her sally, but the end of it was that Ernest received a very cordial invitation to visit his old acquaintances at their station, distant about twenty miles, and mentally resolved to take an early opportunity of availing himself of it. The society of young ladies had been entirely out of his line since he had parted with Antonia Frankston, on the verandah at Morahmee. The effect was agreeable in proportion to the period of compulsory withdrawal from such pleasures and recreations.

Truth to tell, he was commencing to weary somewhat of the eternal, never-ending merino drill. He could understand a lad of seventeen or eighteen, like Charley Banks, spending two or three years profitably enough in the Garrandilla grind, and being better so employed than anywhere else. But he, Ernest Neuchamp, was a man whose years and months were of somewhat more value in the world than those of a raw lad. He thought, too, that he knew about as much of the not very abstruse and recondite lore necessary for the average management of a station as he was likely to acquire in another year, or any greater length of time. He resolved that, after shearing, he would state his case fully to Mr. Frankston, and secure, if possible, that paternal elder's consent to his purchasing a station of his own with his own money.

From time to time at long intervals, whenever by no possibility could any excuse be found for working among the sheep, would Mr. Doubletides summon him, the other youngsters, and any unoccupied individuals that were handy, and crossing the river, proceed to 'regulate the cattle a bit,' as he expressed it. Jack Windsor being a first-class stockman, and handy with the roping-pole, was always invited to join the party. Then they would have a week's mustering, branding, drafting, weaning, fat cattle collecting, what not—and then every one would come back much impressed with the heroism of the whole expedition, and the cattle would be left to their own devices for three or four months longer. These muster parties were extremely congenial to Mr. Neuchamp's tastes and tendencies. He found the country, which was wild and hilly in places, more interesting than the uniform, monotonous, but profitable campaign, where roamed the carefully-tended merino. There were Alpine gorges, tiny streamlets, masses of foliage, botanical treasures, and above all, a mode of life more irregular, more volitional, than the daily mechanical regularity with which the machinery of the 'merino-mill,' as Barrington profanely called it, revolved diurnally at Garrandilla proper.

Moreover there was occasionally trials of speed, of bottom, of horsemanship, in thus tracking the half wild cattle to their fastnesses, in which Osmund distinguished himself, and which were more akin to the noble sport of hunting than anything which Ernest had met with in Australia. The driving of the great herd into the stockyard, the drafting, the roping, the branding, the cutting out, all these were novelties and excitements of a very high order, as they then appeared to the ardent mind of Mr. Neuchamp.

So keenly did he appreciate the general work among the cattle, that upon a recommendation from Mr. Doubletides, who thought all time not absolutely devoted to sheep and wool thoroughly wasted, he was promoted to be a kind of cattle overseer. Then from time to time, in company with Jack Windsor, for whose services he formally petitioned, he was despatched on short but pleasant missions to the cattle station when any particular duty of an outpost nature was required to be done.

Then the friends were in their glory. Jack Windsor had been brought up on a cattle station, and had a strong preference for them as stock over sheep. He always took care to provide an ample commissariat in case of accidents, while Mr. Neuchamp armed himself against the perils of a long evening or two at the hut of the cattle manager by bringing a book. Thus fully accoutred they would start off amid the congratulations of Barrington and Charley Banks for a week's perfect happiness.

Why Mr. Neuchamp esteemed himself to be favoured by fate in being especially selected for this department, was chiefly on this account—that it opened a prospect of change and comparative mental leisure. I have described my hero carelessly and faintly, but the judicious reader will ere this have discovered that Ernest was essentially less disposed to action than contemplation. Not that he disliked or avoided work, but he liked it in large quantities rather than in small, with spaces for consideration and preparation duly interspersed.

For instance, at Garrandilla it was one constant succession of calls and appointments and engagements. 'Would Mr. Neuchamp get something out of the store? Would he make out So-and-so's account? Would he go down and draft So-and-so's flock? Would he be sure to be up before daylight and count the sheep at the Rocky Springs? Mr. Jedwood was returning from the farthest back station, and would he lead a fresh horse to meet him at the fifteen-mile hut? Would he take out a fortnight's rations to old Bob, and be sure to bring in all the sheep-shears? Would he calculate the number of cubic yards in the Yellow Dam, just completed, and check the storekeeper's account with the contractor?' and so on.

Now, all these things Ernest could do, and did do—as did his fellow-cadets—still the endless small succession troubled him. Small wonder, then, that a feeling of relief and satisfaction possessed him when he got the route for Warbrok, and he and Jack packed up their effects and necessaries for a week's comfortable, steady, solitary work among the cattle, where no complications existed, and where they saw no one but a couple of stockmen and old Mr. Hasbene, the manager, from the time they left Garrandilla till they returned.

In the long days of tracking the outlying 'mobs' or small subdivisions of the main herd, in the unrelieved wandering through 'the merry greenwood,' with its store of nature's wonders—hidden watercourses, mimic waterfalls, rare ferns, plants, and flowers, strange birds and stranger beasts—Ernest felt the new delight and enjoyment of a born naturalist. Then the sharp gallops, 'when they wheeled the wild scrub cattle at the yard,' were exciting and novel.

The evening, too, spent in the rude but snug building that had served the cattle overseer—a laconic but humorous old man who had once been a prosperous squatter—for a habitation for many a year, story-telling, reading, or dozing before a glowing fire, were pleasant enough in their way.

In the ordinary yard work—drafting, branding, roping, throwing, etc.—Mr. Neuchamp felt a strong and increasing interest. When they returned to the merino metropolis of Garrandilla, old Mr. Hasbene expressed his regret emphatically, while Jack Windsor loudly lamented the necessity of going back to school.

'Sheep's all very well,' that gentleman would observe, 'but my heart ain't never been with them like the cattle. There's too much of the shopkeeping pen-and-ink racket about 'em for me. Look at our storekeeper, he's writin' away all day, and sometimes half the night, to keep all the station accounts square. There's Mr. Doubletides, he's always away before daylight, and home at all hours of the night. There's some blessed flock for ever away or having to be counted, or drafted, or shifted, or tar-branded, or sold, or delivered; and it's the same story all the year round. There's no rest and no easy time with sheep, work as hard as you will. Of course the wool's a fine thing, but give me a mob of a couple or three hundred head of fat cattle on the road for market with a good horse under ye and a fourteen-foot whip in your hand. That's a job worth talking about—a couple of thousand pounds on legs in front of ye—and precious hard work in a dark night, sometimes, to keep it from cuttin' right off and leavin' ye with your finger in your mouth.'

'By George, Jack, you're a regular bullocky boy,' said old Mr. Hasbene; 'you had better get Mr. Neuchamp here to put you on as stockman when he buys a cattle station, as I expect he will when he leaves us. If I was a young man I'd go with him myself, for I see he's got a real turn for the roans and reds, and there's nothing like 'em.'

'Well, we'll see,' said Ernest. 'I have a great fancy for a cattle run; and I must say, I think Jack is right about the sheep. They are a great deal too much trouble, especially with shepherds. I came away from England to lead a quiet life in the wilderness, to have a little leisure and time to think, and not to be hurried from one engagement to another like a Liverpool cotton broker or a stock exchange speculator.'

'I don't say there isn't money made by sheep,' remarked Mr. Hasbene, 'but cattle, to my mind, have always been the most gentlemanly stock. A man does his work; it's sharp sometimes; but then he has it over. He knows what he's about, and hasn't to be always "hurried up" like a Yankee dry goods clerk. I wouldn't change lives with Jedwood for all the world. I live like a gentleman in my small quiet way, but I'll be hanged if he does.'

'Quite right, Mr. Hasbene,' said Ernest. 'The characteristics of "the gentle life," in my estimation, are occasional strenuous, useful, and dignified exertion, seconded by unquestioned leisure, more or less embellished by letters with the aid of the arts and sciences. All this keenness to amass money, land, flocks, and herds, is merely the trading instinct pushed to excess, whether the owner lives in a street, in a city, or a hut on a plain. However, we must be off. Good-bye.' Away they went at the rapid pace so dear to unthinking youth, all heedless of the capital of human as of equine bone and sinew, secure of a vast endowment to their credit in the future, good for endless drafts and extravagant cheques, while the grizzled senior rode back to his lonely lodge to contest, as best might be, with three months' loneliness, three months' absence of human face, of human speech, laughter, or tears. It was not a gay life, certainly, but such as it was, he had lived and outlived twenty odd years of it. In all human probability—he was failing now—he would remain there until he died. So best—where else should he go? Geoffrey Hasbene had once possessed money, friends, a good station, a fair position. But indifferent luck, combined with an easy, careless, liberal disposition, had caused his property to drift away from him. For a time he had suffered some of the evils of neglect and of poverty. Then this prospect of employment was offered and thankfully accepted, and for many years he had been exercising for another the qualities of vigilance and economy that, in the long past years, would have gathered and secured a fortune for himself.

The season wore on. The mild Australian winter, far different from the stern season that Mr. Neuchamp had associated with that name, changed almost imperceptibly into glowing spring—into burning summer.

The ordinary work of the station advanced. Men came and went; were hired, verbally; retained, paid off, and so on, with an undeviating regularity that savoured of machinery.

With spring came all the bustle of washing and shearing. Herds of men arrived at Garrandilla, and were employed as sheepwashers, shearers, extra shepherds, watchmen, engineers, fleece-rollers, and people to do anything that may be required and nothing in particular. Much Ernest marvelled at the apparently profuse and reckless manner in which men were engaged at high wages, until it occurred to him one evening to reckon up, with the assistance of Malcolm Grahame, the probable value of the wool crop. Then he admitted that a few hands or a few pounds, more or less, were not much to be considered in view of such a large quantity of so high-priced and so promptly convertible a commodity.

The general tone of the establishment was altered. Mr. Windsor had completed his colt-breaking business, and having enrolled himself as a shearer, was living in a state of luxurious freedom from any kind of work, and waiting with twenty or thirty other gentlemen, apparently of independent means, the important tocsin which tells of the commencement of shearing.

Barrington and Grahame were galloping about all day long, from the shed to the wash-pen, looking important and mysterious, while Mr. Banks was permanently located at the latter place, and evidently considered himself as in a great degree responsible for the reputation of the Garrandilla clip in the forthcoming wool sales.

For Ernest, to his great satisfaction, employment had been found at the cattle station, an unusual number of fat stock having been sold and delivered at this particular season, so that he and Jack Windsor had been mustering and drafting and partly delivering the said beeves, until it was time for the latter gentleman to take his place among the braves, who, when on the war-path, on the far plains of the north west, are, sometimes inaccurately enough, styled and designated shearers.

Thus it came to pass that Ernest grew to consider himself more immediately connected with the 'cattle side of the run' than the sheep ditto, and insensibly began to imbibe those prejudices in favour of one description of stock, which, though not capable of logical justification, are often found to be sufficiently powerful to influence a man's whole life.

At last, after many minor combats and skirmishes, a strike among the sheepwashers, a demand for more pay from the shearers, a short supply of carriers, a threatened superfluity of clover-burr and grass seed—the great shearing campaign was completed.

The men were paid off; the teams wool-laden departed; the shepherds returned to their homes—save the mark; Mr. Jedwood departed for town; and for a little space it really seemed as if the genius of bustle would revisit Garrandilla—'nevermore.'

Mr. Jedwood had told Ernest, before leaving, that if he particularly wished to visit town before he returned he was fully at liberty to do so, as Mr. Doubletides would be able to manage all there was to do for the next three months, with the other youngsters, or even without them.

Before he left town, Ernest would have scouted the idea of leaving Garrandilla under a full twelvemonths. But circumstances, it is said, constantly alter and affect cases.

The circumstances were—extreme heat; waveless uniformity, not to say monotony, of existence; the lack of fresh companionship; and finally, a strong, impetuous, sudden desire for civilised life, coupled with an undefined, unrecognised longing for the criticisms of Antonia Frankston upon his new and thrilling experiences.

# CHAPTER XIII

In no way does the proof more plainly reach us of the sadly shortened space of mortal life than by the distinct stages of experience and mental growth.

Looking back upon the ideal fruition of a few years, we are startled to find how far we have progressed from a given starting point. The store of ripened experience would almost overwhelm with its garnered richness, did not fate, with a malicious pleasure, forbid our profiting by it.

A few lustra have rolled over, marked by fast whitening or receding locks, and lo! we have attained to exact conclusions concerning many things. No further fees are necessary. Cautious are we now who once were so heedless. Regular and methodical in business, erst unpunctual and dilatory, we preserve our acquittances. We are industrious without spasmodic energy, cool with the discretion, not the madness, of valour! But one bright-haired goddess has departed with our golden youth. Hope lends no gladness to the summer breeze, gilds not the glowing eve, smiles not on the flowers, beckons not from the cool shadows of the murmurous glade.

Mr. Neuchamp was far on the hither side of these autumnal effects, so it chanced that on one fine day— there had been no rain for about two months—he found himself mounted on Osmund with his face turned towards the Sydney road, and with an unwonted feeling of exultation in or about the cardiac region. He was accompanied by Jack Windsor, who had invested a portion of his shearing cheque in the purchase of Ben Bolt, on favourable terms, as that interesting animal had thrown every other one who had ever ridden him, causing Mr. Jedwood to be honestly glad to be rid of him.

Mr. Windsor had completed what he called a very fair spell of work, for him, and having secured a prominent cheque and a high character at the settlement, after shearing, was in charity with all men, even the police, and much minded to have a pleasure trip 'down the country,' as he phrased the transmontane towns. Hence, when Ernest invited him to accompany him to Sydney, having extracted a confession that he had never seen that 'kingdom by the sea,' or indeed had been a stroller by the 'poluphloisboio thalasses' at any time, he readily and gratefully accepted the offer.

'Seems queer, sir, doesn't it, that I've never seen our main city or the big waterhole, as the blacks call it. Somehow I've always had the luck to miss it. Not that I had any powerful great longing to go. I've always had some pleasant place nigh home to spend my Christmas in, after I'd made a bit of money; and somehow, when I was once comfortable I didn't care about stirring.'

'But I wonder that an active, intelligent fellow like you, Jack, never made up your mind to go all the way to Sydney, out of curiosity.'

'Well, it *is* a wonder, sir; only, somehow I've had no eddication, as I told you before, and chaps like me, as don't know much except about bush things, haven't as much curiosity, I think, as other people. Sydney's only a bigger town than Campbelltown, or Yass, or Goulburn, and what's there to see in them if fifty of 'em was rolled up together? That's the way I used to talk.'

'But the sea, Jack, the sea! you haven't the sea in Yass or Goulburn.'

'Oh! I know that, sir. Bless you, now I am quite different, since you took the trouble to learn me to read and write a bit.' (Mr. Neuchamp had so utilised the evenings at the cattle station and other quiet places.) 'I'm always thinking what a stupid beggar I've been to have been contented with the life I used to lead. Just like an old working bullock in a lucerne field, grubbing away and never raisin' his head till it was time to lay down. You've made a man of me, sir, that's what you have. I hope I'll be able to make you think some day—"Well, he wasn't a bad fellow after all."'

'I think so now, Jack; I always have thought so from the first time I saw you.'

Mr. Windsor here groaned out a curse upon some one of Eve's daughters unknown to this chronicler.

'What a regular more-pork I was to be sure, to go and run my neck agin' a roping-pole, and all for a—false jade, who'd have come to see me hanged, I believe, and laughed at the sight—blank her.'

'You are not the first man, Jack, and will not be the last,' quoth Ernest, 'who has been started on the downward road by the same agency. But I hope you will always perceive, when accusing another, that unless you had been that particular sort of fool that bad luck is exciting one to turn into a rogue, her influence would have been quite insufficient. We may as well drop the subject, for ever; but it will do you no harm to look sometimes, without witnesses, at the precipice you passed so closely.'

Mr. John Windsor, naturally one of the cheeriest of mortals, for which temperament he had to thank a Milesian ancestress, showed no inclination to revert to this painful topic. On the contrary, as they approached the more settled country which lay between Garrandilla and the railway terminus, he entertained Ernest much by his *naïve* and acute observations. His companionship was always valuable in other respects. He knew all the by-tracks and short cuts, by availing themselves of which the road was materially shortened.

At nightfall, wherever they happened to be, Jack took all charge and responsibility as to the horses out of Ernest's hands. He saw that Osmund received full justice in the inn stables, if they happened to stay at one of the village hostelries; or if compelled to turn out he affixed the hobbles, and following the track (slotwise) at dawn of day, regularly and efficiently produced the hackneys saddled and accoutred at the proper after-breakfast hour. Full of anecdote, flavoured with the purest Australian slang, all unconsciously used, he was a never-failing mine of interest and amusement.

They passed the railway terminus, as Ernest had decided to ride down the whole distance, being not unwilling to exhibit Osmund, now 'prompt in his paces, cool, and bold,' and after the summer grasses of Garrandilla, sleek and 'on his top' in point of condition. He pictured himself cantering along the pleasant seaside ways around Sydney, and if a vision occasionally mingled with his reveries of a fair girlish shape, all the more graceful in the riding-habit of the period, not far from his side, was it not the natural outcome of the double summer time, the pleasant season of the land, and the fairy-time that comes but once—the thrice golden spring of youth? With these 'companions of Sintram' not ominous and threatening, but full of high hope, of purpose, and of all mighty dreams, pleasantly he paced on over the rocky, fast descending mountain tracks.

'Rum road this, sir, for coaching,' said Mr. Windsor. 'I've been up and down here many a time, by night and day, good weather and bad, in the old times, many years before the Zig Zag was chopped out of the sidelings. I've been glad enough to see the bottom of the hill at Mount Victoria, once or twice, with a queer team and the brake not over good.'

'I should say if anything happened to *that*,' said Ernest, looking over the sheer drop of a couple of hundred feet which overhung the rugged boulders below, 'the insured passengers would have a chance of realising on their policies, as a Yankee would say.'

'Things went something in that line one night, when I was aboard,' answered Jack, a little thoughtfully. 'I never want to see another start like it. Once is enough of that kind of fun.'

'What was that?'

'Well, sir,' commenced Jack, settling himself on the watchful, untamed animal, who thereupon promptly assumed an attitude of armed vigilance, which caused Mr. Windsor to dig the spurs into him and adjure him to do his worst, 'it was this way—

'It was a dark, wet, stormy night, the roads fearful; we were that heavy loaded that it took all Sacramento Ned could do (he was a Californian, and the best whip *I* ever saw that's seen a few, and that before King Cobb was heard of on the Sydney side) to keep from going over in some of the waggon tracks. I was on the box with him, and we'd made friends like, as he could see I was a bit in the horse line.

'He was a great tall, powerful chap, with a big fair beard, and the way he could rattle five horses and a loaded coach in and out of the creeks and winding bush tracks, was a sight to see. Well, he'd been very downhearted all day about something, and at last he says to me, "Jack, old man, I can't tell what in thunder's come over me this trip; it's my last one on this line, for I've saved up a fairish pile and I'm going back to my people, to turn farmer in the old state for the rest of my days; I suppose it's the infernal weather. Well, here we are; look alive there, you chaps. Hold the reins for a minute, Jack, while I look at the brake."

'Well, the fresh team was waiting by the door; they're desperate punctual those American chaps, and the time was none too much as they had allowed them then.

'I could hear him sing out for the blacksmith, whose forge was nigh the inn—he contracted for their work. When he came, he swore at him in a way *that* man hadn't been used to; by George, he *could* swear when he tackled it, though he was a quiet chap as didn't talk much generally.

'Well, he made him put in another bolt, and said he should report him to the road manager; then he took hold of the reins the three leaders was hitched to, and away we went.'

'He wasn't intoxicated, I suppose?' inquired Ernest.

'As sober as we are now, sir. For when he got up, he says, "I'd have been all the better for a nip, Jack, but just because of the place being risky, and the night extra bad, I wouldn't have one." We had the five lamps, of course—two on each side, two higher up, and one atop of all. Ned lit a cigar, pulled on his gloves, and off we went.

'The team was in grand order, three leaders and a pair of great upstanding half-bred horses at the wheel, all in top condition and fit to pull any fellow's arm off. However, they'd a *man* behind 'em, and when they jumped off he steadied 'em as easy as a pair of buggy horses.

'You know what the road's like. We rattled along a fair pace, but well in hand, though the horses pulled like devils, and I had my foot on the brake, on the near side, just to help him.

'We were about half way down, and I was wondering what time we should make Penrith, when I felt the near wheeler make a sudden rush, and Ned said in a thick, changed voice—

'"By—, the brake's gone!"

'"You don't say so," says I; "it can't be."—"You'll darned soon find out, Jack," says he, gathering up the reins and bracing himself for the struggle with death. "Blast that infernal blacksmith, he ought to be along with us now."

'By this time the team had broken into a wild gallop, and were racing down the narrow, winding road, with a couple of feet, sometimes less, between us and a five hundred feet drop among the rocks. There was no breeching harness on the wheelers; Americans don't use it, but trust all to the brake. Ours was gone. And the pace we were going down that road was enough to scare the boldest man that ever handled leather.

'Ned was as cool and determined as if it was a saltbush plain. He held the mad team true and straight, and trusted, I could see, to pulling them up on the long flat at the bottom of the hill. If we got there. *If!* Of course, the only little chance was to let them go best pace and guide them. The slightest pull up would have sent us sideways over the black rocks, half a mile below.

'It was a strange sight, I tell you, sir. Ned's face was pale but set hard, the muscles of his arms showed like cords, his eyes shining and steady, looking forward through the dark; the great lamps swinging wide with the rolling of the coach. As we turned one corner we hung nearly over the cliff, just shaved it. The women inside kept up a dismal screaming; the men looked out and said nothing.

'"We may do it yet, Jack," he said, "if we can clear those cursed guard-logs near the bottom."

'"Right you are, Ned," says I, to cheer him. I was afraid of them myself.

'Now a'most at the bottom of the hill the road had been new metalled, and as the track was broader and clear of the sideling, the road contractor, damn him, had placed a whole lot of heavy logs on both sides of the metal. I never could see the pull of it myself, except to make accidents easy.

'Well, at the last corner, Ned had to keep as near as he dared to the edge to turn the coach. The pace was frightful by this time, the coach on the swing; and before he could get in from his turn she hit one of these ugly butts and, balancing for a bit, fell over with a crash that I can hear now, dragged for a second or two, then lay on her side with the top wheels still going round and the team struggling and kicking in a heap together.

'I don't know how many rods I was pitched. But when I found I wasn't killed I picked myself up and went to help out the insides. It was an ugly sight. Some were frightened to death, and wouldn't stir. Some had broken limbs. Two *were* dead—one woman with her baby safe in her arms. We got 'em all out of it with the help of those passengers who, like me, were only shaken a bit.

'"There's something wrong with Ned," says I, "or he'd have been among us by this time. There's *one* lamp alight, fetch it along." So we looked about and round, and after a bit we found him lying on his face with his whip in his hand, stone dead. Poor Ned!'

'A sad and terrible accident,' said Ernest. 'What did you all do?'

'We straightened the horses after a bit—there was two dead and one with a broken leg of *them*; and I rode horseback to the next stage and sent a team back for 'em. They got in next day. But I shall always think poor Ned had a kind of feeling beforehand.'

'It was not his fault, poor fellow.'

'Fault, sir? he was the carefullest chap I ever see. It all lay between that idle rascal of a blacksmith and the wooden-headed road contractor that put them guard-logs down.'

'It is safer on horseback, as we are,' remarked Mr. Neuchamp, 'unless we travelled as I did coming up. I rather prefer a horse, though, I must say.'

'Well, it seems more natural like,' said Jack reflectively, giving Ben Bolt a playful touch with the spurs, which caused that tameless steed to jump on one side in a fashion that might have been dangerous to a less resolute horseman. 'Nothing like a good horse under a man; then he's ready for anything or anybody.'

Once more the great meadows and broad river, majestically winding, which needs but the ruined castle on its scarped sandstone cliff to render it in some aspects equal in picturesque beauty to the 'castled Rhine.' Once more the semi-tropical warmth; the soft, luscious, enervating breeze of the southern seas; the half-effaced traces of ancient labour; the patient, plodding industry and general evidence of village life.

Ernest pressed on until they reached Walton's inn, where he took it into his head to stop for the night before they reached Sydney. Drawing rein at the door, he left Osmund in charge of Mr. Windsor, and marched into the clean taproom with a considerably altered air and general expression from those of his first visit.

The old woman was absent, but Carry, hearing some one in the room, came hastily in and stared for a moment in astonishment.

'Well, I declare,' said she at length, 'if it isn't Mr. Newchum! How you have altered; got so sunburned too. I hardly should have known you.

Well, it's very good of you to come and see us again. Mother will be ever so pleased.'

'I thank you for your welcome, Carry,' said Ernest, smiling at the honest pleasure so clearly shown in the girl's face; 'I have a servant with me and two horses—can you put us up for the night?'

'Oh yes. George will be round directly, if your man will take the horses into the yard. So you're not walking now?' asked she, with rather a mischievous look.

'No, Carry, it takes too much time, not that it isn't pleasant enough; but I suppose I shall get into all your lazy ways in time. Mind you take care of my man; he's a capital fellow and a favourite of mine.'

'Is he a native?' asked the girl.

'Yes, a countryman of yours,' said Ernest.

'Then he can take care of himself,' said the damsel decidedly. 'I'll show you your room, sir, and see about your tea.'

It may be safely held that nothing is much more enjoyable in its way than a snug roadside inn, where the host and attendants are cheerfully willing to minister to the comfort of the wayfarer. The food may be plain, the cooking homely, but the prompt and unchilled service atones fully for want of artistic merit; and if the traveller carries with him the inimitable condiments of appetite and reasonable fatigue, the simple meal is a banquet for the gods, and sweet sleep arrives without delay to lull the satisfied traveller into luxurious dreamless rest.

Mr. Neuchamp thought that no club dinner had ever more thoroughly satisfied his every sense than the broiled steak, the fresh butter, the toast and eggs, all placed upon a snowy tablecloth, which the neat-fingered Carry put before him.

Before retiring, Ernest made a point of visiting his horse, as should every horseman worthy of the name. He found that trusty steed and the uncertain Ben Bolt up to their knees in straw, with their racks full of well-saved oaten hay, than which no horse, from England's meads to the sand-strewn pastures where the desert courser roams, can desire better provender.

In returning from his excursion he chanced upon a *partie-carrée* composed of George Walton, his mother, sister, and Mr. John Windsor, who was evidently the lion of the evening, to judge by the way he was holding forth, and the respectful admiration with which his tales of flood and field were received. Among these moving adventures Ernest caught the sound of some reference to a sailing match, in which, as usual, fortune had smiled on the brave. Knowing that the mighty ocean was as yet a wonder unwitnessed by the bold Australian, this experience struck him as improbable, to say the least of it. However, he always permitted Master Jack to encounter his *monde* after his own fashion, not doubting but that his ready wit and fertility of resource would bring him forth unharmed of reputation.

On the following morning, therefore, after a breakfast worthy of the glorious supper which he long afterwards recalled, horses and riders in exuberant spirits, they set forth for the easy concluding stage.

The household turned out to witness their departure.

'It puts me and my good man in mind of old times,' said the aged hostess, 'to have a gentleman stay the night and see horses like them in the stable again. Not as I like that chestnut willin.' (Ben Bolt, by the way, had nearly settled George Walton's career in life, permanently if not brilliantly, as he unguardedly approached the 'irreconcilable.') 'It's done us all good, sir, and I hope you won't forget to give us a call when you're leaving town.'

'It has done *us* good, I can vouch for,' said Ernest heartily, as he observed his follower's bold eyes fixed upon Carry's features with unmistakable admiration. 'I shall always think of you all as my earliest friends in Australia. Good-bye, George; good-bye, Carry—we must pay you another visit when we start back, after our holiday is up.'

'That's something like a place to stop at,' observed Mr. Windsor, in a tone of deep appreciation, as they passed cheerfully onward, after a mile or two's silence. 'Real nice people, ain't they, sir? What a house they must have kept in the old coaching days! One thing, they wouldn't have had time to have waited much on us then, with the up coach leaving and the down one just coming in, and the whole place full of hungry passengers. How did you ever come to find the old place out, sir?'

'It was the first inn I saw in Australia that took my fancy, Jack. I had had many a cruise on foot in England; gentlemen often take a walking tour there for the fun of the thing; you know the distances are not so great, the weather is cooler, and there is every inducement for young strong men to ramble about the green hills and dales of old England, where you may sit under the walls of a ruined castle a thousand years old, or watch the same sort of trout in the brook by the monastery that the monks loved on their fast days centuries ago.'

'That must be jolly enough for a gentleman with his purse full of money and his head chock-full of learning, knowing all the names of the people as lived and died there before he was born. But for one of us chaps, as can't see nothing but a heap of old stones and a lot of out-and-out green feed, why, there's no particular pull in it.'

'But there's nothing to hinder a man like you from knowing as much as other people in a general way, if you can read. Books are cheap, and plentiful, Heaven knows.'

'Well, sir, it does seem hard for a fellow like me to know very little more than a black fellow, as one might say; that's how lots of us takes to drink, just for want of something to think about. Sometimes it's easy to do a chap good.'

'But it always ruins a man in the long run, perhaps kills him right out.'

'That's all very well, sir, only look at his part of it: a man comes in from a long spell of bush work—splitting, fencing, dam-making, cattle-droving, what not—into one of these bush townships. He's tired to death of sheep and cattle or gum-trees; or perhaps he's been in some place, all plains for a hundred miles with never a tree or a stone; all he's seen has been the overseer to measure his work, his mates that he worked with, the regular tea, damper, and mutton, day after day; perhaps flies and mosquitoes enough to eat him alive. Well, he's had a year of this sort of thing, perhaps two; say he's never smelt grog all the time.'

'All the better for him too,' said Ernest; 'see what splendid hard condition he's in; fit to go for a man's life.'

'That's all right, sir, but he's so precious dull and hungry for a change that he feels ready to go to h—l for a lark, as the saying is; so he comes to the public-house bar, in some hole of a bush township, and the first glass of grog he gets makes him *feel like a new man, in a new world*.'

'Well, why doesn't he stop there?'

'He can't,' continued Jack, 'else he'd slip back, so of course he takes another, and the stuff is ever so bad, rough, very like tobacco in it, or some rascally drug, but it's strong, and it's the strength he craves for, from the tips of his fingers to the very inside of the marrow of his bones; when that glass is swallowed he has forgotten that he is a poor, ignorant, working man; he *knows* he's a sort of king; every good thing he's thought of in his life is a-coming to him; he's to be rich, happy, clever, able to marry the girl he likes; if any man looks at him he can knock his head off—ten men's heads off! Drink? Fifty glasses wouldn't make *him* drunk! Capital grog it is too; feels more sober every glass he takes; landlord's splendid fellow; must have some more drink; and so on.'

'But how do you know a man has all these grand ideas? I grant it's enticing.'

'Because *I've passed through it all myself*,' said the henchman grimly, yet with a half air of shame and regret. 'I've been on the burst, as we call it, more than once or twice either, worse luck.'

'I hope you never will again, Jack.'

'I *think* not, sir, if I know it. But a man shouldn't be too sure. It's an awful craving, by—. It drags you by your very heart-strings, once you get it right.'

'But you don't mean to say there's any fun in a week's drink at a wretched pot-house, even if the first hour is as good as you say. Then the waking up!'

'But there *is* fun in it,' persisted the poor relation, 'else why do hundreds and thousands do it? All these chaps are not fools, much less lazy; it's the hardest workers and best hands among us working chaps that's the worst drinkers, by odds. As to the waking up, as you say, it's bad enough, but a strong man gets over it in a day or two, and tackles his bread and meat, and his work, pretty much as usual till the time of the next spree comes round.'

'But what a fool a man must think himself,' said Ernest, 'at the end of a week, when he finds that he has spent all the fruit of a year's labour, and is obliged to begin another solitary weary year.'

'It *is* bad, as you say, sir. You're quite right; but right's one thing and human nature's another, in the bush, anyhow. I remember coming to myself in the *dead-house* of a bush inn once, and I felt like a dead man too; the parson had been preaching at our woolshed the week before, and that text came into my head, and kept ringing through it like a hundred bullock bells.'

'And what was it, Jack?'

'"In hell he lifted up his eyes." I ain't very likely to forget. He gave us a great dressin' down for drink and swearing, and bad ways, and so on. We deserved it right enough, and his words struck.'

'What did you do then?'

'I just crawled into the bar, sir, and when the landlord gave me a nip I put it on the counter and bent down to it; blessed if my hand wasn't too shaky to hold it.'

'"How much is left of my cheque?" says I. "Forty-three twelve six, it was."

'"Not a blessed shilling," says he; "you've been treating all round, and having champagne like water; it ain't likely a small cheque like that would last long."

'"Give me a loaf," says I, "and we'll cry quits." A bushman never disputes his grog score. If he's been a fool, he's willing to uphold it. So off I went and walked straight along the road, and slept under a tree that night.

Next day I was better; and the third day I got a billet, and was as well as ever I was in my life. I had one or two sprees after that, but never such an out-and-out desperate one again.'

Ernest Neuchamp looked at the clear eyes and healthy bronzed skin of the man as he spoke, noble in all the marvellous grace and strength of godlike youth, and thought how deep the pity that such a spirit, such a frame, should sink into the drunkard's nerveless, hopeless, shapeless life in death.

He rode onward more than a mile in silence and deep thought, then he spoke—

'I cannot say with truth, Jack, that I feel inclined to abuse and condemn wholesale everybody and everything connected with intemperance, casual or habitual. I see in it a habit—say a vice—to which the most energetic, intelligent, and industrious of our race have been prone since the dawn of history. Where circumstance is invariable there must be an underlying law. I forget, you don't understand this sort of talk. But, you will admit that it's a bad thing—a thing that grows upon a man till it eats out his will, like a grub in the root of a plant, and then, man or plant withers and dies. Now you're a practical man of wide experience, you know that I mean what I say chiefly, and I want to see my way to do good in this matter. What's the likeliest cure, in your opinion?'

'As to that, sir,' said Mr. Windsor, settling himself so suspiciously in the saddle that Ben Bolt arched his back and made ready for hostile action, 'I should be cock-sure that having an empty cobbra, as the blacks say, was on the main track that led to the grog-camp, only that the best eddicated chaps are the worst lushingtons when they give way at all. Perhaps they remember old times too well, if they've come down in the world. But I've noticed that a working man as likes reading, and is always looking out for a new book, or thinks he knows something as will alter the pull of money over labour—he's a very unlikely card to drink much. If he gets a paper with a long letter in it, or a working man's yarn in a book, he goes home as happy as a king, and reads away to his wife, or sits up half the night spelling it out. *He* don't drink. Even if he spouts a bit at the public, he talks a deal more than he swipes.'

'I am quite of your opinion, Jack; the more a man knows, the more he wants to know. Then he must read; if he reads steadily all his spare time, he finds his drinking companions low and dull, and thinks it a great waste of time to be shouting out foolish songs or idle talk for four or five hours that would put him half way through a new book. Besides, he has become good company for himself, which your drinking man is not.'

'That's the best reason of all, sir,' heartily assented his follower. 'It is hard lines on those chaps that can only talk about horses or cattle, or crops, or bullock driving. When they're by themselves they can only sulk. It's natural that they should want other men to talk to, and then it's hard work to make any fun without the grog.'

'And there's another very powerful beverage,' continued Ernest, 'that has been known to preserve men from the snare of strong drink, when nothing else would.'

'What's that, sir?'

'The influence of a good woman, John. The hope to win her some day by prudence and self-denial; the endeavour to be worthy of her; or the determination to give the best part of one's life to the comfort and happiness of her and her children, after she is a wife.'

'By the holy poker, sir,' shouted Mr. Windsor, roused out of his usual cool demeanour, 'you've just hit it there; there's no man worth calling a man as wouldn't work himself to skin and bone, and suffer thirst till his tongue hung out, if he could make himself of some account in the eyes of some women I've seen. There's a girl that we saw no later than last night, sir—you know who I mean; by George, if she'd only hold up her finger I'd live on rice and pickles like a Chinaman to the end of my days, and sniff at a glass of grog like old Watch does.'

'Very good resolution, Jack; and Carry Walton is as nice a girl, and as good, I'm sure, as ever tempted a man to make good resolutions. I quite approve of your taste. Indeed, she's a great friend of mine, and if you like to show what stuff you are really made of, I'll see what I can do to give you a helping hand.'

John Windsor did not speak for some time. He looked before him for a few seconds as if watching the far sky-line on the great primeval wastes where his youth had been passed. Then he turned with a grave and sobered expression, very different from the one habitual to his somewhat reckless demeanour. 'I don't like to say much, sir—talking isn't my line, when I mean anything—but if you're good enough to be bothered with me for a year or two, and if I get that girl for a wife, and keep her as she ought to be kept by my own industry, you'll have a man as will work for you, ride for you, or fight for you, as long as you want any one on this side.'

'I know that, Jack,' said Mr. Neuchamp, looking feelingly at the heightened colour and speaking expression of his follower; 'and if I have any claim beyond gratitude, you cannot repay it more effectually, and more agreeably to my mind, than by acting in such a way as to make people talk of you by and by as an industrious, steady, and I am sure they will add, clever and successful man.'

Jack's manly face glowed, and his brown eyes glistened at this encouraging statement; but he refrained from further speech until they reached the broad arterial thoroughfare which, from all the great western and southern provinces, leads into the most beautiful city in Australia.

'This looks something like a crowd, sir. What a mob of houses, people, cabs, teams, men, women, and children! What in the name of fortune do they all do, and where do they all go at night? Well, I never thought the town was as big as this. Confound the horse' (this to Ben Bolt, who lashed out at a passing hansom), 'he'll kill some one yet before he's safe in the stable.'

Perhaps a city is never seen to such advantage as after a considerable sojourn in the provinces, at sea, or in any such other distant or isolated abode, where the dweller is necessarily debarred from the required licenses of civilisation. At such a time the sensations, keenly sharpened by abstinence, do more than justice to the real, even to the apparent, advantages of that aggregation of human atoms known as a city.

The returning or arriving traveller revels in the real and supposititious treasures of this newly-discovered fairyland. The predominance and accessibility of wonders; the daily presence of friends, acquaintances, strangers, and notables, dazzle and deceive the eye long accustomed to the rare presentment of such personages; the public buildings, the parks, the intellectual and artistic treasure-houses, the higher standard of appearance, dress—all combine to excite and animate the mind.

Mr. Neuchamp had been familiar with divers capitals of considerably greater pretensions, and of world-wide historic rank and reputation. London had been his home, Paris his holiday retreat; Rome, Venice, Vienna, his occasional residence. But he thought he had never before felt so high and genuine a degree of exhilaration when returning to any of those great cities after an absence, as he now acknowledged in every vein and pulse, as he rode up the not particularly gorgeous avenue of Brickfield Hill, and passing the railway station, decided to thread George Street and, depositing the horses at a snug stable he knew of, find his way once more to the office of Paul Frankston and Co.

It would be unjust to Mr. Neuchamp to say that this name and its concomitant associations had not been many times unquestioned and sole possessors of his thoughts. Many a time and oft had he wondered whether the household remained exactly *in statu quo*. Did the old man return nightly to his dinner, his cigar, his seat in the verandah, and his unfailing request to Antonia to play and sing? He could fancy her pleasant smile as she sat down to the instrument, and her cheerful performance of the somewhat old-fashioned tunes and melodies that her father loved.

And had she made any fresh acquaintances? Were any other newly-arrived colonists kindly greeted and put upon terms of familiar hospitality like himself? That sort of thing might be carried too far. Extremely entertaining young fellows emigrated, and a few that he could name were unmistakably 'bad eggs.'

However, he would very soon see if anything of the kind, any shadow of the falcon, was imminent. He had heard from time to time from old Paul, who occasionally furnished a message from Antonia of a new book she had been reading, a visit she had paid, a sailing excursion that she and her father had enjoyed together; and lastly, something had been said about an Austrian nobleman—Count or Baron, or of some such objectionable rank—who was the acknowledged lion of Sydney just then, and who had been several times at Morahmee.

This piece of information did not cause any of the pleasure almost visible on the letter relating it to be conveyed to Ernest Neuchamp. 'Count be hanged!' he was English enough to say. 'I hate these foreign fellows. Ten to one there's something not quite correct about a foreigner on his travels. Not that there's any logical necessity for it. I trust I am not sufficiently insular to deny a foreign nobility all the graces and virtues that add lustre to our own. But we can always find out and trace our "heavy gunners." But in the countless (I mean no harm) multitude of Counts and Barons, Grafs and Vons, who can possibly tell whether the bowing, broken-Englished, insinuating beggar that you introduce to your wife and daughters is Von Adelberg himself, or his valet or courier levanted with the cash and purloining the title as well as the clothes of his master?'

Osmund and Ben Bolt were safely bestowed in a snug but unpretending stable not a hundred miles from Bent Street, and Mr. Windsor, as a man who 'knew his way about,' even in a strange city, was left temporarily to his own guidance, merely being requested to report himself at Morahmee.

Every Englishman knows what important step Ernest took next. His hair reduced to the smallest visible quantity, and the luxuriance of his beard, which he had lately permitted full liberty of growth, rationally restricted, he betook himself to the well-known counting-house.

The grave head clerk, who had acquired such solemn doubts as to Mr. Hartley Selmore's final destination, smiled, under protest, when he announced 'a gentleman on business,' by Ernest's request. Old Paul looked up with his usual good-natured expression, then stared in unrecognising blankness at the bronzed and bearded figure before him, finally to burst into a perfect tempest of laughter and chuckling, shaking Ernest's hands violently with both of his, and making as if he could throw himself on the neck of his safe returning *protégé*.

'Ha! ha! ha! so you're back again, are you, Ernest, my boy? By Jove, I'm glad to see you; burnt brown enough too—shows you've been working; like to see it—none the worse looking for it, either, I know the girls will say. But, I say—ha! ha! ha! known by the police, eh? Captain Jinks, alias Gentleman Jack, and the *other prisoner*, eh, my boy? How I roared at that till Antonia was quite savage—for *her* you know. Didn't take your photo, did they? generally do, you know. Got an album, for reference, at all the chief police stations. You're coming out, of course, to-night. Antonia will be awfully glad; don't tell her I said so.

'Look here, my dear boy, I was just bothering this old head of mine about some business matters—hang them. You run away out to Morahmee, and tell Antonia to have dinner ready to the minute, or I'll murder the whole household. Now off with you!'

Ernest departed, nothing loath, and as he whirled out, hansom-borne, along the well-remembered road, and gazed once more upon the blue waters, the frowning headland, the green villa-dotted shores of the unequalled harbour, he mentally contrasted these with the gray monotonous plains of Garrandilla, or the equally monotonous waterless woodlands.

'By Jove!' he said, 'I feel like a schoolboy home for the holidays, or a sailor back from a cruise; and all for the pleasure of returning to Sydney, a place I had scarcely heard of a couple of years since. Am I the same Ernest Neuchamp that knew Paris pretty well before he was of age, and Vienna to boot?

'However, all this sort of thing is like your club dinners. The menu goes for little except you have the appetite; if you have *that*, you can renovate soul and body upon bread and cheese.' Here he deserted the region of philosophic parallels, and began to picture the expression of satisfaction, perhaps of unrestrained pleasure, that would illumine Antonia Frankston's countenance upon his arrival. 'What a charming thing a perfect friendship between two persons of different sexes might be made!' he thought, 'if people would not insist upon complicating the highest, noblest, and most exalted sentiment of which our nature is capable with that ridiculous, half instinctive, undignified, inferior passion which men call love. Of course inferior. Why, friendship must necessarily be based upon an equality of culture, of social aims, principles, and sympathies, while the other violent, unreasoning, and unreasonable monopoly may exist between persons of the most widely differing ages, positions, standards of refinement, and intellectual rank; between the dotard and the maiden, the duke and the dairymaid, the peeress and the parvenu, the rustic and the courtier, the spotlessly pure and the incorrigibly base.'

From this it may be gathered that Mr. Neuchamp was not a man addicted to falling violently and promiscuously in love. In point of fact, he had a stupendously high ideal, which, not expecting to realise it in everyday life, seemed to keep the subject a good deal out of his mind. Then he thought a man should do some work under the sun first, and set about a quest for the 'sangreal' afterwards. He regarded Antonia Frankston with a deep feeling of interest, as a dear and highly sympathetic friend. He had given her the advantage of many criticisms with respect to the course of reading, very unusual for a girl of her age, that she was pursuing when they first met, and since then had advised and directed her intellectual progress.

Insensibly the natural sympathy between the master and a promising pupil was quickened and intensified by the originality of mind which Antonia evinced. When Ernest Neuchamp magnanimously departed for the interior, he had commenced to notice the awakening of an unacknowledged feeling that the hour's talk and make-believe school at Morahmee was the period of the day he was most eager to seize, most unwilling to relinquish.

And now how altered and strengthened as to her intellectual grasp must she be—this unsophisticated, unwon child of the fair south—with the brooding fancies and absolute simplicity of a child, the instinctive dignity, the curious aplomb, of a woman. As he reached this not unpleasing stage of his reverie the wheels of the hansom ground viciously the matchless gravel of the drive at Morahmee, and grazed perilously close the snowy sandstone steps in front of the portico.

Ernest recalled the old delicious sense of stillness, the

> beautiful silence all around,
> Save wood-bird to wood-bird calling,

broken only by the calmly murmurous rhythmic plash of the wavelets on the beach.

It was not a house where people were always coming and going, and he did not remember often to have found Antonia otherwise than alone, on the occasion of his former visits. What was she doing now? Should he find her reading in the library, that pleasant room with the bay window, in which slumberous calms the smiles and storms of ocean were pictures set as in a frame? in the drawing-room? in the shrubbery? in the rose garden? in the morning-room, which she usually affected, and which, having a davenport, her favourite authors, and a cottage piano, was able to supply, indifferently well, the distinguishing features of three more pretentious apartments?

As he passed through the hall the notes of the piano, not of the boudoir, but the grand Erard, with a bass of organ-like depth of vibration, informed him that in the drawing-room he would probably find the youthful *châtelaine*.

Almost simultaneously he heard the rich, deep notes of a strange male voice accompanying the instrument, and recognised the concluding words of a duet which he himself had sung with Miss Frankston full many a time and oft.

As the second performer dwelt with perhaps unnecessarily tender expression upon Heine's thrilling 'Bis in den tiefsten Traum,' Mr. Neuchamp became conscious of a distinct change of feeling—of a sudden painful sense of disenchantment.

There was no tangible cause for uneasiness. A young lady was merely singing one of Mendelssohn's loveliest duets with an accredited musical acquaintance. By the merest accident, no doubt. Still, let but a single cloud darken the summer sky, the chill breeze once sigh, how faintly soever, and the heart, that sensitive plant, shrinks instinctively at nature's warning. So smote the melody, albeit effectively rendered, upon Ernest's highly-wrought mind with a savour of bode and of dread. And as he entered the open door of the apartment he knew himself to be deeply changed from the eager visitor who had but a few moments since so joyously alighted at the portals of Morahmee.

# CHAPTER XIV

The attainment of pure and permanent happiness, by either of the attached persons, has always been held to be a leading aim of true friendship. Mild surprise at the nature of the implements chosen for such attainment is, perhaps, admissible. But no selfish disapproval can be justified for a moment, if only the appreciative partner elects to adhere fixedly to the new plan or newer friend.

Still, human nature is ever more philosophical in theory than in practice; and the wayfaring Damon, *de retour*, rarely reaches that pinnacle of sublime abnegation which glories in being superseded, or expresses gratitude that Pythias has provided himself with another Damon, 'whose Christian name was John.' Some natural distrust must ever be felt, must be exhibited, let the fresher friend be in the highest degree justifiable, heroic, adorable.

All the essayists on friendship notwithstanding, Mr. Neuchamp felt distinctly aggrieved. There was he, rushing back upon the wings of—well—intelligent and sympathetic friendship, willing to resume the delightful æsthetic intercourse which compulsory absence had alone interrupted, and now, apparently, he needed not to have come at all. Antonia was fully occupied, no doubt interested, by the first frivolous foreigner that came in her way, and was singing duets and so on, as if she had no higher aspiration than to listen for ever to a German band.

Entering the drawing-room, Ernest presented himself just as the Count (of course it was the Count, confound him!) was singing the *dich der folgen* portion of the melody with, as Ernest thought, ridiculously exaggerated emphasis. He made the most of his eyes—which were really fine—rolled them in an excess of admiration, and throwing the fullest expressive force into the concluding stanza, sighed and bowed low with admiring respect to the fair pianist. She smiled not wholly with displeasure, and as she turned she met the somewhat grave and fixed regard of Ernest Neuchamp.

'Pray excuse me for disturbing your musical entertainment, Miss Frankston,' he said, with a coldness unlike anything she had ever observed in his manner before.

Antonia's colourless face, which had flushed slightly at the suddenness of the *contretemps*, regained its habitual serene delicacy of hue, as she calmly observed—

'The Count von Schätterheims and I have been practising German duets for a *matinée* that Mrs. Folleton gives next week, and that all Sydney is wild about. It is quite a treat to have the aid of one who understands the genius of the poetry and music so thoroughly. Permit me to introduce you to the Count, Mr. Neuchamp.'

The foreign nobleman, a tall, fair man, with a moustache like a Pandour, bowed graciously, and resumed the musical subject.

'Ah! I did know Mendelssohn so well as mine fader. He lif at our house when he come to Munich. He always say I was born for a *maestro*.'

'And why did you not fulfil his prediction, Count?' asked Antonia, much interested.

'De sword,' said Von Schätterheims with a grave, sad air. 'You vill comprehent, he vas too moosh for de lyre. I join de movement of freedom. I haf commant, wit poor Körner. He die in dese arms.'

'The lyre—ahem!' said Ernest, smiling grimly at his utterly unjustifiable *mot*, 'has reasserted his right, I should say. Did not Körner die in 18—?' (Here he quoted the memorable 'Sword Song' in the original.)

'Ha!' said the Count, a new expression, not only of satisfaction, pervading his features, 'thou hast seen the Faderland. No Englander ever learned a so *heimlich* acsend who drank not in youth the beer at *Studenten-Kneipe*—we must have *Brüderschaft*. Is it not so?'

'Do you think we can manage "Die Schwalben," Count?' asked Antonia.

'But I haf bromiss to be at the house of Madame Folleton, to hear mademoiselle bractise dat leedle Folks-lied. Besites, we read Heine togeder. She is aisthetig—yaas—to de tips of her finkers. Adieu!'

'And now, Mr. Ernest Neuchamp, what have you to say for yourself?' said Antonia, in a tone between jest and earnest, 'in that you have been in my presence for half an hour and have only smiled twice, have called me Miss Frankston, and have looked at that delightful creature, the Count, with an air of stern disapproval? Where do you expect to go to?'

'Really,' said Ernest, 'I am unconscious of having done or looked anything peculiarly unsatisfactory. But I thought you were so exceedingly well contented with the Count's society that I doubted whether I was not making an undesirable third. And who is this Count?'

'Well, he had letters to papa and old Captain Blockstrop; and all Sydney is wild about him. No party is worth going to where he does not come. He is the most accomplished and charming person—plays, sings, paints, has been a soldier and desperately wounded. All the young ladies of Sydney are wild about him. He is enormously rich, and gives such parties on board his yacht!'

'And is Miss Frankston one of the young ladies whom this broken-Englished invincible has conquered?' asked Ernest. 'May I be permitted to congratulate her?'

'You must judge for yourself,' said the girl, with so merry a look and such a genuinely amused expression that Mr. Neuchamp's slight experience of the ways of womankind assured him that no great damage to his pupil's heart had as yet taken place. 'But there is just time for a stroll on the beach before dinner, and a slight sketch of your adventures since you left us. You look quite a bushman now. How sunburned you have managed to get!'

Mr. Neuchamp was but mortal. The best of us, under certain conditions, are weak. As Antonia shut down the piano and ran to get her straw hat with girlish freedom of manner, he felt his justifiable wrath evaporating. Long before they had finished that pleasant ramble in the cool twilight, with the stars one by one appearing, the surge voices whispering low and solemnly kind, the cool briny savour of the ocean—a sea of enchantment to Ernest, but of yesterday from the inner deserts—long before the somewhat emphasised dinner-bell rang, Ernest repented of his pettishness. He knew that his friendship had suffered neither wrong nor change. He felt that there were still feelings and aspirations in that fresh, unspoiled, girlish heart to which he alone had the password. He answered Mr. Frankston's boisterous hail from the verandah in a surprisingly nautical and cheery manner, and passed into the enjoyment of dinner, and dinner talk, much relieved in mind.

'What's become of the Count, Antonia?' said the old gentleman. 'Try that Chablis, Ernest, my boy; imported it since you were down. Old Jedwood didn't give you anything like that; thundering old screw, isn't he? good man for all that; trust him with your life. I thought you were going to make the Count stay to dinner, Antonia.'

'Well, it would have been pleasanter for Mr. Neuchamp, perhaps,' said the young lady demurely. 'But he said he had to go to Mrs. Folleton's.'

'Oh! that was the attraction then,' said Mr. Frankston. 'They say he admires Harriet Folleton tremendously. She will have twenty thousand down; but as he is so wealthy himself, of course the cash can't matter.'

'You all seem to take it for granted that he is so very rich, and a wonderful fellow in all respects,' said Ernest. 'He's good-looking enough, I admit; but who is to know whether he is really the man he represents himself to be?'

'Why should he not be himself,' said Antonia, 'more than any one else?'

'For this reason,' replied Ernest, 'that it is much more easy for a foreigner to impose upon English people, in a community like this, than for an

Englishman to practise a similar deceit. He has but to bring manufactured introductions, and the whole difficulty is over to a man of ordinary address and qualifications for sustaining such a part.'

'Well, I must say,' said Mr. Frankston, 'that the letters I received might have been written by any corresponding clerk in a German counting-house. I took him and his letters for granted, and so did old Blockstrop, just as we should have taken his bills properly endorsed. But let me ask you, Ernest, my boy, doesn't he look and speak like the real thing?'

'You must not be offended with me,' said Ernest, conscious of a certain flash in Antonia's eyes, 'or think me ungenerous, if I say that I should like to take a little more time and have some opportunities of intercourse before giving my opinion. You must remember that habitudes of ceremonious behaviour pervade *all classes* in continental countries to an extent unknown in British communities. By superficial observers a count and a courier, for instance, will not be perceived to differ in manner or language; and the courier is often the more picturesque personage of the two.'

'And why not?' inquired Antonia; 'is there no difference between the manners and the conversation of people of upper and lower rank, except in England and English places?'

'I do not say that; the contrary is the case, but the discrepancies are sufficiently minute to escape British people not thoroughly acquainted with the language. For the same reason no foreigner would discover the difference between a good-looking, decently-educated Britisher who dropped his aitches, and the real article. Thackeray somewhere gives a case in point.'

'Well, I suppose we shall be all at the great ball next week,' said Antonia, 'and you will then be able to analyse Count von Schätterheims to your heart's content. They say he admires Harriet Folleton extremely.'

'It's nothing to me whom he admires,' said Ernest, 'as long as he leaves a certain independent-minded young lady friend of mine alone. I should not like to see her carried off by any privateer hoisting false colours.'

'You are all jealous; that's the truth, if you would but own it,' laughed Antonia; 'and indeed, if one thinks of the commotion the Count has created among the Sydney young ladies, it seems reasonable enough. If he had been a whole man-of-war compressed, he could not have been more flattered and run after. And that is saying a great deal *here*, you know.'

'I am aware of that,' said Ernest, with a slight bow; 'short as has been my experience, I have noticed so much.'

'Well, I agree with Ernest to a certain extent,' said old Paul reflectively. 'It's as well to be cautious with these wonderful strangers, especially foreigners. We haven't quite forgotten Senor Miranda yet, eh, Antonia?'

'Yes, I did see him once, if that's what you mean,' said the girl, looking at Ernest; 'and I have always been very sorry that he should have come to shame. He was a bad man, of course; but he was really so very grand-looking, and when he spoke he had such a sweet, grave, deep voice that you would have done whatever he asked you at once.'

'What did he do, then?' inquired Ernest.

'Do?' said Mr. Frankston. 'Why, with forged letters of introduction he commenced a business transaction with one of the banks; he placed to his credit a large balance, which he took care to draw out; and the end of it was that he walked off with five-and-twenty thousand pounds in exchange for bills not worth *that*, and has never been seen or heard of since.'

'How many Germans are there?' asked Antonia innocently.

'Forty odd millions,' answered Ernest.

'And there are twenty-two millions of Spaniards,' continued she, 'for I saw it to-day. Well, that makes so many—sixty millions, or more, altogether. And we are to suspect and distrust all these people just because Senor Miranda was a swindler. I wonder if foreign nations are equally just to Englishmen on their travels.'

'Come along and let us have our cigars,' said the old gentleman. 'Antonia, we must get you made Austrian consul. What—you haven't learned to smoke in the bush, Ernest? Never mind; come along all the same. Cigars have more flavour in company, and the music will sound better too.'

It was a superb night—one of the units of that wondrous wealth and prodigality of perfect weather by which we should set greater store were we compelled to undergo a quarter of the austerity of northern Europe. Not a cloud was visible. The large and lustrous stars glowed all unheeded by an accustomed world. All the intricacies of the harbour seemed stretched and illumined by the glowing lights from the various vessels outward, homeward bound, or at anchor. And yet all invisible as was the sea, the presence of the majesty of the deep was manifest in the salt savour of the air, in the half-heard murmur of the tide ripples, in the far indistinctly wondrous tones of the surge upon the distant beach.

As the old man lit his cigar and looked seaward, mechanically, the first notes of a brilliant aria floated out upon the air from the piano, and Ernest musingly realised the unostentatious luxury of the household, the exquisite beauty of the scene and surroundings, and contrasted them with the rude adjuncts of Garrandilla and its environs.

Next morning Mr. Windsor made his appearance immediately after breakfast at Morahmee, and awaited commands.

'What a pretty horse!' said Antonia; 'is that yours?'

'That is Osmund, my first Australian hackney, and a great favourite,' said Mr. Neuchamp, with a certain pride.

'Well, you've done credit to your knowledge of horseflesh,' said the old gentleman; 'he would fetch fifty pounds now in Sydney. And what about my countryman who is on his back? I can tell his parish without twice looking. He's like the horse, a good-looking, upstanding young one; but we can't be so sure about *his* value from appearance only.'

'Jack Windsor is mine, too,' said Ernest, 'a good, clever fellow, I think. It's rather a long story how we first became acquainted. I'll tell it you some day. When I buy a run he will go with me as stockman and right-hand man generally.'

'So that's the arrangement. I hope he will turn out a credit to you, like the horse. He's the cut of a good man, and I should have been very glad to have shipped him in old days for a whaling cruise. You will have to exercise your horse, now you have him stabled. Antonia would like a canter, I daresay.'

'I should, of all things,' said that young lady. 'My poor Waratah has not been out for a week; she looks ready to fly over the moon with nervousness. We might go this afternoon, if Mr. Neuchamp can spare the time.'

Mr. Neuchamp declared that all his time was spare time now, and that he should be charmed to be at Antonia's disposal for any and every afternoon as long as he remained in town.

So Jack and the gray horse were sent back to their stable, with orders to return at three o'clock punctually.

'And after the ball,' said Mr. Frankston, 'I shall take a holiday, so I think we'll have a sail and do a little fishing. At any rate we shall see the harbour, and I can show you something choice in the way of bays. How do you like the idea?'

Both of the young people protested that it was the exact thing they had been longing for for months. And so, that arrangement being settled, the old gentleman departed for town in his dogcart, and Ernest, having a few things to do bordering upon business, accompanied him.

One of the minor perplexities which assail the student of human nature arises from the fact that all, or nearly all, of the persons who arrive in a colony conduct themselves after the same fashion. For a season, which includes the first few months, they are wildly capricious, and even reckless, in the matter of raiment. The idea is always uppermost that, in a new country, it is not of the slightest consequence how anybody dresses. That to no one, the newly-landed in particular, can it possibly matter whether his fellow-mortals array themselves in broadcloth or sackcloth, tweed or canvas, spotless linen or red shirt.

Another strongly implanted idea is, that the subdivisions of society, set up by colonists among themselves, are vain, weak, and unnecessary. These severely linear distinctions are adhered to in the old country, and are *there*, doubtless, right and expedient. But, ye gods! in this land, inhabited by the wandering savage but of yesterday, by the confused crowd of hard and anxious colonists (all colonists are necessarily rough and unceremonious), why revive these absurd, exaggerated, old-world ceremonies?

Thus, during his little day of nonage, the emigrant Briton disports himself, rejoicing in his newly-found emancipation from conventionalities. He goes to a dinner party in a morning suit, and finds himself the sole person not in evening dress. He pays visits in a pilot's jacket, and feels a thrill of pride and defiance as he observes the young ladies of the house look wonderingly at him. He bears himself as he would not dream of doing in his own country town, perhaps a more primitive and deplorably dull neighbourhood than he could easily find in the older districts of Australia. And for all this refusal to pay the simple compliment of conformity to the kindly people among whom he is entertained and made welcome, he has no better reason to give himself or others than that it is a colony, and that it would be absurd to expect the same social observances as in an old country.

Nothing could be more amiable than the general toleration which obtains of this youthful eccentricity, were it not so thoroughly understood that it is the ordinary early phase of griffinhood, and that it is certain to wear out in time. It would be mortifying to the pride of the contemner of social customs, could he but fully understand how every one, from the mild uncritical senior to little miss in her teens, holds these clothes-philosophical eccentricities in good-humoured contempt, and relies upon the wearer becoming like everybody else, in a year or two at farthest.

We know that much of this spirit possessed the aspiring soul of Ernest Neuchamp when first he stood upon the balcony of the Royal Hotel and gazed upon the crowd that passed below. But though he had abated not a jot of some points of his original charter, he yet could not but acknowledge that he was a very different individual, in opinion and in feeling, from the ardent emigrant of only a year ago.

As one consequence of this altered tone of mind, he cheerfully accepted Mr. Frankston's offer of arranging his admission as honorary member of one of the clubs. He began to feel a longing for the society of his equals; and, as he could not be always lounging away the day at Morahmee, and did not contemplate an immediate return to Garrandilla, he saw the necessity of having some recognised place of temporary abode wherein he might take his ease, in the society of gentlemen, and keep himself *au courant* with the progress of the world.

This transaction having been formally carried out by the ever-zealous and kindly Paul, he was placed in receipt of a missive, signed by the secretary, and announcing that he had been elected to be an honorary member of the New Holland Club.

He was introduced next day by Mr. Frankston himself, and discovered that he had the *entrée* to a handsome commodious building, with a larger extent of lawn and shrubbery than he had ever seen attached to an institution of the nature before. The internal arrangements were familiar, being precisely the same as those of the London Club, to which he had been elected about five years after nomination.

There were the same grave, decorous servants, the same silent appreciation of the same style of highly respectable cookery, the same comfortable sitting-room, with—oh, pleasant sight!—good store of magazines, *Punches*, *Saturdays*, *Pall Malls*, and all the priceless luxuries of refined, if ephemeral, journalism. There was the same deserted library, the same populous smoking-room, with billiard-room ditto. To a few members old Paul had introduced him, and for the rest he was aware that he must take his chance.

He found, after a day or two, that he had small reason to fear of isolation. A gentlemanlike stranger needs but the evidence of this quality to procure friendly acquaintances, if not intimates, at any club.

He was soon known as 'a young fellow who had been sent out to old Frankston, and was going to buy a station. A decent sort of fellow belonging to swell people, and so on. Going to do wonders, and make important changes. That will wear off—we've all passed through that mill. He'll settle down and take to wool and tallow kindly, like all the rest of us, in good time.'

Mr. Neuchamp made the discovery that, if he had been less obstinately bent upon separating himself from the presumably prejudiced society of the new land, in the fervour of his philanthropy, he might possibly have met with other colonists, who, like Paul Frankston, would have shielded him from harm, and proffered him good and true advice. In his new home he made the acquaintance of more than one silver-haired pioneer, who, while gently parrying the thrusts of his eager and somewhat communistic theories, quietly put forward the dictates of long experience and successful practice. Every one was disposed to be tolerant, agreeable, even friendly, to the frank youngster, who was, in spite of his crotchets, evidently 'good form.' And Ernest realised fully, and rather unexpectedly, that even in a colony it is possible for a stranger to fall among friends, and that colonists are not invariably all stamped out of one pattern, whatever anticipations may be compounded in the fancy of the emigrating critic.

In another respect Ernest found that his club privileges were valuable as well as luxurious. Among the squatters, who composed the larger proportion of the members, he had the advantage of hearing the question of pastoral property discussed with fullest clearness and explanation, in all its bearings. No one evaded giving a decided opinion upon the chances of investment, though, according to temperament, and other causes, the answers were various. All agreed, however, in one respect, namely, that stock had touched a point of depression, below which it seemed wellnigh impossible to fall. The great question, of course, was whether such properties would ever rise, or whether such profits or losses, as the case might be, must be accepted as permanently fixed.

'I believe that cattle and sheep never *will* rise a penny higher during our lifetime, particularly cattle,' said a slight, elegant, cynical squatter, with whom Ernest had made acquaintance. 'It's of course nothing but what any one ought to have expected in this infernal country. What is there to keep stock up, I ask? As for wool, South America will grow three bales to our one directly; and cattle and horses will be slaughtered for their hides, as they are there.'

'What a grumbler you are, Croker!' said a stout cheery-looking youngster, with a long fair moustache and a smooth face; 'you run down the country like a rival agent-general. Why do you stay in it, if it's so bad?'

'I'd leave to-morrow if I could get any one fool enough to buy my runs; take my passage by the mail and never be heard of here again.'

'Well, you wouldn't make a bad immigration agent, if the Government wanted to appoint a prepossessing advertiser for Europe.'

'Agent! why, what do you see in me to make you think I should accept any such office?'

'Only, this strikes me, that if you went on talking there in your dissatisfied strain, the acute common people would be certain that you had some reason of your own for dissuading them from embarking, and, so thinking, would pour in by crowds.'

'Likely enough,' sneered the *avocat pour le diable*. 'There are only two sets of people in this rascally country—rogues and fools.'

'And to which division of society do I belong, may I ask?' inquired Ernest, rather amused at the uncompromising nature of the denunciation.

'Well, perhaps it's not very polite, but, as you wish for the information, I look upon you as a fool, for wishing to invest and waste your life here; upon

Compton as another, because he thinks well of the place and people; and upon myself as the biggest one of the lot for staying here, when I know so well what lies before the whole rotten sham which calls itself a prosperous colony.'

'Are matters then so bad?' inquired Ernest, with some solicitude. 'I thought that the country was sound generally.'

Mr. Croker bestowed upon him a look of pity, mingled with contempt, and in his most acid tones replied—

'If you knew half as much as I do about the banks and mercantile transactions, if you were a little behind the scenes as I have, perhaps unluckily, been, you would know that a crash must come—*must* come—within the next two or three years. I expect to see all the banks in the hands of official assignees—they'll be the only solvent people. As for the merchants—'

'Well, Mr. Jermyn Croker, "as for the merchants"?' said a jolly voice, and Paul Frankston's rubicund and reassuring countenance appeared in the little group which had gathered to listen to the lamentations of this latter-day seer—'how about the merchants?'

'Why,' returned Mr. Croker, totally unabashed, 'I expect to see you, and Holder Brothers, and Deloraine and Company, and the rest, begging in the streets.'

'Ha! ha! ha! capital. Well done, Jermyn; put a half-crown or two in your pocket against that day; I know you'd like to relieve honest poverty. In the meantime come and dine with me on Thursday, will you, and Compton, and Neuchamp? Better come soon, you know, while that Roederer holds out. "Let us eat and drink," you know, etc. I say, what will you take for that cattle station of yours at Lake Wondah? No use holding, you know, eh?'

'Two pounds a head, for three thousand—calves given in.'

'What dates?'

'Cash down! Do you think I'd take any man's bills now? No, not if Levison himself were to endorse.'

'Hem—ha—I learn the cattle are baddish, but the run is understocked. How long will you leave it open?'

'Oh! a month; three months if you like. Send me a cheque at any time for six thousand and I will send you an order to take possession; that is, as soon as I find the cheque all right.'

'Ha! ha! not bad, Croker. It would be the first cheque of Paul Frankston's that ever was unpaid, so far. But you'll not forget Thursday, all of you, boys.

We must try and shake Croker out of the blues, or he'll ruin the prospects of every squatter in New South Wales.'

Mr. Neuchamp's spirits were not so permanently affected by the alarming vaticinations of Mr. Jermyn Croker as that he was prevented from exhibiting Osmund's figure and paces past the club verandah that afternoon, followed by Mr. Windsor on Ben Bolt, on his way to keep tryst with Antonia.

There may be a pleasanter species of locomotion, on a fine day, than that afforded by a good horse in top condition over a smooth road, in the immediate vicinity of a valued lady friend; let us say there may be, but we have yet to discover it. The yacht, sweeping like a seamew over the rippling, gaily-breaking billow, with courses free and a merry company aboard, holds high excitement and joyous freedom from the world's cankering cares; the mail-phaeton with a pair of well-bred steppers, or, better still, a high drag behind a fresh team, well matched and better-mouthed, has its own peculiar fascination as one is whirled through the summer air, or borne fast and free through the gathering twilight homewards and dinnerwards; even the smooth, irresponsible rush of the express train yields not wholly disagreeable sensation of a victory over time and space, as we whirl down the flying grades and round the somewhat *risque* curves. But the personal element which the rider shares with the bonny brown, or gallant grey, that strides with joyous elasticity beneath him, had a thrill, in the 'brave old days of pleasure and pain,' that dwarfed all other recreation. If anything can intensify the feeling of joyance, it is the presence, similarly equipped, of the possible princess. Then the fairy glamour is complete—in the forest glades are the leaflets hung with diamonds, the half-heard music is full of unearthly cadences—and as the graceful form sways with movement of her eager palfrey, the good knight's head must be harder than his casque if heart and sword and fame, past, present, and to come, be not laid, then and there, at the feet of that ladye-fayre.

Miss Frankston rode, like most Australian girls, extremely well, and with an unconscious grace and security of seat only to be attained by those who, like her, had enjoyed the fullest opportunities of practice from earliest childhood. Her dark bay mare was thoroughbred, having been carried off by Mr. Frankston five minutes after she lost her first race at Randwick. She had been indifferently brought out, and, as a sporting friend said, was not fit to run for a saddle in a shearers' sweepstakes.

Antonia had taken a strong fancy to her personal appearance, and Paul, as usual, had then and there gratified his pet. Waratah, which was the filly's name, proving after trial high-couraged and temperate, had been installed at Morahmee as the description of dumb favourite for which, in the springtime of life, the heart of a woman is prone to crave.

On this particular afternoon it was proposed by Antonia that they should ride to Bondi. 'One of our show places, you must know,' she said; 'and as the wind is coming in strong from the south, we shall have the surf-thunder in perfection.'

'Don't ride *into* the breakers, that's all, as you tried to do last time we were there; if you and Waratah were carried off your feet, your poor old father would never see his pet again.'

'How do you know? You silly old papa. Can't we both swim?' said the girl, laying her hand tenderly on his weather-beaten cheek; 'you will make Mr. Neuchamp think that I'm as wild as a hawk, instead of being the sober-minded damsel that I really am. However, you need not be afraid of my running any foolish risks to-day.'

The morning had been clear, with that suspicion of chill which told that at no great distance from the coast there had been a strong change of temperature. In and around Sydney the atmospheric tendency had been softened into a composite of warmth, tempered with freshness wonderful to experience and exhilarating past all description.

The girl slacked the rein of her eager mare, and the excited horses swept along the smooth, winding, dark-red road. Before them lay the dark blue plain of ocean, fading into a misty, troubled haze which met the far horizon. Gradually they increased their distance from the gay gardens and villas of the more populous suburbs, the spires and terraces of the city.

'This has always been a favourite excursion of mine,' said Antonia. 'From the moment we pass Waverley and front the ocean in all his wondrous strength and beauty, I feel as if I could shout for joy. Morahmee is very pretty, but the harbour has always a kind of lakelike prettiness to me; like the beds in a flower garden, while here—'

'And here?' said Ernest, smiling, as the southern maiden fixed her earnest gaze upon the wide glory of the unbounded sea, with a passion and tenderness of regard which he had never observed before.

'Here,' said she, 'I feel lifted from my daily small pleasures and *very* minute cares into a world of thought and vision, exalted, infinite in grandeur and richness of colouring. My mind travels across that region of mystery and wonder which the sea has ever been to adventurous and practical minds, and all my heroes stand visibly presented before me.'

'Please to introduce me,' said Ernest.

'I see Walter Raleigh, courtier, poet, warrior, sailor, statesman, and can mourn over him, as though I had seen that noblest of heads upon the cruel block but yesterday. I see Francis Drake with his crisp curls and dauntless spirit; I see Columbus ever calm, watchful, indomitable; Ponce de

Leon, pacing up and down his lonely beach at Hispaniola, and can fancy him setting forth upon his half-melancholy, half-ludicrous expedition to *la fontain de jouvences*; even Bimini—oh! the many, many friends and companions that have ever been associated with the sea in my mind since my earliest childhood.'

'I am afraid,' said Ernest, translating an unacknowledged thought, 'that you must be something like a cocoa-palm, or your own Norfolk Island pine, unable to exist out of hearing of the sound of the sea.'

'I never thought about that,' answered the girl with a half-curious look, as if back from the unreal world. 'I have always fancied that I would do whatever other people would do. But we all have our pet fancies, which we spoil like children, or which spoil us, and the prosaic part of our life has to go on notwithstanding.'

'Have you ever seen anything of the bush?' inquired Ernest.

'Nothing more than a very hasty visit to one or two of the inland towns. I have always wished to go to a real station and see something of bush life, but papa never could spare me sufficiently long. What is it like? All riding about, from morning to night, and being very sleepy in the evening?'

'There is a good deal of that,' said he, 'but not quite so much as might be thought. There is a great want of books, and of the habit of reading, in many places, though I know of course that it is not universal. But I think when I have a place of my own that I can manage to unite work and play, real exertion with an intellectual alternation, and this should be the perfection of existence.'

'I don't see why it could not be managed,' said Antonia. 'Many of the young squatters have told me that they could not get books, and that they were becoming frightfully ignorant; but I always said it must be their own fault. Any one who *must* read will read, no matter what their circumstances are.'

'So I believe,' answered Ernest, with most appreciative accents. 'When young people, or people of any age, say they have not time to read, it sounds in my ears as if they said that they had not time to eat their dinners, or to bathe, or say their prayers, or to talk to their friends. For these duties and other distractions they generally find leisure, and if the time be really fully occupied, a quarter of an hour almost in converse with some authors would provide the mind with new and instructive thoughts for the whole livelong day.'

'Well, we must see how Mr. Neuchamp carries out his ideas when he has a station of his own,' said Antonia archly. 'He must have everything very nice, very superior to the ordinary ways of colonists, and must make money also; *that* is indispensable.'

'I will answer for his trying to have things pleasantly and perhaps artistically arranged,' said Ernest, following out the sketch; 'but as for the making money, I have so little interest in it as one of the fine arts, that I may fail in that.'

'But that is the foundation of all the good deeds that you may do, so at least papa says. If a man doesn't make money, I heard him say once, he shows all the world that there is some quality lacking in him, and any little that he can say or do will not have its just weight; he is regarded only as an unpractical, unsuccessful enthusiast.'

'I hate the word enthusiast,' said Mr. Neuchamp, 'or rather the sense of disparagement in which it is generally used. It has come to mean, a man who is obstinately bent on a course of conduct which is wrong, or who exaggerates the degree or importance of his practice in what is right.'

'I cannot say that I am particularly fond of the word or of the idea myself, woman as I am; and you know that we are supposed to be full of enthusiasm on every conceivable subject from parasols to politics.'

'And why does Miss Frankston add her powerful influence to the world's Philistinism, already sufficient for its needs?' asked Ernest, with a slight tinge of satire.

'I don't say that I deny or distrust enthusiasm in men; and I can imagine a sincere respect and liking for the individual to go with a distrust of the quality, and for this reason. We may have the greatest admiration for this lofty feeling and generous self-denial which go to compose the character of the enthusiast; but we may smile at the likelihood of any of his great schemes issuing in glory and success.'

'But, surely,' pleaded Ernest, 'many of the great deeds which embellish history and which have ennobled our common natures have been nurtured in the brains, wrought out by the hands of men whom the world call enthusiasts.'

'Of that fact I am not so sure,' answered Antonia. 'I should rather say that the successful heroes were men of steadfast nature, not particularly acted upon by joy or despondency, whom success did not exhilarate, nor adversity bow down; through good and evil report, failure, or the harder trial of success, they bore themselves calmly and strongly.'

'But how about the sea—and the mysterious intoxication communicated by its very appearance?' asked Ernest mischievously. 'Is there no enthusiasm about such a feeling?'

'All those sensations,' laughed the girl, 'belong to the ideal Antonia Frankston, of which only a glimpse is permitted to any one from time to time. The real Miss Frankston—'

'What does she do?'

'Makes puddings, keeps the household accounts, orders dinner, and has distinct ideas on the subject of the main chance; *very* prosaic this last. Is not that a lovely nook, and *such* a pretty house?'

At this turn of the subject, and the turn of the road, they had unexpectedly come upon a villa embosomed in an almost Alpine fir grove; the trim lawns and delicately-coloured parterres, amid which it was placed, giving the whole place the appearance of a Watteau, framed in sombre green.

'It is a living picture,' said Ernest; 'how that wonderful Bougainvillea has draped the whole height of the north wing of the house; it is in full and splendid bloom, and mingled with it are the snowy flowers of the delicate myosotis. How charmingly secluded it is; they can look straight from their parlours across those dwarf-walls—across the Pacific Ocean. But where is the shepherdess?'

'There she is; do you not see that young girl sitting reading by the fountain? Calm and untroubled she looks; she reclines upon the low terrace facing the sea; by her side is a great vase filled with flowers. A child with a wide sash runs out from the house towards her. Can anything more closely realise a deep dream of peace?'

'Nothing, indeed,' assented Ernest admiringly. 'I could live all my days in such a nook, with one fair spirit to be my minister, and perhaps defer finishing my own and other people's education indefinitely.'

'Look!' continued Antonia, ignoring the personal element, 'with what a bold, sweeping curve the coastline recedes; leaving the loveliest little landlocked bay, with silver sands and a grand sandstone bluff guarding and walling-in the farther point like a grim jealous giant. But now we have such a piece of road, before we reach Bondi—smooth, soft, and slightly ascending. We *must* have a gentle breather.'

She took Waratah by the head, and slightly bending forward on her saddle, the eager thoroughbred went away at once, causing the heart of Mr. Neuchamp to palpitate with a nervous dread of accident. Of course Osmund followed suit, though it gave him quite enough to do to keep pace with the bounding, elastic stride of the well-bred flyer. In a three-mile race he could have run Waratah hard. However, for the half-mile spin it took a little hustling to prevent his being distanced. At the steep ascent of the hill above the far-famed beach, Antonia reined in her steed, which possessed the rare compromise, good temper with high courage.

'I suppose that our stupid scientific men will never find out any way for us to fly,' said she, 'but a good gallop must be as near the sensation as we can hope for. What a glorious feeling it is! I envy men their hunting, perhaps more than any of their exclusive pastimes.'

'But ladies hunt, at any rate in England,' said Ernest, 'and very straight they go too.'

'So they do, I have been told; but in Australia there are hardly enough of us to keep one another countenance; and besides, papa does not like it; the fences are so very dangerous.'

'All things considered, I agree with Mr. Frankston.'

'But what a view of views!'

They had now reached the crest of the hill, the deep-toned ceaseless roll of the surf-billows had long been in their ears.

'That is Bondi,' said Antonia, pointing southward. 'I have heard that sound at intervals all my life. I used to dream of it when I was a little child.'

Ernest looked southward over a rolling, rugged down, flecked with patches of low underwood and heath, to where a broad, milk-white beach received the vast rollers of a boundless ocean. No point or headland broke the continuous distance of the immense dark blue plain which stretched to the utmost boundary of vision.

It was no day of gale or tempest, but there had been sufficient wind on this and the previous day to set in motion the unresting surges which failed not the year through to moan and thunder upon this broad clear shining beach. Great crags lay to the westward, shutting off this bay from the other portions of the coast, while a projection to the eastward tended to isolate the bay of surges. Far out, from time to time a shining sail came from the under-world and swept placidly towards the city, or a stately ocean steamer, with throbbing screw or mighty paddle, left a long line of smoke trailing behind her as she drove haughtily against wind or tide on her appointed course.

'How one drinks in all this grandeur and loveliness of Dame Nature,' said Ernest. 'An instinctive constitutional craving seems satiated only by gazing at a scene like this.'

'I fully comprehend the condition of mind,' said Antonia. 'You have been shut up at Garrandilla, where in time, except from information, you would begin to doubt the existence of the sea altogether.'

'It is an astonishing contrast,' assented Mr. Neuchamp. 'How awfully hot it must be there now. I daresay old Doubletides is just coming in, half melted after his day's work, looking for lost sheep—counting one flock, and ordering another to come in to-morrow.'

'Surely it must be a terrible life,' said Antonia apprehensively. 'Is that why people in the bush go mad sometimes?'

'It's hard to say. I really don't think he or Jedwood are even dull or distrait, or unduly impressed with the nothingness of existence. I think very energetic people have certain advantages. Their tuglike, unremitting habit of doing something keeps the machine going, until some fine day a cogwheel catches, or a rivet breaks, and one more human unit mingles its dust with the forgotten millions.'

'Contemplation is very nice,' said Antonia, 'but I think it tends to lower the spirits, whereas work of any kind, with or without a purpose, tends to raise them; and now we must ride for it, or we shall be late for dinner, which I know from experience does not tend to raise papa's spirits.'

The roads were perfect, and the kindly twilight as they swept past the line plantations of Randwick, and adown the noble avenue which in the future will be one of the glories of Sydney, through the wide half-redeemed expanse of Moore Park, and so home by Woollahra, gave them every opportunity of lengthening their *tête-à-tête*, and yet arriving at Morahmee in time for dinner. It necessitated a hasty toilet on both sides, but at the last notes of the bell Antonia appeared, looking very fresh and animated after the expedition, and Ernest, whose appetite had not yet relapsed into metropolitan apathy, looked forward to dinner with feelings of almost youthful anticipation.

'Well, what do you think of Bondi?' asked the old gentleman. 'I was nearly drowned there when I was a youngster swimming in the surf. In fact I *was* drowned to all intents and purposes, except that I am here now. I was sucked back by the undertow time after time, till I was quite beaten. I had a few minutes' awful struggle; then collapse and half a minute's choke; then lovely music in my ears; and I left the world—as I thought—for good.'

'You dear old naughty boy of a father,' said Antonia, with tears half gathering to her eye, 'I am sure you were bathing unlawfully, like the boys in the story-book. But what restored you to life?'

'Well, a Maori, who happened to come up at the time in a fishing-boat. He could *swim*.'

'But I thought you said that you were swimming in the surf and did your best to fight through it?' inquired Ernest.

'Maoris and Kanakas can *swim*', repeated the old man sarcastically. 'White men like you and me can only paddle. Anyhow, he dived and brought me up, and ten minutes after I was suffering the frightful torture, "coming to." So, as perhaps you may have guessed, I did not die that time.'

'Oft in danger, yet alive,
We are come to, fifty-five,'

quoted Ernest. 'I daresay you have had all sorts of hairbreadth escapes, if you would only tell them to us.'

'Escapes! well, I have had a few,' chuckled the old man. 'Some day I must make Antonia write them out, and we'll publish the *Surprising Adventures of Paul Frankston*. I wonder if I could put in some of my stories? Ha! ha! ha! How they would laugh.'

'I think your life would make a capital book,' said Antonia, 'and you could afford to leave the stories out.'

'Ha! well, I don't know; some people might object; but I have seen some queer places and people, and had some very narrow squeaks. I was a ship boy in the *Lloyd* when the Maoris took her at the Bay of Islands.'

'What did they do?' asked Ernest.

'Do? Only murdered every living soul except a little girl and myself! Old Parson Ramsden came down months after and ransomed us. He could go anywhere. That little girl is a grandmother now. I could show you such a splendid bit of tattooing just—Antonia, my dear, you needn't be afraid.'

'Don't be foolish, papa,' said Antonia, blushing. 'Mr. Neuchamp, he is only joking.'

'Joking,' said the old man; 'if you'd only had those patterns printed out slowly and indelibly, like me and Mrs. Lutton, poor thing, you'd have known it was no joke.'

'Well, they didn't eat you that time, at any rate,' said Ernest, coming to the rescue; 'a hero can't be killed in the first volume; and what was the next narrow escape?'

'Years afterwards I was cast away in the south seas, and came ashore on a spar at an island where they'd never heard of a white man. They had sacrifices and prayers and made a kind of lottery about whether they should eat me; when, as luck would have it, the chief had lost his eldest son a year before, and the priests said I was him come back. So I was turned into a Kanaka Prince of Wales.'

'And was the rank properly kept up?'

'Jolliest place I ever was in, before or since; I had been starved and shipwrecked, and I tell you it was a pleasant change; I was the second man in the island. I had a palace, partly leaves, but cool and pleasant. I had thirty—well—hum—ha—more attendants than I knew what to do with. I cried, I know, when a Yankee whaler took me off six months after. But come, this won't do, Master Ernest, you mustn't keep me spinning sea-yarns all night about myself. You haven't half told us about your doings. Was Captain Jinks really a pleasant sort of fellow? And how about the lock-up?'

'Come, papa,' said Antonia, 'it's hardly fair to Mr. Neuchamp to laugh at him about that little mistake—any one might be taken in by a nice-looking, clever, plausible man.'

'Well, I confess,' said Ernest boldly, 'I *was* taken in, though I ought to have known better. If I had seen a seedy aristocrat in my own country, I should not have made a travelling companion of him. But he was very clever and good-looking, and I thought there was nothing wonderful in such a man being out of luck in a colony.'

'Never mind; fault on the right side,' said Mr. Frankston—'anything's better than being suspicious; you'll cut your wisdom teeth before you've done with us.'